Dreaming in
CHOCOLATE

Center Point
Large Print

**This Large Print Book carries the
Seal of Approval of N.A.V.H.**

*D*reaming in CHOCOLATE

SUSAN BISHOP CRISPELL

CENTER POINT LARGE PRINT
THORNDIKE, MAINE

The text of this Large Print edition is unabridged.
In other aspects, this book may vary
from the original edition.
Printed in the United States of America
on permanent paper.
Set in 16-point Times New Roman type.

ISBN: 978-1-68324-752-4

Library of Congress Cataloging-in-Publication Data

Names: Crispell, Susan Bishop, author.
Title: Dreaming in chocolate / Susan Bishop Crispell.
Description: Center Point Large Print edition. | Thorndike, Maine :
    Center Point Large Print, 2018.
Identifiers: LCCN 2017061393 | ISBN 9781683247524
    (hardcover : alk. paper)
Subjects: LCSH: Mothers and daughters—Fiction. | Large type books. |
    GSAFD: Love stories.
Classification: LCC PS3603.R5738 D74 2018b | DDC 813/.6—dc23
LC record available at https://lccn.loc.gov/2017061393

for my mom, who taught me
to love with an open heart
(and let me take
the apothecary table)

ACKNOWLEDGMENTS

This book has tried to be so many different things since these characters first came to me. And I am so grateful to everyone who helped me finally get the story right.

Thank you to my fabulous editor, Kat Brzozowski, for loving my quirky, magical books and for sticking around to help me finish this one! Fingers crossed we'll work together again on some magical YA. And extra thanks to Laurie Chittenden for taking me on and guiding my books into the world. My books would be nowhere without the support of the whole St. Martin's Press team, including Jessica Lawrence, Karen Masnica, Kristopher Kam, and Lisa Bonvissuto.

A lifetime of gratitude and exclamation points to my rock star agent, Patricia Nelson. Thank you for always seeing what I'm trying to do with my writing (especially the magic!) and showing me how to do it so much better. There's no one else I would rather have on my side.

Mark, thank you for keeping me well-fed and in clean clothes, for holding my hand at doctors' appointments and on the beach, for countless concerts and distillery tours and beers at Bombers (where one day we'll get our name on a stool!), but most of all for loving me back.

I would not be where I am without the support of my family (all the Bishops, Schwartzes, Johnsons, Harrisons, and Crispells). Thank you for believing in me and encouraging me to follow my dreams. And for talking up my books to everyone you meet. All the love to my oldest niece, Caroline, for bringing Ella to life in my head (even though you outgrew her by years). My mantra for this book was "What would C do?" You have my heart forever, kid.

Rebekah Faubion, Jessica Fonseca, Courtney Howell, and Zoe Harris: you brilliant ladies give me life. There will never be enough thank-yous for your friendship and spot-on writing advice.

Extra hugs to Anna-Marie McLemore, Alisha Klapheke, and Carrie Brown-Wolf for reading a partial early draft and steering me in the right direction; to Hayley Chewins, Jaime Questell, Melissa Roske, Kathryn Rose, Laurie Elizabeth Flynn, and Marci Lyn Curtis for being bright spots in my writing journey; to Nova Ren Suma for all of your encouragement and wisdom; and to Beth Revis and Cristin Terrill for making this book fall apart at the first Appalachian Writers Workshop and then teaching me how to put it back together (when I was supposed to be working on my YA instead).

So much love to my friends who keep me sane on the rare occasions I come out of my writing cave: JoAn and Stacy Shaw, Suzanne Junered, Sarah Collier Southern, Ashley Williams, Krysti Wetherill, Lindsay and Eli Smith, Erin Capps, Thalia Simmons, and Jeff Lee.

Always, thank you to Karma Brown for your steadfast cheerleading and friendship. I'm also eternally grateful to Kristy Woodson Harvey, Amy Reichert, Kimberly Brock, Colleen Oakley, and Louise Miller for reading this book early and for saying such lovely things about it.

I'm so lucky to be a part of a few wonderful writers' groups, especially the Tall Poppy Writers, who are some of the smartest, funniest, and most supportive women I know, and the Pitch Wars 2014 Table of Trust, who remind me that I will never have to go it alone.

To all of the amazing online book-pushers who have supported me, most notably Stacee Evans at *Adventures of a Book Junkie* (a fellow fangirl who also shares her books with me), Jenny O'Regan at *Confessions of a Bookaholic*, Tamara Welch at *Traveling with T*, and Kristy Barrett at *A Novel Bee*; your devotion to books and authors is better than cake for breakfast. I adore you all.

And a special shout-out to The Hot Chocolatier

in Chattanooga, TN, and French Broad Chocolates in Asheville, NC, for providing delicious inspiration while I was writing this book.

1

If there was one thing Penelope Dalton knew for certain, it was that every day offered up at least one magical moment. A taste of sheer happiness that was sweeter than her favorite dark chocolate caramels. Too many moments had slipped through her fingers before she'd known to look for them, but over the past month, she'd made it her mission not to miss any more.

This was today's—knees-down in the snow, shivering from the cold and wet that soaked her cotton leggings and the hem of her dress, building a snowman while her daughter chatted nonstop about her day at school.

Penelope had thrown on just enough outer layers as she left work to keep her comfortable on the ten-minute walk to and from Malarkey Elementary. But when she and Ella had approached the park in the middle of downtown, all white and winter-wonderlandy, she could practically hear it begging for them to be the first to leave their mark.

And since memories didn't make themselves, they'd walked hand in hand into the fresh snow, inadequate attire be damned.

"What was the best thing that happened at school today?" Penelope asked. She shoveled an armful of snow into a pile and began molding it around the ball Ella had formed.

"Besides the snow?"

Snow wasn't unusual in the northwest corner of North Carolina, but this early in the season they rarely got more than a smattering of flakes at a time. The couple inches that had fallen since lunch were a delightful surprise.

"Yes, besides that."

"At recess I got to play tag with the other kids," Ella said, her gap-toothed smile taking over her face. She skimmed her fingers over the cat ears sewn into the top of her knit hat, then continued. "At first Mrs. Shutters said she wasn't sure if I should play because she didn't want me to get hurt, but then one of the other teachers said it was just tag and running around would probably do me some good after being sick. So Mrs. Shutters said okay. And then, guess what happened? I got to be It, Mama!"

Penelope locked her eyes on her daughter, her smile freezing into place and breath catching in her throat, a vain attempt to hold on to the moment. But not even Ella's excitement about playing the position in the game no one ever wanted could keep reality from rushing back in at the word "sick."

Exhaling, Penelope relaxed her face. Ella had

12

gotten to play at recess like a normal third grader. That in itself was a reason to be happy. For now, she would make it be enough. "That's great, sweetie. Did you get to tag someone?"

"Yep. This girl in my class. Her name is River. She's really good at tag. She almost never gets caught," Ella said. She scooped her mittened hands into the snow then dumped it right back out. "Hey, wait! We can't make our snow family without Grams. Let's go get her so she can help."

"It's going to be a little tough for her to make snowmen while she's working."

"She can take a break. She'll be sad if we make them without her."

"You know she can't take a break without closing the shop. Somebody has to help customers when they come in, and since I'm here with you, Grams is there by herself."

Ella set a hand on Penelope's to stop her from packing another handful of snow onto the lopsided sphere sitting on the ground between them. "I know. But can't she just come for an hour? Please? I'll make a note for the front door so anyone who wants some hot chocolate will know when to come back."

Penelope hesitated. She had never been one of those moms to give in to her kid's every demand. But lately the word "no" had abandoned her, and she couldn't bring herself to go looking for it. Making Ella smile, hearing her laugh with

13

delight—that's what mattered now. Guilt from all of the no's over the years—and all of the experiences Ella never had because of Penelope's decisions—burned at the back of her throat. Giving in to it, she said, "You're right. Grams wouldn't want to miss this."

"Yes! Okay, let's go." In her haste to get a move on, Ella chucked the handfuls of snow she had collected into the air, showering Penelope's face with a flurry of snow as she stood.

Startled by the shock of cold on her cheeks, Penelope lost her balance and went sprawling backward in the snow.

"Sorry, Mama!"

"It's okay," she said, still staring up at the gray-blue sky. *Maybe,* she thought, *on days when you really need it, you can steal a second perfect moment.* Then she crooked a gloved finger at Ella. "Come here, kid."

When Ella leaned over her, Penelope wrapped her arms around her daughter's too-skinny waist and pulled Ella down on top of her. A chorus of giggles burst out of Ella at the sudden shift from standing to being draped across her mom's torso. Penelope kissed Ella's temple, where a wisp of light-brown hair had escaped the hat. She twisted to the side, careful to cradle Ella's head with one of her hands, then laid her daughter next to her.

"Since we're both down here, we might as well have a little fun," she said.

Penelope scooted a few feet away and dropped to her back again. Turning her head toward Ella, she matched her daughter's grin with one of her own. On the count of three, they both spread their arms and legs wide and made angels in the snow.

They sacrificed a half dozen dark chocolate truffles for the snowmen's eyes. The truffles—formed by hand in the chocolate cafe Penelope owned with her mom—made for more convenient eyes than lumps of coal, which would have required a separate stop at the market a few blocks away on the opposite side of the park. Since they only had an hour before they needed to reopen the Chocolate Cottage, Penelope agreed to pilfer snowman supplies from the shop's inventory. In place of carrots, they fashioned noses out of white-chocolate-dipped pretzel sticks as thick as two of Ella's fingers. The pink, red, and green sprinkles set in the chocolate complemented the colorful aprons Penelope's mom, Sabina, draped around the snowmen's rotund waists.

The mouths proved more difficult. Ella had searched the apothecary table tucked into a nook in the back of the kitchen for a serendipitous stash of red licorice or even the whole dried cayenne peppers used to make the spicy hot chocolate she wasn't allowed to drink. She found neither. In the end, Penelope convinced her daughter that chocolate-covered espresso beans were a good substitute. And the three snowmen smiled at the passing cars with unpainted lips.

"Are you finished yet?" Ella asked.

Penelope drained the last of her hot chocolate, grateful for the extra hit of warmth and the sugar rush it provided. Unlike her snow doppelganger, Penelope's lips were stained a deep red and left a ring on the plastic lid. She handed the disposable cup to Ella, who was taking her time with her own drink. "What are you going to do with it?"

"You'll see."

Which in Ella-speak meant Penelope might have vetoed the idea if Ella had asked permission.

But Penelope was curious enough to let it slide. "Okay, well, we've got about ten more minutes before we need to get back. So whatever you're planning, better make it quick."

"I will," Ella said. Then she turned away, tossing a smile over her shoulder, and raced off. Her boots kicked up snow behind her with each step.

A handful of other kids, all around Ella's age, had made their way to the park and were building their own snowmen and amassing an arsenal of snowballs. None of them had parents with them. None of them would need immediate supervision with Mrs. Lehman in the antique shop across the street and Old Mr. Harvey sitting out in front of Malarkey Hardware on the corner to keep an eye on them.

"You two can stay, honey," Sabina said, pinching a tangle of flyaway hairs between her fingers and tucking it behind her ear into the mass of dark curls. "Ella's having so much fun. She shouldn't have to stop just because I need to leave."

"Believe me, she's crammed a lot of fun into the day already," Penelope said.

They both shifted to watch Ella. At first Penelope thought Ella was trying to overcome her shyness by talking to the other kids, but Ella bypassed them in favor of the line of trees separating the park from Hawthorne Street. Then she crouched beneath the barren limbs of a magnolia tree. Her hat snagged on one of the branches and twisted so the gray cat ears sat sideways on her head. When she crawled out, her smile rivaled the brightness of the snow blanketing the ground.

Penelope turned back to her mom, trying to remember her reasons for why they should pack it in too. It was easier when Ella's happiness wasn't her only focus. After a moment, she said, "Ella has homework to do and all this running around is going to catch up to her at some point tonight. I'd rather her crash at the shop than in the snow."

Sabina tipped her head in Ella's direction. "Doesn't look like she's slowing down anytime soon."

Ella headed back to them, arms crossed over her chest to keep the long sticks she'd gathered from tangling with her legs and tripping her.

"Not as long as she can help it," Penelope agreed, ignoring the cold ache deep in her chest that had little to do with the chill in the air. They'd had such a good day. She wouldn't ruin it by letting the sadness get a stronger hold.

"I'm almost done," Ella said, bending over to lay the sticks on the ground in front of the snowmen. After a short inspection, she handed two of the sturdier ones to Penelope. "Hold these, please."

And just like that, Penelope's smile returned. It was impossible to feel bad when Ella was happy—her good moods were infectious. "Your ears are crooked." She spun Ella's hat back to straight with her free hand.

"Thanks." Ella picked up the remaining sticks and jabbed them into the middle sections of two of the snowmen, creating arms. One stick pointed up and the other reached for the ground. She stepped back, hands on hips as she looked them over. Nodding, she said, "Okay, Mama, I'm ready for those."

Penelope handed over the sticks. "This one gets special arms, huh?"

"Yep. You'll see why in a minute," Ella said.

Penelope and her mom exchanged amused looks over Ella's head.

18

Ella placed the sticks in the same position as the others. The forked end overlapped with the arm of the snowman next to it as if they were holding hands. Then Ella picked up Penelope's empty hot chocolate cup and balanced it on the end of the snowman's other arm.

"Ta-da! They're us."

"They certainly are," a voice said behind them.

Penelope turned to find Malarkey's mayor, Henry Jameson, walking toward them. He wasn't quite six feet but was built like a small fridge. At just shy of fifty, he was in better shape than most people half his age thanks to his commitment to reduce his carbon footprint, which resulted in him tarping his car in the garage and walking everywhere he needed to go in town.

"I can't tell you how good it is to see the three of you out here together," he said.

"We couldn't resist the fresh snow," Penelope said.

He pointed to the cup in the snowman's hand and chuckled. "That hot chocolate's not gonna bring those snowmen to life like Frosty, is it?"

"No, I used the magic-free hot chocolate," Ella said. She frowned at the cup as if it had let her down. Then she whipped her attention back to the adults, her lips unfurling into a smile again. "The table wouldn't give me anything when I looked. That would be so cool, though. I'll try again when we get back to the shop."

Penelope wrapped her arms over her daughter's shoulders and pulled her in so Ella's back pressed into Penelope's stomach. "I don't think animating snowmen is the best use of magic."

Ella tilted her head back to look at Penelope. "Don't say that, Mama. It would be so much fun."

"Yes," Penelope conceded. "It probably would."

But the recipes and ingredients that mysteriously appeared in the drawers of the antique apothecary table at the Chocolate Cottage came of their own accord. Penelope could ask for a magical fix to a problem, but there was no guarantee it would ever come.

2

Penelope learned long ago not to trust the chocolate's magic. At least when it came to her own life.

And the recipe for truffles that would mend a broken heart she found in the apothecary table's top right drawer further justified that stance.

She tucked the recipe card into her apron pocket. It was safer there than left in the table for her mother to find. Or worse, Ella. They would both encourage Penelope to use it—her daughter because she would be the cause of the heartbreak it promised to alleviate and her mom because Sabina held fast to the belief that their chocolates were some sort of magical cure-all drug. With one taste of their chocolates, people dreamed of their futures and reveled in temporary bouts of happiness and luck to get them through the rough times.

Though the magic had been utterly useless when it came to curing Ella.

Penelope slid the drawer shut, only the slightest scuffing of wood on wood giving her away. The mother-of-pearl knob warmed beneath her fingers, as if the table wanted her to know it wasn't finished giving unwanted advice.

"Next time, give me something worth having," she whispered.

Then she gave the drawer another little shove for good measure. Bottles of extracts and flavored salts and dried lavender petals in some of the other drawers rattled against each other traitorously. She threw a quick glance over her shoulder and met her mother's curious gaze as Sabina leaned around the doorframe separating the front counter from the kitchen. There was no use pretending nothing had happened. Her mom was attuned to the table's quirks and always knew when it had gifted a new recipe or ingredient.

When they'd first opened the shop, it had been like Christmas every day, both of them giddy with excitement to see what new bite of magic they'd be able to offer their customers next. Now it was a daily disappointment.

Penelope walked out front, opting to get the impending argument out of the way as quickly as possible.

"Did it give you something new?" her mom asked. A fresh wave of hope curved the corners of her mouth up. "Something that might help Ella?"

"Yes, it did. But it's not for Ella."

"Let me see it."

Penelope curled her fingers around the card in her apron pocket. With just a little pressure she could crush it into a tiny knot of pointless words and numbers. "It's not for you either."

"Something new for the shop then?" Sabina asked.

"No, this one's for me. And since I don't plan on using it, there's no need for you to get worked up over it." It didn't do Penelope any good to let it affect her either. The magic of the apothecary table could only do so much. This was just its way of reminding her of its limits. She relaxed her grip, letting the paper fall back out of reach.

Her mother cupped the side of Penelope's face with one hand. "But maybe it's—"

"Mama, you really have to stop hoping that the chocolates will fix everything. If there was a way to save her, the doctors would have found it," Penelope said. She laid her hand over her mom's and squeezed.

"There is still so much life in her," her mother said, the whisper stealing the ends of her words. "I think you stopped too soon. Gave up."

Since Ella's first seizure almost two years ago, Penelope had tried everything to make her daughter well. Neurologists at Duke. Acupuncture. Recipes for healing truffles made with fennel seeds and white chocolate. Writing the future she wanted for Ella on a piece of paper at last year's Festival of Fate and tossing it into the bonfire along with the futures of the rest of Malarkey's residents.

Deciding to stop Ella's treatment was the hardest decision Penelope had ever made. And as a twenty-seven-year-old single mom, she'd had her fair share. But she and Ella agreed it was the best choice out of the crappy ones they'd been given. And she wouldn't let anyone guilt her into questioning it.

"A point you've made abundantly clear over the past week," Penelope said. "But this is what Ella wants."

"She wants a lot of other things too. Her list is proof enough of that. She adds something new every day. And when you both realize she deserves more time to do it all, it will be too late."

Penelope flicked her eyes to her daughter who was tucked into the corner of the sofa at the front of the shop. With her notebook leaning against her propped-up legs, she scratched out a list in pink magic marker of all the things she wanted to do before she died. In her case, the list was necessity, not daydreaming.

Bucket lists should've been reserved for over-achieving teenagers and people in the throes of midlife crises. Not eight-year-olds. Yet there they were, left with only six months—a year if they got lucky—all thanks to an inoperable tumor embedded deep in Ella's brain. On a good day, it caused nausea and migraines that sent her home from school. On a bad day, Ella suffered from

24

localized seizures and prolonged hospital stays.

"It's already too late." Penelope pressed her lips together and took a steadying breath. Falling apart so soon after the final diagnosis would only make things harder. She had to stay focused on Ella. "So I'm going to do whatever it takes to make her life as happy and full as I can. If you can't do that too, I need you to tell me now."

"Of course I will do that. That's all I've ever wanted for her. And for you." Sabina's voice wobbled as the first tears fell. "I just wish we had more time."

"I do too, Mama." If the apothecary table had given Penelope a recipe that would allow her to trade years of her life for Ella's, she would've started collecting ingredients as soon as she'd finished reading. But it hadn't. And it wouldn't.

This time when her fingers slid over the smooth surface of the recipe in her apron pocket, she crumpled it in her fist.

Ella's happy shouts of "Mama!" and "Grams!" had them both smiling before the words had even completely left her mouth. There was now a limit on how long they would have to hear her call their names. And they both cherished every one.

"Do you want to see what I've added to my list?" Ella asked.

"You didn't put *get a tattoo* back on there again, did you?" Penelope asked.

"Nope." She scratched the marker back and

forth on the paper to cross something off the list. "It's something even better."

The list had been the doctor's idea. A way to ensure Ella's final months would be filled with all the things she loved. Which meant most of what Ella wanted were typical eight-year-old requests: eating cake for breakfast, going to Disney to meet Elsa and Anna, and adopting a kitten and naming her Truffles. A few were on there simply because they were things Penelope would normally say no to, like piercing her ears or dyeing her hair purple. And Ella was smart enough to try and play the terminal illness card to get everything she could.

Penelope crossed the room and leaned over the back of the couch, resting her chin on Ella's fair hair. Ella's handwriting was oversized and sharp-edged. A few letters were adorably missing, as Ella had sounded out the words she didn't know how to spell and improvised. She skimmed the all-too-familiar list until she found the newest entries at the bottom.

16. Go to scool with zro sick days for one hole month.

"I think it's the best one yet," Penelope said.

But if Ella managed to do that, it would be nothing short of a miracle.

Just as predicted, Ella's full day of school and snowman-building wiped her out. She was sound asleep within minutes of being tucked into bed. Penelope tried to tell herself it was a good kind of tired, the kind that meant her daughter had enjoyed every second of the day. But looking at how thin and pale Ella's face was against the pillow, all Penelope could see was how the day had taken its toll.

Penelope watched for the subtle rise and fall of Ella's chest before leaving the room. Even then, she lingered in the hallway before finally shaking loose some of the worry and going downstairs.

With just the two of them in the house, Penelope had never seen a need for a formal dining room. They ate most meals at the island in the kitchen and on some lazy Saturday mornings they cuddled together on the couch in the living room with a shared plate of French toast dusted with powdered sugar to finish watching whatever movie Ella had fallen asleep during the night before. So the open area off the kitchen that would have been the dining room had become Penelope's sewing space.

Like the rest of the house, it was an eclectic mix of antique and modern. Two wingback chairs in a palm green and cream damask pattern flanked the sewing table she'd made by attaching a thick slab of dark-stained oak to her grandmother's early-1900s cast-iron sewing machine base. Her sewing machine, built within the last decade, sat gleaming white on top. The room had become her sanctuary when she couldn't sleep. Which was more often than not these days.

Penelope turned one of the chairs and scooted it over to the table. Sinking into it, she scrolled through the playlists on the iPod attached to a speaker dock on the far corner of the table. The mixes were categorized by mood to create the perfect soundtrack to her current state of mind. She bypassed Frustration—loud, passion-fueled hard rock that temporarily drowned out her own problems—and paused on Melancholy—mostly indie singer/songwriters with acoustic guitars and pianos that called for sitting in a dark room and pretending the outside world didn't exist. Then she backtracked to Inspired. It was a compilation of her favorite songs and could trick her into smiling and singing along as quickly as three songs in.

That was exactly the kind of distraction she needed tonight.

So was the stack of half a dozen triangular hair scarves she and Ella had cut and pinned together the weekend before. They'd picked a mix of fabrics in vibrant colors and patterns to bring some much-needed brightness to the pediatric oncology unit where they were donating the scarves when they were done.

She pressed Play on the iPod, letting the first few notes of the Athenaeum song chase the rest of the tension from her shoulders. Grabbing the coral chevron fabric from the top of the pile, she secured it in place beneath the machine's presser foot and applied pressure to the pedal under the table. She guided the fabric past the needle, pivoted when she reached the corner, and started up the next side. Penelope could just make out the music over the steady buzzing of the sewing machine. She bumped the volume up a notch. Then she eased back on the pedal to slow the needle and her progress.

Like Ella, Penelope was determined to get as much happiness out of the day as she could.

3

Penelope had found all of her recipes in the apothecary table's drawers. Espresso truffles that gave a jolt of energy. Jasmine tea caramels that calmed frenzied nerves. Spicy hot chocolate that sparked dreams of true love. The recipes came in different languages with ingredients and measurements that were indecipherable to everyone but the owners of the apothecary table. When her granddad had acquired the table at an estate sale to put in his antique shop, no one in the previous owner's family mentioned its unique traits. The first recipe her grandparents discovered was for the Kismet hot chocolate, a dark-chocolate-and-lavender mixture that gave the drinker the ability to change their future on just one night a year—the winter solstice.

No one in town believed them, of course. Not until her grandparents held the first Festival of Fate and invited everyone to share in the magic. *What could it hurt,* they all said. At worst, it was a night spent sharing their dreams and drinking hot chocolate around a bonfire in the town park with their neighbors. But at best, they might all be able to decide their own fates.

After a few months, when all of their wishes for the future came true—or so the story went—there wasn't a doubt in anyone's mind about the power of the chocolates.

Penelope's grandparents had an open-door policy when it came to sharing their chocolates. Whenever someone in town needed a boost of magic, all they had to do was ask. It wasn't until Penelope wound up pregnant at eighteen that she and her mom decided to use the recipes as a source of income. And the town had rallied behind the idea of having access to the magic every day. In the nine years since, the Chocolate Cottage had become an indispensable part of life in Malarkey, North Carolina.

When the shop door swung open, Penelope pasted on a smile so her anger at the festival's magic failing to save Ella didn't show. Pretending that everything was fine was the only way to ensure Ella got to live like a normal, healthy kid. She would deal with the fallout of her lies . . . after.

Eliza Rose tamed her copper hair with both hands as she stepped inside out of the wind. "Hey, Penelope. Is your mom here?"

"No, she's off today. Is there something I can do for you?" Penelope asked.

"I wanted to tell her the chocolates were a success," Eliza murmured. She pressed a hand to her mouth to stifle a giggle. "Like, a major success. Philip only ate one before he asked me out. Can you believe it? The guy I've had a crush on since freshman year just asked me out. And it's all because of you and your mom. I feel like I owe you our firstborn or something."

The girl's enthusiasm was impossible to ignore. Penelope grinned back. "Lucky for you, we don't take children as payment," she said. The teen giggled again. "And I'm happy it worked out for you. Be sure to come back in after the date. I know my mom'll want to hear all about it."

Eliza tugged her hair over one shoulder, twisting it a few times as she looked back at the door as if she could will Sabina to walk in by sheer determination. "Oh, I definitely will. If I could bring Philip by on the date I would. But I don't want him to know about the chocolates, you know? I mean, not that using the chocolates on him was wrong or anything 'cause I did dream about him, so it's totally legit, right?"

Sighing, Penelope nodded. "Don't worry. The chocolates didn't make him ask you out. They just put him in the right mood to finally make a move. So, you're off the hook."

"That's what I thought!" She slid her phone out of her back pocket and pulled her ID and a couple of folded dollars from the card slot built into the case. "While I'm here, can I get just a normal hot chocolate?"

"Sure." Penelope handed her a to-go cup and

pointed her to the pantry. "You want the jar with the white label. Grab one of the caramels too. They go really well with the dark chocolate."

The open-air pantry was a small, octagonal room between the kitchen and the sitting area with built-in cabinets and shelves in a vibrant white that ran from floor to ceiling. Customers ordered at the front counter and took their cups to the pantry to select the hot chocolate base and add-ins, such as individually wrapped bite-sized caramels; mini marshmallows; jumbo chocolate-dipped marshmallows; hazelnut rolled wafer cookies from Uprising Bakery down the street; and fresh peppermint leaves picked from a potted plant on the second shelf. A tiered chandelier hung from the center of the ceiling, which was painted a metallic gold to complement the deep chocolate paint of the rest of the shop. Despite the hazy gray light pushing in through the front windows, the shop was bright and cozy.

Eliza prepped her cup and brought it back to the counter to finish. The steam wand on the espresso machine screamed when Penelope submerged it in the milk. She tilted the metal pitcher and dipped the wand in and out of the liquid until the sound settled into a low rumble. She let it bubble for a few more seconds, stirred it into the hot chocolate powder, then sent Eliza off with a wave and a promise to tell Sabina the good news.

And this time when Penelope smiled, she had no ulterior motive. Just the simple joy of knowing her chocolates had done their job.

As far as hole-in-the-wall towns went, Malarkey took the cake. Nestled in a valley in the Appalachian Mountains, the town was one where people found themselves in one of three ways—they were born there, they knew someone who was born there, or they'd gotten themselves good and lost.

Penelope considered herself one of the lucky ones. She was Malarkey born and raised. The uneven brick roads that mapped out the heart of town and the bells of the old wooden church that chimed a few minutes early or late, but never on time, were as much a part of her life as the townspeople who offered their opinions as quickly as their smiles. With a population of thirteen hundred—give or take a dozen—she knew most of the town's residents on a first-name basis. The rest she knew by sight.

It was rare that anything happened in Malarkey without it becoming common knowledge within ten minutes. The current topic of most conversations was how Tucker Gregory had crashed his motorcycle late the night before. Penelope had heard half a dozen different accounts of how bad his injuries were and figured the truth was somewhere in the middle.

If it had been someone other than a Gregory, she might have sent a get-well care package over. But the less interaction she had with that family, the better. For both her and Ella.

So Penelope left her mom to chat with the customers while she spent the better part of two hours holed up in the kitchen replenishing the inventory of chocolates. Every so often, Sabina would swing into the back to give Penelope a triumphant smile from making another customer happy.

"Your turn," Sabina eventually said. She nodded toward the front when the next pair of customers entered.

Of course Penelope would get to help two of the biggest gossips in town. Though to be fair, almost everyone in town talked about everyone else. That was just how small towns worked. Or at least how Malarkey worked. Penelope had never been anywhere else long enough to know if things—or people—were different there.

"Karma," she muttered and went out to greet the women.

Ruth Anne Lockrow bustled up to the counter, the collar of her wool coat pulled up over her chin to keep the cold out. Her gold-shadowed eyes flicked to Penelope, a smile tugging at her lips in lieu of a proper greeting. She turned back to her companion, continuing their conversation without missing a beat. "It's a shame Noah doesn't live closer. I'm sure Tucker could use his brother's help right about now."

Noah's name rarely came up in conversation these days. He'd been gone for so long there was little reason for people to gossip about him. So when they did talk, it was hard to ignore. No matter how much Penelope wanted to.

"I took a casserole over there this morning and Layne said they'd asked Noah to come home to help with the bar until Tucker's up and moving again," the second woman, Delilah Jacobs, said as she looked over the menu written on blackboards behind the counter.

The possibility of Noah Gregory coming back to town nine years after walking out of Penelope's life for good was not even something she wanted to consider. As she brewed a pot of tea for the women, she had to remind herself there was no point in getting worked up over something that would never happen.

She was grateful for the distraction when another customer came in.

Penelope passed off the tea and plate of assorted chocolates to the customers still talking about Noah then turned her attention to the woman with a wide-eyed nervousness, which manifested in fingers that worried the hem of her coat as she made her way to the front counter.

"Can I help you?" Penelope asked.

The woman dropped her hands to her sides.

She looked equal parts desperate for and wary of the magic. Her round face was pale—freckleless cheeks, a dab of colorless lip balm, eyes so light blue they almost seemed unnatural. But her features sparked to life when she said, "Oh, hi. Yes, I hope you can."

"Me too." Having dealt with countless first-timers over the years, Penelope offered the woman a smile. A little getting-to-know-you chit-chat went a long way to ease people into talking about magic and what they hoped it could do for them. "I don't think I've seen you in here before."

"I came in the other day. Your mom helped me with some Enlightenment hot chocolate."

"Ah, okay." So not first-time jitters. This woman had dreamed of her future, and whatever she'd seen, it had her on edge.

"Is it possible for the chocolates to go wrong somehow? For what I dreamed to be wrong?"

"I've never seen it happen before," Penelope said.

The chocolates that affected emotions kicked in almost immediately and lasted for no more than a few hours. The ones that gave visions of the future resulted in one very vivid dream the next time the person went to sleep. And what part of the future they saw depended on the type of hot chocolate they had used.

Sometimes the magic could simply not work. But work wrong? Never.

A few customers asked for their money back or for a do-over. But only a handful actually received a second chance. And those were only granted on the rare occasions when the magic hadn't worked at all.

The woman gripped the berry-colored scarf double-looped around her neck with both hands. She didn't look at Penelope when she said, "So, you're saying I'm screwed."

"Not necessarily. Do you mind telling me what you saw?"

"If you think you can help, sure." She dropped her hands to the counter, locking them together as if in prayer. As if Penelope could save her from a future she didn't want.

Penelope wanted to tell her not to get her hopes up. That there was likely nothing anyone could do to change her fate. But she knew all too well how heartache could make you blind to logic. That it could steal your breath and leave you hollow inside. Even if only temporarily.

"Okay. But first, I feel like I should know your name before I know what's supposed to happen to you."

"I'm Zan. Or Suzanne, if you want." She smiled, and for a second the fear retreated. "Zan Maslany."

"Oh, right. You bought the cafe over on Orchard Street."

"Yep. That's me."

"Sorry. I should have known that. My head seems to be somewhere else today. So, what did you see in your dream?" Penelope asked.

Zan curled her fingernails into the wooden counter as the memory of what she'd dreamed flooded her. Taking a deep breath, she said, "I saw my ex-boyfriend. He was in the cafe, drinking a cup of coffee and smiling at me. But he shouldn't know where I am. Nobody knows for that exact reason. I gave up everything to get away from him but he's going to find me anyway."

Penelope's insides twisted at the thought of what else her chocolates had shown Zan. "Did he hurt you?"

"Not in the dream." She shivered and pulled her coat tighter around her waist.

But he had before she'd run away from him. The fear of it happening again was written all over Zan's face.

"What were you hoping the chocolates would show you? Not what you wanted to dream about specifically, but what you wanted to learn."

The hot chocolate worked best when the drinker thought about a specific thing they wanted to know. For the Enlightenment hot chocolate, it could be anything that would happen at any point in the future. People, places, emotions. But for the Corazón hot chocolate, it was always a question of who was their true love.

"I wanted to know if I'd be safe here," Zan said.

"How did you feel in the dream? Were you scared of him?" Penelope asked, keeping her voice low and soothing. She checked to make sure her other customers were still engrossed in their tea and gossip so this story didn't spread around town too.

Zan shook her head. "No. I felt relieved. And that's what really scares me. What if some stupid part of me still loves him and makes me forgive him? I don't want to pack up and have to start over again someplace else, but I can't stay here if he's going to find me. If he's going to smile at me like nothing ever happened."

But Zan would stay in Malarkey. And her ex would find her here. Even if she decided to leave town, he would show up just like he had in her dream, before she set foot outside of the town limits. Because that's what her future held.

Maybe if the Kismet hot chocolate worked the way they'd always believed it did, Penelope could tell Zan to stick it out until the Festival of Fate. Then she'd be able to change what she'd seen. But the festival now felt like a sham and she couldn't give Zan false hope that things could be different.

Penelope reached out and patted Zan's arm. "I wish I could take back what you saw so you don't have to remember it or tell you it'll all turn out okay. But that's not how it works. The future is what it is and now that you know, you'll have to find a way to live with it. Not having a choice in how things turn out is the one flaw with our chocolates."

"Oh, Penelope, you know that's not true," Sabina said, waving a dismissive hand in the air as she joined them at the counter. "People always have a choice. And you, honey," she added to Zan, "don't listen to all her pessimism. Why don't you try one of these hazelnut pralines and see if you don't gain a little more clarity within a few hours."

"Mama, she doesn't need more magic," Penelope said.

Zan shifted her focus to Sabina. "Do you have anything that will keep him from coming here? Or something that will guard my heart against him?"

"No, you'll just have to trust in yourself to be strong enough to handle him. But take these. I do think they'll help in the short term." Sabina removed two of the Clarity pralines from the display case and boxed them up.

"What will they do to me?" Zan asked.

"They will help you focus on a solution to your problem."

There was no point arguing with her mother. Sabina's belief in the magic was infectious. And most people were more than ready to believe right along with her. Penelope forced a smile. "Good luck."

When Zan left, bag clutched to her chest, Sabina turned to Penelope and said, "I know you've always been a little cynical when it comes to the Corazón hot chocolate, but since when are you against all of them?"

"I'm not, Mama. But I don't see how giving that woman more magic will help."

"Well, for one, it would clear her mind so she can see the situation for what it is. And two, it might help her remember something from her dream that she didn't before. Something that makes it seem less hopeless." Sabina smoothed a hand over Penelope's short crop of hair. Her sigh was bone-deep. "Maybe if you used a few of the chocolates, you'd remember how good the magic feels. And you might forget to be so scared of what the future may hold."

Penelope pulled away from her mom, her cheeks burning with a flash of anger. "I don't need magic to tell me what's in store for my life. Ella's doctors painted a pretty clear picture of how the next six months are going to go. And past that, I don't even want to think about it."

What Penelope couldn't say was that she'd already dreamed of her true love. For a time, she'd thought it had been Noah. But he had wanted nothing to do with the future she offered him, and it wasn't until she'd found out she was pregnant that she realized maybe he hadn't been the one she'd been waiting for at all. Maybe Noah had just been in her life to bring her Ella.

4

Whispers of true love and destiny and happily ever after floated into the kitchen of the Chocolate Cottage a few mornings later. With the Festival of Fate just over a month away, people were coming in daily to see what their futures held—and if they'd need to wish for something different at the festival. Penelope rolled her eyes at the line of lovesick customers out front. Sure her chocolates helped people find true love, but did women really have to pin all of their happiness on finding their soul mates? Especially when there was no guarantee they'd even want the fate the confections showed them.

She let out a slow breath and scowled at the dark chocolate that had scalded in the double boiler. It clung in thick chunks to the bottom of the glass bowl, as if annoyed by her cynicism. She twisted the stove knob and killed the flame.

"So, it's gonna be that kind of day, huh?" Grabbing a towel from a hook on the wall, she wrapped it around the lip of the bowl to protect her fingers from the heat. Steam licked at her skin as she dumped the clumps into the trash. A familiar voice grew louder out front, wishing the customers good luck with their love lives. Like luck had anything to do with it.

Megha Ghelani poked her head around the doorjamb a few seconds later. Her sharp cheekbones jutted out even farther when she flashed a wide smile at Penelope. "Have you seen him yet?"

Penelope froze. The rumors must be true. She'd hoped like hell Noah wouldn't come back, but apparently she hadn't wished hard enough.

"Seen who?" she asked.

"I know you know, so don't play dumb with me. Just because you were never hung up on Noah like the rest of us doesn't diminish how effing gorgeous he is. And yes, that is present tense, 'cause damn that boy got even hotter with age."

"Of course he did," she muttered. Her fingers still gripped the edge of the bowl, the heat seeping through the towel to burn her skin. She set it aside and rubbed her fingers on her apron. "And you can't blame me for being the only one smart enough not to fall for his bad-boy charm."

The lie was so smooth she almost believed it herself.

Whatever Penelope had had with Noah had been over and done with almost as soon as it started. There hadn't been time before he was out of the picture to tell Megha she'd fallen for him.

Megha leaned her hip against the wood trim

and crossed her ankles so the toe of one black stiletto shoe rested against the floor, as if she could stay there all day gossiping. "I wish I knew how you do it. Hell, it's been nine years since we graduated and just the mention of his name had me all flustered. Teach me, antilove guru. Show me how to resist him."

Penelope remembered the dream she'd had about Noah back when she was eighteen and stupid enough to believe in true love. It was so vivid, even after all this time, she could still hear the absolute certainty in his voice when he told her he loved her.

No. Just no. She would not think about him that way. The chocolate was wrong.

She shook her head and forced a smile. "Now *that* would be a good chocolate to make. A bad-decision repellent."

"You can't seriously stand there and say that Noah Gregory wouldn't be the best kind of bad decision," Megha said.

Penelope knew better than anyone just how bad a decision he was. And it was one she had no intention of ever repeating. Or admitting to.

She shrugged, ignoring the nerves jumbling in her stomach at the thought of running into him after all this time. "Shouldn't you be at the salon instead of over here bugging me about Noah?"

"Yeah, yeah. I'm going." Megha lifted her hand in a half wave. Then she pointed her index finger in Penelope's direction and walked backward out of the doorway. "But when you see him, we'll find out if you're really as immune to him as you say."

"That'll be difficult since I don't plan on seeing him," Penelope called.

Megha sang out, "Stubborn!" just before the front door closed behind her, and Penelope chuckled.

They'd been friends before their ages hit double digits—plenty long enough for Megha to know just how stubborn Penelope could be.

She turned back to the mess she'd made of the chocolate coating for the lavender caramels, set the bowl in the sink, then moved to the apothecary table to start again. The L-shaped table contained twenty-four hand-cut drawers, which were all slightly different sizes. The mother-of-pearl knobs gleamed against the dark reddish wood. The smooth rosewood gave off a faint sweet scent despite the lingering aroma of burnt chocolate permeating the air.

Opening the top drawer on the short part of the L, she removed three bars of dark baking chocolate. They were cool to the touch despite the heat of the kitchen, and she slipped them into her apron pocket. Two drawers over, she pulled out the bottle of lavender extract that had refilled itself since she'd used it half an hour before. She trailed her fingers over the top of the table in gratitude. Then she snatched her hand back as she realized that if she believed in this magic, some small part of her also believed what she'd dreamed about Noah being her one true love.

"I can keep from running into him, right?" she asked the empty room. "I'll just stick close to home and it won't be a problem."

"Did you say something?" her mom said when she glided into the room. Her gauzy red skirt danced around her legs and her shoes made the barest of scuffing sounds on the old wood floor. She continued without waiting for a response. "Love is certainly in the air lately. Every other customer who comes in, it seems like, wants to know who they are destined to love. The girl who just left even took home a half dozen of the Spark truffles to nudge her dream boy into making a move."

"Not that I mind the extra sale, but why doesn't *she* just make the first move?"

"Some girls like to be romanced, honey."

Penelope shot a look over her shoulder at her mom as she submerged her hands in the hot water. "Ah, yes, romance. I keep forgetting about that." She grinned and then turned her attention back to the stubborn burnt chocolate she had to pry from the sides of the glass with her nails.

"One of these days you're going to fall madly in love, even if I have to use charmed chocolate to make it happen."

"Mama!" The bowl clanged against the metal sink basin when it slipped from her soapy fingers. She turned around and suds dripped from her hands onto the floor. Though her mother was only five three—barely an inch taller than Penelope—she could be downright immovable when she set her mind to something. "You wouldn't dare."

Her mom closed the distance and patted both of Penelope's cheeks. "If I had a recipe, I would've done it years ago. You're too young to spend the rest of your life alone. You deserve to be happy, honey."

"I am happy. All things considered. And I won't be alone. I've got you to keep me company. Plus, the last thing Ella needs right now is some new person coming into our lives and throwing everything off-kilter." And the last thing Penelope needed was for her mom to know how close that was to becoming a reality. She gave a small smile and told herself that just because Noah was back in town didn't mean he would ever find out Ella was his. Leaning in, she pressed a kiss to her mom's cheek. "Now, I've got to redo this batch of chocolate for the caramels, so take your romance-pushing self back out front and stop distracting me." She smiled and gave her mom's shoulder a playful nudge.

"Fine. But tomorrow I'm candying and you are

on helping-couples-fall-in-love duty," her mom said.

"As long as it's not me, I'm all over it."

"I know falling in love is the last thing you want to think about right now. But I refuse to believe that's not something you want eventually. So whatever is keeping you from wanting it, you've gotta let it go, honey."

Penelope nodded, knowing it was pointless. For her it wasn't a what, but a who. And she'd let him go a long time ago.

Penelope was early to pick up Ella from school, but she'd needed to clear her head. All the talk about Noah and love that morning had her nerves buzzing. Despite the chill in the air, she stood halfway down the sidewalk, eyes closed with her face tipped up toward the sun, letting its warmth calm her.

"Penelope Dalton," someone said from behind her, more amusement than question.

A hand nudged her elbow, and she turned at the light pressure. Noah dropped his hand after a second too long. Her skin warmed beneath her thick cotton shirt as if the contact had been skin to skin. He had grown into his broad shoulders, and the former boyishness in his face had sharpened so the line of his jaw was hard even under the layer of stubble. His blond hair had darkened into something closer to caramel but still had the wild, messy look she'd once found endearing. The whisper of a smile tugged at the corners of his mouth.

Penelope's lips automatically twisted into a frown.

"Yep, definitely Penelope," he said with a short laugh.

He was nearly a foot taller than her so she spoke to his chest. "Hey, Noah," she managed past the tightness in her throat. She forced herself to look at his face again.

He let his murky hazel eyes roam over her, rubbing his knuckles back and forth on his jaw. "I wasn't expecting to run into you today."

"It wasn't really on my agenda either."

"Whoa, I didn't mean seeing you is a bad thing. It's just a surprise, that's all." He shrugged, but when he looked at her, his gaze held steady. "You look just the way I remember. Except the hair. Why'd you ditch the teal?"

She smoothed down the paisley head scarf hiding most of her dark-brown hair. "Teal hair wasn't exactly business-friendly around here." Not that anyone had really cared about her hair color. They were all more shocked that a good girl like Penelope, who always volunteered to help with town functions and planned to be a teacher after college, had ended up pregnant out of wedlock. And that she claimed the father was just some nameless guy she'd shared one careless night with.

"Depends on the business. The bartenders and servers in my brother's bar get away with all kinds of crazy shit."

"Yeah, well, I'm not exactly the bar type," she said.

Noah shoved his hands in the back pockets of his snug jeans. His lips parted just enough for breath to slip through. The silence built between them, pulsing in time with her rapid heartbeats. He watched the main door of the school over her shoulder. She resisted the urge to check her watch.

"How's Tucker doing?" Penelope asked after another few moments of strained silence. "I heard about his accident."

"He's one lucky bastard. Broken rib, broken leg, concussion. Beat the hell out of his bike too, but he's gonna be okay."

"That's good. I'm sure it's not fun right now, but it's good that he's got you to look after things for a while."

"No big deal. It's just what you do for family."

He'd only been back to Malarkey a handful of days since he left for college. Penelope wondered if he really meant that or if he just thought that's what she'd want to hear.

"How's your mom?" Noah asked. "Tucker said y'all opened some kind of crack-den-like chocolate shop that my niece is obsessed with."

"Crack den?" she asked. She clenched her

jaw to keep from calling him an asshole on elementary school grounds.

He shrugged, the leather on his well-worn jacket swishing with the movement. "Yeah, you know, because your chocolates are addictive or give you hallucinations or something. Maybe he just didn't explain it well."

She shook her head and cut her eyes toward the school entrance. She crossed her arms over her chest and dug her nails into her biceps.

"Let me try that again." He stepped around her so they faced each other. "What I meant was that I heard your chocolates are amazing and that people can't seem to get enough of them. Though I'm fairly certain that part about the hallucinations was true too."

If only he'd believed in the magic years ago.

The school-ending bell inside was tinny and faint from the distance, but it was enough to catch her attention.

While other kids raced down the sidewalk, rubber soles scraping on the concrete in their haste to get to their parents' cars, Ella stared at her mismatched shoelaces: one pink, one orange. A small smile played on her lips. She'd spent twenty minutes the night before swapping them out so they'd coordinate with the rainbow-colored tulle skirt and pink-and-white polka-dot shirt she wore today. Her palms traced the edge of the skirt from front to back on each side as she walked.

"It didn't get flat, Mama! Do you see? It's stayed poufy!" She twirled in a circle still primping the skirt. Her tongue poked through the hole left by a missing tooth in her bottom row when she grinned.

"I do see. And I'm betting it's a good thing you wore leggings underneath too so you could pull it up every time you sat down and not squish it."

"How did you know that's what I did?"

"I know you, sweetie."

"Holy shit. You have a kid," Noah said, his voice lazy but amused. "Tucker didn't tell me that."

Penelope cupped her hands over Ella's ears and held the girl in place. His gaze dropped to her lips and then down to her hands before whipping back up to meet her glare.

"Holy shit, could you not talk like that around my kid?" she mocked. "And, hello? We're waiting outside a school. Did you think I was just here for fun?"

"Mama! Be nice to him," Ella gasped, dragging Penelope's hands from her head. She narrowed her deep brown eyes at Noah, studying him with pouted lips. "Who are you?"

Noah pointed a long finger at his chest and raised an eyebrow at her. "Me? I'm a friend of your mom's."

"Friend?" Penelope asked.

Noah winked at Ella. Before he could respond

to Penelope, a girl ran down the sidewalk and launched herself at him. He caught her under her outstretched arms and hugged her. She wrapped her skinny legs around his waist and planted a noisy kiss on his cheek.

"Hey, Fish. How was school?" he asked.

The girl giggled and leaned back, her curly blond hair dancing in the air as she tipped upside down with Noah's hands clamped around her wrists. "Uncle Noah. It. Was. So. Long," she said.

His face softened when he grinned at her. Years of late nights working a bar and later nights spent drunk drained away, revealing the charming, quick-to-laugh boy she'd caught glimpses of in high school when no one had been around but Penelope. Her lips curved into a smile without her permission.

She pressed the back of her hand to her mouth, smudging the smooth red lipstick against her skin.

"I'll switch with you. You can go to work for me and I'll go to school for you. Deal?" Noah said.

"Can I go to work for her?" She turned her blue eyes to Penelope. Her smile was lopsided when she spread her lips wide. "She has the best job. In. The. World. Doesn't she, Ella?"

Ella's head jerked up when the girl said her name. Her mouth popped open in wonder as she nodded. Penelope's chest ached at how removed

Ella was from other kids. Like she was always surprised when they acknowledged her. Her tumor had kept her out of school and ballet class and every other normal kid activity for so long she barely knew anyone her own age. Penelope smoothed Ella's hair down, tickling her behind her ears to jolt her out of her shyness.

"The best," Ella said, her voice just above a whisper.

"I told you River was obsessed," Noah said. He swung River out and dropped her to her feet. He ruffled her hair, his deep rumbling laugh mixing with his niece's lighter one.

The sound twisted knots in Penelope's stomach. His laugh haunted her dreams, offering a life she was all too willing to succumb to in her sleep. She didn't want to think about what it meant that she had remembered it so precisely. She darted her eyes away when he caught her watching him and smiled at her.

Tipping her head back, Ella narrowed her eyes at him. She held her breath as she studied him. He raised an eyebrow at her, and she took it as an invitation to ask, "Why do you call her Fish?" Her voice was loud, sure.

Noah, face as serious as Ella's, looked her in the eyes. "Because when she was born I told her dad that River was a noun, not a name. That it was like naming her Fish. And she's been Fish ever since."

"Oh," Ella said.

"I like being Fish," River said to Ella. She turned to her uncle and tugged on his hand. "We could go with them to their shop and then I could be Chocolate Fish."

Penelope smiled at her despite the panic building in her chest at the prospect of spending more time with Noah. She needed time to regroup her thoughts. She wasn't ready to believe Noah was no longer the same jerk who'd showed up on her doorstep in the middle of the night—wasted—just to tell her the future she'd dreamed about them was a joke. That there was nothing in Malarkey worth sticking around for. She felt his eyes on her, like he knew he made her uncomfortable, like he'd always known she had to talk herself out of liking him. She stuck her hands in her vest pockets without meeting his gaze.

Just because he was adorable with his niece didn't mean he had changed. And it certainly didn't mean he deserved her and Ella.

"Not today, okay?" he said.

Penelope let out her breath. It clouded in front of her, a thin mist of white in the cold air. Noah chuckled beside her. She shook her head and turned her attention to Ella, who had yet to look away from Noah, as if the Earth's gravitational pull had shifted and now everything revolved around him instead of the sun.

The thought of Ella being sucked under his spell scared Penelope almost as much as the thought of losing her daughter altogether. Penelope might not have control over Ella's fate, but steering her clear of Noah was definitely something she could do.

5

Noah tried to ignore the fact that he'd had an actual conversation with Penelope Dalton that afternoon. But after he and River collapsed into a heap on the living-room floor from their impromptu dance party, he couldn't take it anymore.

Turning down the volume on the stereo, he said, "Hey, Fish. You know the girl we talked to after school? The one whose mom makes chocolate?"

"Yeah. Everybody knows Ella."

"Are you friends with her?" He rolled onto his back so his expression didn't give away how interested he was in her answer.

"Not really," River said. She twisted on the floor until she was perpendicular to him then plopped her head down on his stomach. "She doesn't come to school much and last year she lost all of her hair and she didn't even wear a hat to try and hide it. She just went around town bald like it was no big deal. But my mom said it *was* a big deal because it meant Ella was pretty sick. But everybody wished she'd get better at the Festival of Fate last year and now her hair's growing back and everything."

Poor kid had definitely gotten the crap end of the stick. Penelope too, for that matter. He wouldn't wish that kind of misery on his worst enemy. But at least Ella seemed to be on the mend.

"Hey, do you think her mom used some of her magic chocolates to make her better?" River asked.

"I'm pretty sure if she had chocolates that could cure whatever Ella had, everyone would know about it by now. That's not something you keep to yourself," he said.

River tilted her head back to look at him. "If anyone could do that, I bet Ella's mom could." Her voice held the kind of reverence normally reserved for rock stars or the Pope.

He wasn't surprised by that kind of adoration. The Penelope he'd known growing up was surrounded by this overwhelming sense of belonging. Everything about her—her genuine smile, her willingness to offer help before anyone even asked, the way she could be the quietest person in the room yet be the only one with anything real to say—had lured people in. She treated everyone like a friend, whether she knew them well or not. Though based on the cold shoulder she'd given him earlier that day, he didn't even rate that now. Not that he could blame her after the way he'd ended things between them. But admitting her hot chocolate was right about them having a future together meant giving up his ability to choose how his life would turn out. And true love or not, at eighteen it wasn't even close to a fair deal. "What about Ella's dad?"

"She doesn't have one."

Well, that was an interesting turn of events. After all this time, Penelope Dalton was still single. And there was someone else on the planet just as stupid as Noah had been. "Since when?"

Tucker clomped into the room, still incompetent at walking with his crutches. "Are you seriously pumping my kid for info on Penelope Dalton?" He jabbed Noah's ribs with the end of one crutch.

"Just making conversation," Noah said.

"All you need to know is that it's a bad idea, bro."

Tucker didn't even know the half of it.

Noah grabbed the crutch before it connected with his side again and grinned at his brother. "So's hitting me with this," he said, yanking the crutch out of Tucker's grasp. He let his brother flail for a few seconds as Tucker tried to regain his balance. Point made, Noah pushed up from the floor, propped his shoulder under his brother's arm, and lowered him down onto the sofa.

River continued her dance party solo.

Tucker hefted his cast onto the coffee table and dropped his head back on the cushions. "I know you carried a big effing torch for her before you moved away, but Penelope's been through a lot with her kid being sick and she doesn't need you trying to restart something that never had a chance to begin with just because you're in town for a while."

"That's not what I'm doing."

"No?" Tucker asked.

"No," Noah said.

Even if he'd wanted to pick things up with Penelope where they'd left off, he'd have a hell of a time convincing her to forgive him for leaving her—and the future she'd seen—behind.

The cold seeped through the cotton covers, making Penelope shiver. The temperature alone wouldn't have woken her, but the gentle pressure of a small, clammy hand on her shoulder jolted her eyes open before her mind was clear of the haze of sleep.

"Ella, are you okay? Are you feeling sick?" Her hands groped for the warm face in front of her, fingers gliding over soft, tangled hair and down to the flannel penguin-print nightgown.

"No. I'm okay. But it's snowing," Ella whispered. She slid her hand into Penelope's and tugged. "You're cold."

"Sorry," she said and rubbed her free hand over their joined ones. "Better?"

"Yeah."

"Good. Now you might want to get under the covers before the rest of you gets cold."

"Don't you want to see the snow?"

"I thought you were making that up so you could come sleep in bed with me." Penelope climbed across the mattress and followed Ella to the window. "We're only going to watch for ten minutes, okay? Then you need to get back in bed and go to sleep. Unless you've changed your mind about not missing any school."

"I haven't. Only ten minutes," Ella agreed.

Penelope had had the bench built a month after moving in, though she rarely used it as a reading nook like she had planned. It had become a late-night snuggle spot for her and Ella. Full moons, bad dreams, thunderstorms, snow—they both latched on to any excuse Ella could come up with to leave her boring backyard view, as she called it, and watch the night crawl by nestled together on the plush cushion.

Just one more thing to add to the list of what Penelope would miss most when Ella was gone.

She sat and tucked her legs under her. Ella stood over the floor vent so her nightgown filled up like a hot air balloon. Strands of her light-brown hair floated around her ears where the air shot out of her collar.

"Don't burn your feet."

Ella grinned at her and jumped from one foot to the other and back again.

Penelope rested her head on the window, and her breath fogged an oval on the glass. The flakes were translucent, only noticeable in the sphere of light from the streetlamp in front of the neighbor's house. It wasn't coming down heavily, just enough to leave a thin layer on the grass. She kept her arms wrapped around her middle to fend off the shivers that crept along her skin and leaned closer to the heating vent pumping straight into Ella's pajamas.

"Want me to warm you up?" Ella asked, pulling Penelope back from her thoughts. She wiggled her eyebrows up and down.

"I'd love it." Penelope caught her as she threw herself onto the bench and snuggled into Penelope's side. She wrapped her arms over Ella's and hugged.

"Do you think we'll see Noah again tomorrow after school?"

"What made you think of him?"

"You'll need someone to keep you warm when I'm not here anymore."

Penelope's eyes went instantly wet. She looked at the ceiling to keep the tears from welling up and spilling down her cheeks. She'd cried so much over the past year she half expected her tear ducts to give out at some point. It hadn't happened yet. She held her breath until she was sure her voice wouldn't shake when she responded. "You don't need to worry about me, sweetie. I've got a closet full of blankets. They'll keep me nice and toasty."

And she'd take mild hypothermia over Noah any day. At least she knew what she was in for with the cold.

"But blankets can't hug you when you're sad. I don't want to leave you all alone." Ella squeezed her arms tight around Penelope's waist. "So, will we see him?"

"I'm not sure." Definitely not if she could help it.

"I hope we do. I like him."

Could Ella somehow tell that he was a part of her? Not just in the way she laughed or charmed everyone she met with just one smile, but that she wouldn't exist without him even when neither of them knew the other existed? Penelope's heart beat out a panicked rhythm against Ella's cheek, but her daughter remained oblivious. "What in the world did you find to like about him in the five minutes you talked to him?"

"I don't know. I just like him." Ella turned her gaze up to meet Penelope's. Her thick dark lashes fluttered as her eyes grew wide. "Did you see him catch River and flip her upside down? I want someone to do that to me. Do you think it would be something good for my list?"

"I don't think you should put Noah on your list, sweetie. We're not really going to see him much, okay?"

Ella's lip jutted out in a pout. "Why not? He said you were friends."

"Yes, he did say that," Penelope said.

"We're friends with Megha, and she comes over for dinner every week."

It was clear she wouldn't be able to talk Ella out of liking Noah. Those feelings, for whatever strange reason, had taken hold of Ella instantly and completely. So she'd have to settle for logic and pray it worked. "That's different. Megha is practically family. I haven't seen Noah in years. So long ago, in fact, that you weren't even born yet. I don't expect that to change just because he's in town for a little while."

"Maybe he would come over if he knew we wanted to see him," Ella said. She scooted away from Penelope, pulled her legs up onto the cushion, and tucked her nightgown over her knees.

Penelope didn't miss her daughter's use of the plural. "Well, 'we' don't want to see him. That's all you. But you don't need to worry that River won't be your friend if her uncle and I aren't really friends."

"I'm not. I think I can make her like me. But he's special, Mama. Didn't you feel it? I want us to be friends with him."

"He's something all right," Penelope said under her breath.

It wasn't quiet enough.

"But he's ours. He's supposed to be with us, I know it," Ella said, not even a hint of doubt tainting the words. The stubborn set of her mouth and the twitch in her left eye matched the defiant expression Penelope had seen in the mirror too many times to count.

She took a deep breath to keep her next words calm and soothing. "No, Ella, he's not. He's just here to help River's dad while he's sick and then he's leaving. End of story. So please just forget about it, okay?"

"What if he wants to spend time with us while he's here?"

"He won't," Penelope said. She was mostly certain of that.

"But if he does, I can ask him about the upside-down thing, right? And then I can put it on the list and check it off all at the same time."

Penelope just nodded. They both knew there was no way she could say no to that.

Penelope woke up the next morning in a cold sweat from a dream she couldn't remember. She was only vaguely aware that it involved Noah. She rubbed her eyes, as if that would make the image disappear, and silently told her sub-conscious to lay the hell off.

As she stood at the kitchen sink an hour later slicing an apple for Ella's lunch, a trail of goose bumps crawled up her arms. She wouldn't let him do this to her again. Get under her skin and into her thoughts. It was a slippery slope from there to him working his way back into her heart. And he had no place there, no matter what Ella thought. She dumped the apple slices into a zip-top bag and the paring knife into the sink. Dropping to her elbows, she blew out a breath.

He'd only been back a handful of days and he was already driving her crazy. How was she supposed to last a few months?

Penelope flicked a stray seed into the sink where it landed with a soft *plink*. Then she reached for her coffee cup and took a sip. Over-sugared, it was almost too sweet to drink now that it had cooled to room temperature. Whatever the case, she'd have to find a way to tell him to stay away without making it seem like his presence was getting to her. That would just pique his interest and she'd have an even harder time avoiding him.

And there was still Ella's infatuation with him to contend with. Penelope would have to get a handle on that before it snowballed.

She pushed away from the counter and walked to the foot of the stairs. Music from Ella's alarm hummed just loud enough for her to know it was still going off twenty minutes after Ella should have gotten up. She rested her hand on the newel post, wiping away a thin layer of dust, and called, "Ella, if your cute little butt isn't in the kitchen in ten seconds I will drag you out of that bed by your toes."

"But it's cold," Ella whined back.

"I know it is."

If the drab light eking in through the tall, skinny windows flanking the front door was any indication, today would be the kind of spit-freezing day that would take most people the better part of a week to forget. Penelope shivered again and walked back to the kitchen.

Then she started counting.

By eight and a half, Ella was skidding on the tile floor in her sock feet like a champion skier, though she'd never stepped foot on the slopes. Learning to ski was on Ella's list, but the antiseizure medication she took daily messed with her balance. So skiing was a disaster waiting to happen. "That was close."

"Yes, it was," Penelope said, turning away so Ella wouldn't see her trying not to laugh.

"I thought maybe it would keep snowing." Ella's bottom lip jutted out as she scooted onto a stool at the island. "School would've closed and I could've gone to work with you and maybe River would've come in and I could've invited her for a sleepover."

"I thought you wanted to go to Grams's tonight?" Penelope asked. She poured milk over the bowl of oatmeal she'd prepped earlier, stuck it in the microwave, and set the timer.

"I do. River could come with me. And maybe if Grams gave us as many chocolate chip cookies as we wanted, River might want to be my friend. I even put River on my list, that's how much I want it to happen. And I'm gonna use my wish at the festival to make sure we'll be BFFs."

Her chest constricted at the hope in Ella's voice. This girl, who always seemed happy playing alone in her room, who had a constant smile despite the limitations her illness put on her life, who spent her free time sitting in front of the apothecary table just to see what new surprise it would give up, was lonely.

Penelope forced a smile and said, "Maybe next weekend. I'll call her mom and ask, okay?"

She would even put up with spending time around Noah if it meant making her daughter happy.

6

Any snow that had fallen the night before had either already melted or turned to gray slush on the side of the roads, but Penelope wore her sky-blue snow boots anyway. They were lined with thick magenta fleece, and Ella, who had a kid-sized pair to match, insisted they both wear them. The three inches of skin between the hem of her navy cotton skirt and the top of the boots tingled when she walked inside the shop. She shrugged out of her coat. Folding it, she set it on one of the empty work tables.

Her mom's gaze swept over the coat before focusing on Penelope. Her eyes were large and dark, dark brown. "You're here early."

"Not really," Penelope said. Though it had taken a week or so to get used to getting Ella to school before eight instead of going to the hospital three days a week for treatment.

She swapped out her boots for a pair of navy flats from her bag and donned an apron. The air in the shop was cool, as much to keep the chocolates from melting as to entice more customers to sit and enjoy a steaming mug of hot chocolate—either the dream-inducing kind they made or the

71

gourmet powdered stuff they bought in bulk.

"You look a little pale. Are you sure you're feeling all right?" Sabina asked in a thick voice that drawled out slower than usual.

"Yeah, I guess."

Sabina's laugh shook her shoulders and made her eyes crinkle at the corners. "That's a very noncommittal answer."

"Well, nothing's wrong. I just feel off."

"What's going on with you?"

"Ella and I had a rough night," Penelope said, not wanting to go over it all again.

Her mom finished rolling the truffle between her palms and set it on the silicone sheet. Her hands had a thin layer of chocolate coating them. "I'm going to need a little more than that, Penelope. You've been acting weird since yesterday."

"I'm fine. It's just—" She caught herself. How was she supposed to tell her mom that the magic had been wrong about her having a future with Noah? That she was a hypocrite for telling others to believe in a magic that had failed her? Or worse, that she was denying Ella her father?

She settled for a version of the truth. "We couldn't sleep. The house was really cold. I think I need to get the heat checked."

"This coming from the girl who plays in the snow in short-sleeve shirts and no gloves?"

That had only happened once in high school

when she and Megha experimented with a recipe for hot chocolate bonbons and it backfired, leaving them perfectly warm for days no matter the temperature outside. That was when Penelope had learned the consequences of tasting anything she made from the recipes the apothecary table gifted them. The magic was twice as potent and lasted considerably longer when they used it on themselves.

"I'm going to call your dad and see if he can fit you in between other patients today. You need to be checked out," Sabina said.

Penelope deflated at the mention of her dad, as if he was still alive. She turned and laid a hand on her mom's shoulder, digging her fingers in just hard enough to make her mom look up from the chocolates she was dusting with cocoa powder. "Mama, what did you eat?" The words almost sighed out of her.

Sabina smiled. Too wide, too happy. Too like someone who was living in a fantasy world instead of reality. "I might've tasted a few things as I was working. It's not a big deal."

"Are those the Bittersweet truffles?" The 75 percent dark cocoa truffles promoted happiness, and her mom's version of happy involved her dad still being alive. With as much stress as Penelope and her mom had been under since Ella's diagnosis, she could see how her mom might get distracted around the magic—or tempted by it.

"You can't do that, Mama. You know it messes with your head. How much have you had?" She let her hand fall.

"It was just a bite or two. Not enough for the chocolate to affect me. I can still work."

No, you can't. Not when you think Daddy is still alive. Who knows what you'll say to customers? Penelope cupped her mom's elbow and said, "Why don't you go take a break? You can sit on the settee and rest until we open. Sound good?"

Her mom moved with her, shuffling her feet as they walked out front. "I still think you need to let your father check you out. You know how he worries about you."

"I will. Later this afternoon," Penelope agreed. She kept her grip firm on her mom and eased her down onto the plush velvety seat by the front window. "I'll go finish the truffles. Do you want some water?"

Her mom's eyes fluttered closed as she laid her head back on the curved headrest at one end. She tucked her legs under her, fanning her long skirt over her knees so it grazed the floor. "Maybe just a sip," she said. She stretched her fingers out, groping for Penelope's. When she found them, she squeezed once, twice. "Don't tell your father you saw me like this."

"I won't," Penelope said and went back to the kitchen as the magic lulled her mom to sleep.

• • •

Most of the chocolates wore off within a few hours. But since her mom ate ones she had made, the effects could last infinitely longer. Penelope finished rolling the last two dozen truffles from the batch her mom had started. Then she made enough Enlightenment hot chocolate and spicy Corazón hot chocolate mixes to refill the depleted glass jars in the pantry.

Over the next hour, Penelope served customer after customer while Sabina slept off her magical overdose on the settee.

Penelope had always believed their magic helped people. That it gave them hope. She felt it like a current of electricity running beneath her skin. When she looked at her mom, that spark fizzled, leaving a trail of numbness along her arms. She rubbed them to coax some feeling back.

After the last customer in line left, with a half dozen espresso-filled Red Eye truffles to help him stay awake during his overnight rotations at the firehouse, she added a lemon wedge and lavender honey to a mug of hot water for her mom. But the settee was empty. And her mom was on the sidewalk out front talking with Noah.

Penelope set the cup on the table on her way out the door. They both turned and smiled.

"Noah was just telling me that his niece and Ella are friends. You might have been right about her going back to school. It's good she has a friend her age to play with. You two will have to get them together soon," her mom said.

Penelope shook her head before Sabina tried to play matchmaker for her and Noah. "Actually, Ella and I were talking about that this morning. I need to call River's mom and make plans."

"If you could set up a play date for Tucker at the same time as River, Layne would be eternally grateful," Noah said.

"It must be hard for him to get out of the house with a broken leg. Penelope's dad was in a bad car accident once. He broke all sorts of things, but I didn't mind having him around more. It was much better than the alternative," Sabina said.

Penelope would have preferred her mom's alternate version of history in which her dad had only been hurt in the crash instead of killed. But not even their magic could make that come true. Penelope rubbed her mom's back. "Mama," she cautioned, "maybe you should go lie down for a little longer."

Sabina looked between Penelope and Noah, her dilated eyes glinting with a hint of reality. "Okay. That's probably a good idea."

"I'll be right in." She watched through the window, waiting for her mom to settle onto the settee before turning her attention back to Noah. He was still looking over her shoulder, focusing on her mom.

"Is she okay?" he asked.

"She's not quite herself this morning, but she's fine." Or she would be once the chocolates wore off.

Noah shrugged. He settled his gaze on hers and stuffed his hands in his back pockets. "Hey, so I'm pretty sure one of my brother's customers has a thing for your mom."

"Marco?" she asked.

"Dr. Wiley? Pretty much the epitome of the Southern Gentleman, with impeccable taste in bourbon and women?"

"I can't vouch for his taste in alcohol, but the other descriptions are spot-on."

Since Ella had gotten sick, Marco had been coming into the shop at least twice a week, always when Sabina was working. He'd order two bourbon truffles and a black coffee to go, and then he'd linger at the door, a wistful smile lighting up his face as he wished her a good day. Sometimes Penelope had to prod her mom in the back to get her to notice him. And even then, Sabina only saw a longtime friend who liked his chocolate.

"How do *you* know he likes my mom?" she asked.

Noah grinned at her, enjoying that he was right. "He came in last night and we had a nice little chat about you and your mom. It was a full-on Dalton-girl lovefest. He said she was the most exquisite woman he'd ever seen and then something about how he'd been waiting for Ella to get better before asking your mom to go to dinner with him. He talked like landing a date with her was his Holy Grail or something."

Penelope sighed. How a woman who dealt in love on a daily basis could miss it when it was smiling right at her boggled her mind. "It probably seems like an impossible quest. She's not always attuned to the world around her."

"No," Noah said, shaking his head. He dragged a hand through his hair to wrangle the pieces that had fallen across his eyes. "I think it's more that he feels he needs to prove he's worthy of her love before he can actually have it."

"He'd be better off just asking her and not taking no for an answer."

"I'll be sure to pass that along next time he's in."

A little real-life romance had to be better than relying on the Bittersweet truffles to hold on to the love she'd lost. At least Penelope hoped her mom would see it that way if Marco ever got up the courage to ask her out. And with a little push from Noah, that might happen sooner rather than later.

She turned to see her mom watching them, and the smile Sabina sent Penelope—or possibly Noah—was purposeful, as if to say she approved of whatever was happening between the two.

Penelope tried to project the words *nothing is happening* directly into her mom's brain with one long stare. When Sabina looked away, Penelope allowed herself a small victory smile.

"Okay, so what's up with Ella?" Noah asked. "Dr. Wiley didn't really say much other than she'd been sick and is better now."

The whole town assumed that because Ella was back in school that the latest round of radiation had worked. And Penelope hadn't bothered to correct them. She caught enough flack about her decision from her mom. She didn't need the whole town telling her how to let her kid die. Because not dying wasn't an option anymore. The only say she had in the matter was whether or not Ella's final few months would be spent stuck in a hospital pretending the doctors could do something for her.

A sliver of guilt snuck in anyway.

It didn't matter that Noah didn't know Ella was his. That he didn't even care he and Penelope slept together in the first place. His daughter was dying, and a small part of Penelope thought he deserved to know.

She shoved the guilt down—even farther down than the feelings for Noah she'd never quite been able to rid herself of—and wrapped her fingers around the ends of her shirtsleeves, pulling the fabric into her clenched fists. "She's just had some issues with headaches," she said. Not a complete lie. "Nothing you need to worry about."

"Hey, no need to get all territorial. I just wanted to make sure she's okay. Just thinking about something serious happening to Fish makes me nauseous, so I can't imagine living through it."

Living through it wasn't the hard part. It was the living after it that made Penelope wish she could just go numb. She hadn't bothered to read the new recipe for curing heartbreak, but maybe the apothecary table had already given her a way to survive. "I hope you never find out."

"Me too," he said. He tapped his fingers to his chest right over his heart. "Your mom mentioned that you're kidless for the night. I'll be behind the bar at Rehab until closing. If you come by, I'll buy you a drink."

"Thanks, but I can't," she said, ignoring the way her stomach jumped in response. Noah had no place in her life, or Ella's, and she intended to keep it that way.

"It's an open-ended offer. At least while I'm in town. But maybe you'd rather sit at home drinking your magic hot chocolate and dreaming of your perfect guy."

A stab of residual heartbreak for the girl she'd once been pierced her chest. How stupid she'd been to believe Noah was her future. "I don't drink our hot chocolate anymore." She took a step toward the door and rested her hand on the knob. The cold metal bit at her skin. "And I certainly don't trust its judgment when it comes to who I'm supposed to love."

Noah dropped his head like her answer disappointed him. When he looked at her, all traces of the emotion had vanished. The muscles in his jaw tensed. "That's probably smart. I mean, you wouldn't want to fall for the wrong guy again. That would be bad for business."

"Just don't, Noah."

"Don't what?"

"Don't act like you know anything about me," Penelope said. She tightened her fingers around the doorknob. "Or like you care about what my chocolates can or can't do."

"C'mon, Penelope. I know you well enough to know that if you didn't believe in the magic of your chocolates you wouldn't be selling them or still using them at the Festival of Fate." He pointed to a festival banner bracketed to the lamppost a few feet away.

It read: YOUR FATE AWAITS.

Dozens of identical banners hung along the old brick streets of downtown in preparation for the festival a month away.

The festival had always been Penelope's favorite time of the year. One day when the whole town came together to celebrate their deepest desires for the future with frothy cups of hot chocolate and marshmallows toasting over the bonfire and enough laughter that the air rang with it for days after. But after the past year, Penelope knew one thing for certain. The Kismet hot chocolate was a lie. It didn't work.

She couldn't reveal that without telling everyone her daughter was dying. But could she continue to pretend the festival would change anyone's future? A sharp pang shot through her chest, and she swallowed hard to relieve some of the pressure. She just needed to get through a few more weeks without letting slip to anyone that the festival was nothing more than praying for things that would never come true. The future was set, and no amount of hot chocolate or wishing otherwise would change that.

"And it would be a waste of perfectly good magic to have it at your fingertips and not use it," he said.

Penelope cocked an eyebrow at him. "I didn't peg you as the believing-in-true-love type. Much less the believing-in-magic type."

"Guess I'm just full of surprises, huh?"

"You're full of something," she said. She ducked inside, letting the door shut between them.

If Noah had believed in love or magic back when they were younger—even if he'd just pretended to for Penelope's sake—they could have been a family. But he hadn't. And Penelope's interest in a do-over with Noah was right up there with getting frostbite on her fingers and scalding the taste buds off her tongue.

7

Her mom hadn't mentioned her dad in an hour, but Penelope continued to watch her out of the corner of her eye. Every time Sabina laughed a little too loudly at something a customer said or teared up when someone asked her for a love potion and she had to set them straight about the limitations of the chocolates' magic, Penelope knew the effects hadn't worn off yet.

And there was no way she could let Ella spend the night with her if she wasn't lucid, a fact that sent Ella to the pantry to pout not five minutes after getting to the shop after school. She sat cross-legged on the floor with her back to Penelope. Her small shoulders tensed whenever anyone tried to talk to her. After the third attempt, Ella jumped up and ran into the kitchen to stare at the apothecary table as if it could magically change Penelope's mind.

"I know you think I'm a little loopy right now," Sabina said, cutting squares of cellophane to wrap the caramels. The plastic crackled with each *snip snip snip* of the scissors. The top few on the pile trembled as she waved the scissors back and forth for emphasis, stirring up the air.

"But I wouldn't let anything happen to her."

Penelope sighed. "I know, Mama. But it's not good for her to see you like this. Not when I'm not around to temper it. She doesn't fully understand what's happening and I don't want her to be scared of what we do. I'm sorry." She set a caramel on one of the squares, tucked the sides in to cover the sticky candy, and twisted the ends to seal it.

"It's coming back. Reality. The memories. Part of me knows your dad isn't here. I feel it pressing in my head to get out but there's a part of me that's resisting still. That doesn't want to believe it. But I know what's real now. I just have to keep reminding myself of that until the magic dissipates. I didn't mean to worry you."

"I know. And I know it might've just been an accident, but if it wasn't—"

Sabina's shoulders went rigid. She stepped back, putting half a foot of space between them. "If I spelled myself on purpose, you mean?"

"Yes, if you did it on purpose. I can understand why you might want to. I miss him too. But if you think you might do it again, can you give me a heads-up before you do?"

Her mom plunked the scissors down on the counter. Her left eye twitched, causing her dark lashes to flutter. "It was an accident. But if I get it into my head that I want a few hours of happiness thinking the man I love is still with me, then, yes, I will tell you. And I might just stay home to keep you from looking at me like I'm crazy or damaged or both."

Penelope covered her mom's shaking hand with her own. "Ella's not the only one who gets scared when you're like this, you know. I'm always worried it will be permanent or you won't want to fight it off and we'll lose you. Promise me you'll be more careful."

Sabina brushed hair back from her face with her free hand, her bangle bracelets clinking out a soft melody. Then she let out a long, unsteady breath. "I will," she said.

"Thank you." Penelope watched her mom for a moment, looking for a sign that she meant it, and finding none. "Can I ask you something?"

Sabina nodded, her lips pressed together as if by not saying yes out loud she could take back her agreement if she didn't like the question.

"Why didn't you ever date again after Daddy died?"

She didn't hesitate to answer this time. "Because he was the love of my life. There was no replacing him."

"So you don't think you could have loved someone else?" Penelope asked.

"I had you to love. That was enough."

Penelope prayed it would still be enough after Ella was gone. If she lost her mom to the chocolates for good, she wasn't sure how she'd find the strength for her next breath, let alone the rest of her life.

Noah's words from earlier came rushing back to her. *Marco.* If he could make her mom happy, they had a chance of surviving this somewhat intact. "But what if there's someone else out there who would love you and make you happy? Don't you think he deserves a chance?"

"I won't say it is not a possibility, but when I fell in love with your dad, that was it for me. You'll understand that when you find the one you're supposed to love."

But Penelope knew all too well what being in love felt like. And if Noah was it for her, then she'd take her chances with loneliness.

They resumed their cutting and wrapping, letting the sounds of the shop fill their silence. Two of their regulars sipped cocoa and cackled at jokes told too quietly to reach the counter from the wingback chairs in the far corner. They came in once a week, one with her dyed red hair that verged on orange and the other with a pure white braid down to the middle of her back. The older women always drank the same thing, and Penelope had stopped herself on half a dozen occasions from asking what they dreamed about. The customers who wanted to share did. All the others, she tried to respect their privacy.

But it didn't stop her wondering.

She looked up when Ella raced out from the kitchen.

"Look, Mama!" Ella called, all traces of her anger obliterated by the excited smile plastered on her round face. "I found a necklace in the table."

A quarter-sized pendant twisted back and forth on a long brass chain as Ella held her hand up. One side was navy blue with white pinprick dots scattered across the enamel in some sort of pattern. The other was a glass-fronted compass. The compass points—red on one end, white on the other—didn't budge as the necklace spun.

Penelope let the necklace dangle against her outstretched palm. The dots on the back, she realized, formed the constellation of the zodiac sign Pisces. Ella's sign. "Very pretty. You found this in one of the drawers?"

"Yeah. The one in the very middle. I've never found anything in that one before. What does the other side do?" Ella leaned around her hand to flip the compass over.

The dial spun around twice before pointing the red end at Penelope. She jiggled her hand, but the dial stayed steady.

"It's how people used to tell direction. The piece in the middle that's stuck, it's supposed to point north, so the person using it can always find where they are and which way they need to go."

"I don't think this one does that."

"No, this one is broken," Penelope said.

Ella shook her head and rolled her eyes as if to say *you don't know anything*. "No, this one doesn't show that. See, it came with a note. It's supposed to help find love." She waved a yellowed scrap of paper in the air between them. Then she traced the word "love" with her finger and asked Penelope to read the whole thing.

Penelope examined the large, looping script that was too precise to be done by an eight-year-old. The paper was gritty and the words bled at the edges from old age. "When it is love you seek, keep this close to your heart and love will reveal itself," she read.

"So, it'll show me who loves me?" Ella asked.

"Maybe."

Why would the table give her this? She doesn't need a necklace to tell her who loves her. But their conversation about River from that morning flashed in her mind.

"And that spinny thing didn't move or anything until I brought it out here to you," Ella added when Penelope didn't confirm that the note was real.

"I guess that means I love you a whole lot then, huh?" Penelope asked. She dropped her hand and let the pendant rotate on the chain.

"Yep. And it means that I love you too. Even

if you won't let me go to Grams's tonight."

"If Grams is feeling better tomorrow, you can spend the whole day and night with her."

Closing a hand around the compass, Ella held it to her chest and took a deep breath, like she was making a wish on it. She bounced on her toes, her eyes wide with delight. "Maybe some hot chocolate would help her. I could make us all some." She took off across the room without waiting for an okay. Her quick footsteps shook the ceramic mugs in the cabinet.

"Make sure you use the plain powder," Penelope said.

"I know."

Penelope heard the eye roll, though she didn't see it.

When they were settled on the couch that backed up to the front wall of the pantry, Ella passed out their mugs with slow, measured steps and two hands wrapped around the bowl-shaped cups to keep the liquid from sloshing out. She had added a large dollop of the hand-whipped cream from the bowl and sprinkled them all with cinnamon powder.

Sitting in the spot Penelope and her mom left between them, Ella carefully clinked her cup to both of theirs and laughed when she took a sip and purposely got whipped cream on her nose. "C'mon, drink up, slowpokes," she said. "I put a surprise in the bottom."

"Is it a caramel?" Sabina asked, sniffing her hot chocolate.

"You'll just have to drink and see," Ella said.

Penelope and her mom smiled at each other over Ella's head and did as they were told.

8

When Penelope walked into her living room, Noah was asleep on her couch, hair mussed just enough that she wanted to run her hands through it. Ella's favorite blanket draped over his chest and stopped above his knees. His bare feet rested against the back cushion. She let her eyes drift to his mouth and wished that he was awake so he could smile his maddeningly sexy smile at her and erase all of her reasons for staying away from him with one desperate kiss.

She sank to the floor and pulled her knees into her chest. She sat there, just watching the rhythmic rise and fall of his breaths, trying to determine when in the hell she'd fallen for him. Then she noticed Ella's stuffed zebra tucked between his arm and his chest and questions like *when* and *how* went right out the window. The only one left was: *What am I going to do about it?*

Pushing up onto her knees, she brushed her fingers over his temple and along his scratchy jaw. He smelled like spicy chocolate and promises of forever. She leaned in to kiss him, knowing exactly where it would lead.

Penelope jerked awake as their lips touched.

She dug her knuckles into her chest to combat the pressure that didn't vanish with the dream. Her lips still tingled from the desire to kiss Noah. She pressed them together and stared at the ceiling.

She'd known from the first sip of her hot chocolate that Ella's surprise had been a spoonful of the spicy Corazón mix. By then, the magic was already in her system. She continued drinking it as much to make Ella happy as to prove to herself she wasn't scared of what it would reveal to her. The sweet cream and cinnamon had masked the scent of the ancho, cayenne, and chipotle peppers that made the drink truly hot. It tasted just as she remembered it. A subtle heat that gathered on the back of her tongue as the smoothness of the chocolate burned away.

When she closed her eyes again, she saw Noah. And something in her chest ached. She held her breath until her cheeks and lungs threatened to explode and the sensation finally passed. But she still saw him. Even when she opened her eyes to stare at the ceiling, he was there. The no-bullshitting, fast-car-driving dream boy who'd called her from a pay phone in the middle of a snowstorm just to tell her he was in love with her and the dangerous-smiled, zebra-cuddling dream man who looked at home asleep on her couch.

No. She would not think about him like that. Noah and "home" did not belong in the same sentence.

But if that was true, why had she dreamed about him a second time?

9

It took Penelope three days to fully shake the feeling that had settled over her after drinking the hot chocolate and dreaming of Noah. Ella had asked her every morning at breakfast if she'd dreamed about anything exciting, and each time Penelope told her "nothing exciting at all," because the possibility of Noah being her true love was just the opposite.

She'd lived happily without him for more than eight years. If they were supposed to be together—supposed to be in love with each other—wouldn't it have happened long before now? The fact that he came back to town right as Ella's life was getting cut short just proved to Penelope that their only connection was their daughter. And that made it easier to ignore the part of her that hoped she'd run into him again.

The dream had also convinced her that canceling the festival—and removing the false hope it gave the town—was the right choice. So Penelope had told Henry the evening before that she wouldn't be able to supply the hot chocolate for the festival this year. Then she hung up before he could ask for an explanation.

When the shop door flew open with a blast of cold air, she took her time looking up from the pile of gift boxes she was assembling.

Ruth Anne hustled to the front counter, her short legs working double time. The hat and gloves she peeled off slipped from her thick fingers to the floor in her haste. She didn't notice. Not even when she slapped her empty hands on the wood in front of Penelope and wheezed out a breath. Her dyed reddish-purple hair stuck up at all angles, teased by static electricity and probably a healthy amount of stress.

"You're not serious about canceling the festival, are you?" she asked.

Of course Ruth Anne already knew. She lived to be the bearer of news, good or bad. If she knew this, there would be no keeping it from the rest of the town for much longer. Now Penelope would either have to come clean and risk everyone trying to talk her out of it or derail Ruth Anne.

Stalling, Penelope collected the knitwear from the floor.

"Who told you that?" she asked when she returned to the counter, trying to keep her voice light, a little confused.

"I went to see the mayor about the never-ending road work over on Coal Mill that has traffic backed up for a good thirty minutes every morning as people try to get into work. And while I was waiting for him, I overheard him talking to Margarete about how you'd told him the festival was off this year. I was sure I'd heard him wrong because I just knew you couldn't be who he was talking about. Not after all the good the festival's done for the people of Malarkey. I didn't wait around for him to confirm it for me either, I just ran right over here to get it straight from the horse's mouth. I even forgot to ask him about the road reopening. That's how much of a hurry I was in."

"I'm sorry you rushed over here without talking to Henry. That traffic backs up right in front of your house, doesn't it? That must be frustrating when you want to get out of the driveway."

"Oh, it is quite frustrating. Some days I've parked my car half in the road to try and secure a way out and people just swing around it and block me in. And then Henry had the nerve to send a police officer over to tell me the next time *I* blocked traffic they'd have to give me a citation. Can you believe that?"

Mission accomplished. Now Penelope just had to keep Ruth Anne riled up long enough to get her out of the shop without realizing she'd left without a response about the festival. "That is awful. He should've come out himself and put up a 'Do Not Block Driveway' sign for you."

"Why didn't I think of that? He owes me that much." Ruth Anne clutched her hat in her fist and shook it at Penelope. "You'd think after a

96

few months of this ridiculousness people would know I have places to go and people to see."

And the news about the festival's cancelation to spread, Penelope thought.

"You've got to have one of the busiest social calendars of anyone in town," Penelope said.

Ruth Anne leaned forward, smiling at what she took as a compliment. "Not a day goes by that I'm not visiting one person or another for tea and a friendly chat or returning lost and found items to their rightful owners. I spend half my time running back and forth across town with every other person waving at me or hollering 'Hey, Ruth Anne.' I wonder what they'd do if I just let that traffic keep me shut up in my house for a day?"

"I hope we won't have to find out." Penelope grabbed the top box from the pile she'd been working on. "Why don't you take some of the dark chocolate toffee over to Henry to help sweeten him up a little? Maybe you'll be able to talk some sense into him that way."

"Maybe you could give me some of the mood-enhancing chocolates instead to really sway him to my side."

"You don't need to resort to that. I promise these will do the trick."

Penelope boxed up a half dozen rectangles of toffee, knowing Ruth Anne would eat one or two along with Henry. Then she rang up the sale and waved as Ruth Anne set off for the mayor's office.

"Wait a minute," Ruth Anne said halfway to the door. She threw her hand with the chocolates into the air and whirled back around. "I almost forgot. You never said whether or not you're not trying to put a stop to the festival. That would've been twice in one day I left a place without getting what I went in for."

Damn it. She was so close.

"Yes, I told Henry I didn't want to do the festival this year," Penelope said.

"Well, why on Earth would you do that?"

"Because it doesn't matter what any of us want out of life. It doesn't matter what future we write down and burn in the bonfire. Fate has already decided how things will turn out. And I think our time would be better spent focusing on things we have control over."

Ruth Anne smoothed a shaking hand over her wild hair and tugged the hat on so hard a small tear split the seam. "That is a very sad way to look at things, Penelope. Especially after so many people added an extra wish last year that Ella would get better. And whether her recovery was fate or some magical intervention caused by our collective happy thoughts, we may never know. So I for one will not be discounting the good the festival does. And you shouldn't either."

The truth about Ella's condition was on the

tip of her tongue. Words that would convince anyone that her feelings toward the festival were justified. That the Kismet hot chocolate didn't do what they'd always promised. But she couldn't let them out to ruin the little bit of normalcy Ella had laid claim to in the time she had left.

The restaurant Ella picked for dinner was next to Noah's bar. Even though Penelope was purposely ten minutes late so she didn't have to wait out front and risk running into him, she still beat her mom and Ella there. The entryway was jammed with people. She pushed her way through them, put her name on the waiting list, and shuffled back out in the cold.

The snow had stopped, but a few flurries still clung to awnings and windshields of parked cars. A gust of wind swept down the sidewalk, swirling thicker pockets of snow into half a dozen funnels before scattering it back to the ground. She jumped when a hand settled low on her back.

"Is your mom doing better?" Noah asked. He was close enough that his breath danced along her neck.

Penelope forced out a breath. The cloud of white in the cold air dissipated, but her nerves continued to hum under her skin. "Yes. Thankfully it didn't last as long this time," she said without turning around. She hated that she couldn't trust herself to be that close to him. That the desire she'd felt for him in the dream had lodged itself firmly in reality. She pulled her coat tighter so the collar hugged her prickling skin.

He stepped around so he was beside her, his hand fingering the wooden button on the cuff of her sleeve. "Will she remember that she thought your dad was still alive? Or will the magic wipe that from her memory too?"

"She'll remember."

"And you'll remember what it's like to see her as if nothing ever happened to him. Shit, that's gotta be hard."

"Every damn time."

Noah met her gaze. Despite their cool greenish-brown color, his eyes burned into hers until she looked away just to break the tension that hovered between them. "Are you meeting someone?" he asked after a moment.

She nodded and smiled when his jaw tightened. "Just my mom and Ella."

"Good."

"Good?" she asked.

The feelings she'd had for him in her dream came rushing back, all warm and tingly. *What if we are supposed to be together, him sleeping on my couch and me so stupidly in love I can't think straight?*

For a second, it didn't seem like the worst idea in the world.

"Yeah. Good, you know, that your mom's

okay enough to go out." He looked down at the sidewalk and rubbed his jaw.

"Oh, right."

His smile was slow, inching up a little higher on the left side, and hopeful. It sent a tingling sensation down to her toes. When he caught her staring at his lips, his grin deepened. She flicked her eyes away from him and they landed on the bar behind him. And it didn't matter that he was working instead of drinking, that he seemed genuinely worried about her mom, or that his smile could tie her stomach in knots if she wasn't paying attention. He was still the guy who'd run away from the life she'd offered him, and she'd be better off if she stopped forgetting it.

"Hey," Noah said, pointing down the street. "There are your dates now."

Ella skipped ahead of Sabina when she saw them, her snow boots clomping on the concrete. She didn't look as small and gangly all buttoned up in her puffy jacket. She waved to them, throwing off her rhythm and listing to the left. She caught herself on the trunk of one of the leafless maple trees lining the street. A dusting of snow rained down around her, making her giggle.

"Careful," Penelope called.

"I am," she yelled back.

Noah chuckled, a deep rumbling that rocked his shoulder against Penelope's. She took a purposeful step forward to break the contact. She caught another smile from the corner of her eye and held her breath until Ella reached them.

Wisps of hair had pulled loose from Ella's ponytail and fluttered around her face. She wiped them away with her mittened hand. "You're coming to dinner too?" she asked.

"No," they both said. Penelope's voice a little harsh, Noah's a little amused.

Ella pierced them both with her dark brown eyes before settling them on Noah. "Why not?"

"I'm working," he said.

"No, you're not. You're standing here talking to my mom."

He nodded to Sabina when she joined them before turning his attention back to Ella. "Well, I should be working. But maybe one night when I'm not we can have dinner. How about that?"

Penelope shook her head, an excuse hot on her lips. "I don't think—"

"Like a date?" Ella asked. She clasped her hands and held them to her chest.

"It's a little awkward to have a date with three people. But you and I can go on the date and your mom can be the third wheel," Noah said.

"What's a third wheel?"

Cocking her head, Penelope narrowed her eyes at Noah. "You're not taking my daughter out. Even as a joke."

"Jealous?" Noah whispered in her ear.

"Just explaining the situation so neither of you gets your hopes up," she said.

"I gave up on hoping a long time ago."

Something about the defeated way he said it made her believe him.

10

The next morning, hundreds of pieces of paper in varying sizes and colors covered the entire front of the shop—the windows, the door, the brick. Not one inch of surface was spared. Penelope should have expected something like this after her conversation with Ruth Anne. As a whole, the residents of Malarkey had a hard time letting go. The last time they had left notes to try and change someone's mind it had been to convince Eileen Morley not to sell the cafe and move to Atlanta to be closer to her son and grandkids. That hadn't worked since Zan bought the cafe not a week later and Eileen was gone within a month.

It wouldn't work on Penelope either.

She located the door's lock on the second try, underneath a piece of thick pink stationery with "SMALL NOTE. BIG THANK YOU" in letterpress across the top. She freed it from the others and scanned the dramatic handwriting that filled the small card: *Just a sampling of why we need the Festival of Fate.*

She walked inside without reading the rest. Slivers of sunlight eked between the edges of the collage into the shop, brightening the room enough for her to navigate to the light switch by the kitchen door. Flipping it on, she hated how artificial everything looked without the natural light flooding the space. The golds and browns of the wall paint came across as flat instead of the usual vibrant hues. Even the chocolates in the case lacked their typical sheen. She dumped her purse and the card on the counter and headed back out front to remove the rest.

For every one she removed, it seemed like two more took its place. It would've been impressive how many people Ruth Anne corralled into helping in less than twenty-four hours if they weren't all in direct opposition to Penelope. She'd known the decision wouldn't go over well. With anyone. But she'd hoped to find at least a few people who agreed with her.

"Man, you sure know how to unite a community over a common cause," Megha said from behind her.

She turned just as her friend stepped out of the street and onto the sidewalk next to her. Reinforcements. That was so much better than Ruth Anne or Henry or one of the nameless other people who had offered up a reason not to cancel the festival. "It's a gift," she said.

"Want some help?"

"Do you really have to ask?" Penelope grabbed at the notes with both hands and ripped four or five free of the door all at once.

Megha pinched the edges of one and peeled the tape from the glass in slow-motion. Then she folded the tape onto the back of the paper, preserving the integrity of the note. "You should at least read them. A couple of them really make you want to believe in fate."

She stared at her friend a moment, trying to decide if she'd heard her right. Megha always laughed at the idea of fate. And Penelope seriously doubted anything written here would change her mind. "When did you read them?"

"Last night. Another blind-date bust, by the way. But everyone in the bar was all worked up about you wanting to cancel the festival. So I came to check them out after I politely faked an emergency. If anyone asks, we found your keys in the freezer."

"Freezer. Got it. And happy I could be your alibi. Sorry it was a dud."

Megha held the notes in her hand, careful not to crease them. "You'd think I would've learned by now. But every time my mother calls, I can't say no."

"She just wants you to find the love of your life. No pressure," Penelope said.

"Speaking of, Noah added a note too. It's over there. The one on the cocktail napkin. It's about you, in case you're wondering."

"I'm not," she said.

She was.

It took more effort than she'd expected not to look for it. She pulled another few down and added them to the stack she'd stuffed in the gold mailbox affixed to the brick. "Did you get up early just to make sure I saw it?"

"Not just his note. I mean someone had to stop you from going all Grinch on the town and taking away our beloved festival." Megha clutched a handful of notes to her heart and chuckled when Penelope glared at her. "Like I said, some of these are damn convincing. It even has me wanting the festival to happen this year."

"I'm pretty sure that's the whole point." Penelope leaned back against the window, the remaining notes fluttering against her jacket as if trying to get her to save them from being ripped away by the wind. "All of this," she said, holding up the handful of paper she'd collected, "is out of my control. And I can't pretend everything's going to turn out okay when I know that's not always the case."

"Maybe not always, but all of these notes, they're the times that it went right. Like this one that says, 'I made the same prediction at every festival for twenty-three years. That I would become a doctor. That wasn't something women did back then and everyone said I was wasting my wish, but I knew it was what I was meant to do. And I did.' And this one. 'I made a promise to myself at the festival last year that I would

107

tell my parents I'm gay. When I did, my mom said she'd been waiting for me to admit it so she could set me up with this guy she met at her yoga class. We have our first date next week.' "

She took them from Megha without responding. There was nothing she could say.

Megha continued. "Or this one," she said, removing Noah's cocktail napkin from the window. " 'At my last Festival of Fate, the only thing I wanted to happen in my future was to kiss Penelope Dalton.' "

He'd done that. And more. But for him to claim it was because of fate was a lie. Not to mention downright insulting.

She snatched one side of the napkin. A jagged line ripped through the middle of the confession when Megha didn't release it. "Was that supposed to convince me to help with the festival?"

"Do you know how many girls we went to school with would have killed for Noah to say that about them?" Megha gave an exasperated sigh when Penelope shrugged. "Okay, fine. How about this one? 'Last year Ella Dalton had a brain tumor and'— Shit." She dropped her hand, letting the note drift from her grip.

"And the festival didn't heal her," Penelope said.

Megha was one of two people outside the family who knew Ella was still sick. She wouldn't keep trying to convince Penelope to support the festival that had failed Ella any more than she would spill the secret she was keeping.

By the time her mom arrived at the shop, Penelope had stashed all of the notes in the filing cabinet in the small office she used to keep up the business end of things. She hadn't been able to throw them away, though that had been the logical choice. The words—the futures that had come true after the Festival of Fate—couldn't get under her skin if they were dismissed as nothing more than garbage.

But they weren't garbage. They were the truths of people's lives. And she couldn't ignore that no matter how much she wanted to.

She still hadn't told her mom about her decision to cut the hot chocolate from the festival. The longer she put it off, the less she believed Sabina would agree with her. They spent too much time at odds already, arguing over what was best for Ella, and the thought of adding another issue to their list made her chest so tight she had to step outside and gulp in lungfuls of cold, biting air.

Penelope stayed outside just long enough to clear her head and drive the worst of the worry away. Then she slipped back inside and locked the door behind her, not yet ready to deal with her neighbors' stories face-to-face.

Sabina watched her with narrowed eyes as Penelope entered the kitchen. "Do you know why the table would have given me these? They're in every drawer and more appear every time I reopen one," she said.

Penelope looked up and there in her mom's small hands were the notes she'd hidden away. Or copies of them anyway, re-created by the apothecary table's magic to show that it sided with the town and not her. She clenched her hands into fists despite the burning sensation that prickled her skin as feeling returned to her fingers. "Because it hates me."

"It's a table, honey. It can't hate you."

"It can. And it does. First it gave me that recipe for curing heartbreak, as if it already knows I won't be strong enough to survive losing Ella. And now it's giving you all of those damn notes so that you can lead the tar-and-feathering mob against me."

Sabina's only show of surprise was her eyes widening into pools of brown as dark as the chocolate she worked with. "You don't know that the recipe is because of Ella." She thumbed through the papers as if expecting to find Penelope's heartbreak cure among them so she could prove her point.

"Yes, I do, Mama. You would too if you stopped living in a fantasy world where bad things don't happen to good people. I hate it as much as you do, but she's dying and we can't save her."

Penelope had thought saying those words would get easier, but every time was as painful as the first. Like reopening a wound before it fully healed. She turned away from her mom and lifted the pan of marshmallows she'd left to set from the baking rack.

"She's not gone yet," Sabina said. "So maybe the recipe cures heartbreak by stopping it before it ever happens."

Flipping over the tray, Penelope slammed it down on the table with more force than was necessary to remove the large block of marsh-mallow. The resulting crash of metal on metal made Sabina jump. Penelope set the empty pan aside and dusted the tops with powdered sugar from a sieve.

It would be so easy to let herself get sucked into her mom's optimism. To ignore reality and pretend everything would be okay. But blinding herself with false hope wouldn't change any-thing. It would just take up precious time and keep Ella from accomplishing everything on her list. So Penelope would have to make the hard decision for all of them.

"It doesn't matter," she said. She kept her eyes focused on the slab of white in front of her to keep her mom from seeing the lie in her eyes. "I don't have it anymore."

Sabina crossed the room and stopped in front of the table where Penelope worked. "What did you do with it?"

"I threw it away." The lie came out smoother than she expected. Her voice wavered only slightly. "You can throw those away too." She motioned to the papers her mom still held.

"What are they?" Sabina shook them at Penelope, the pages flapping and rustling against each other with every quick back-and-forth.

"They're an attempt to convince me the Festival of Fate is something we should keep doing. But it doesn't matter what the notes say. Or what you say. The festival is a lie and putting a stop to it is the right thing to do, even if no one else believes me."

"The festival is not yours to cancel, honey."

Penelope matched her mom's hard look of disapproval with one of her own. "All of the people who left me notes this morning seem to think it is."

"If you don't want to be involved with it any longer, no one can make you. But you cannot stop others from celebrating their futures just because you don't like what is in yours."

"This isn't about me," she said.

But as she sliced the marshmallows into cubes, Penelope couldn't tell if that was the truth or another lie.

11

After years of tending bar in Charlotte, Noah couldn't quite adjust to how desolate Malarkey became on weeknights after 11:00 p.m. By this time of night back home, most people had barely gotten their nights started. And even long after last call when he crawled into bed in his downtown apartment, the streets outside never stopped whispering.

Here, everyone was shut up tight in their houses, lights out, pretending the outside world didn't exist.

The upside was speed limits didn't matter as much when there was no one else on the road.

The fastest he'd gotten from the bar to Tucker's house was six and a half minutes. Tonight he was shooting for five flat. Just to see if he could.

He rounded the corner leading out of downtown and revved the engine with a quick twist of his hand, his Ducati tilting so close to the ground he half-expected his knee to scrape asphalt. Running into Penelope a handful of times had provided the bulk of his excitement since being back in town, and if he didn't do something to keep his heart rate up, he ran the risk of turning into one of the sleepers in the houses he passed.

His brother managed to make it look not so bad. But he'd gotten the girl and had the best kid on the planet, neither of which Noah had.

Don't even think it. He whipped his gaze back to the road in front of him and swore at the woman walking down the middle of the lane. He swerved and somehow managed to keep control of the bike. The tires screeched, rivaling the deep growl of the engine as he jerked to a stop.

She studied him with a guarded expression so like her daughter's he felt compelled to try and win her over.

Hopping off the bike, Noah walked to her, adrenaline sending his thoughts a dozen different ways at once. But they all spiked from the same source: he'd almost taken out Penelope's mom.

"Mrs. Dalton?"

She blinked at him, her eyes dilated and unfocused. "Do I know you?"

He stopped a foot away to keep from scaring her more than he already had. "I'm a friend of Penelope's. Noah Gregory."

"Oh, yes. I recognize you now."

"Are you okay? You look a little . . . cold." What she really looked like was lost. Stuck in the past without a clue that she was walking the streets in thirty-something degrees in nothing more than a cotton nightgown and robe.

She tightened the cords of the robe at her waist.

"I guess it is a little chillier out than we—than I—thought."

"Should I call Penelope?" Noah asked, his fingers already pulling his phone from the pocket of his motorcycle jacket.

"No, no," she said. She blinked at him a few more times. "I'm okay. Just a little turned around is all."

"Okay. Well, how about I call Dr. Wiley instead? I can take you home and have him meet us there."

"Marco is—*was*—my Ollie's best friend and partner. A sweet, sweet man. Neither of them should have to see me like this. Do you really need to call someone?"

Not sure if she meant Marco and Penelope or Marco and her dead husband, Noah said, "For one, I'd feel better if you got checked out. You know, just to make sure everything's okay. And two, if you want to keep this from Penelope, it might be best to keep your husband out of it too. You know he'd have to tell her and then they'd both drive you nuts with worrying."

Sabina patted his arm. "You're nice. She gets mad when I'm like this and tries to pull me back to reality before I'm ready. Before the chocolates have worn off."

"So you know what you did? That not everything you're seeing or feeling is real?" At least he wouldn't have to explain why her husband

and daughter weren't at home when he finally convinced her to let him walk her there.

"The chocolates don't last as long as they once did. Or maybe my body is just too used to them now. So, yes, I know. It's easier to pretend the magic is still working when it's just me in here." She tapped a finger to her temple. "But I'll be okay. No need for you to go out of your way."

"It's not out of my way." He'd already missed his shot at beating five minutes anyway. And there was no way he could just leave her to get home on her own when her brain was at least partially trapped in another decade. "And I still want to get Dr. Wiley to check you out. It's that or I'm calling your daughter." He held up his phone, though he didn't have Penelope's number, hoping she didn't call his bluff.

"Are you trying to get me in trouble?"

"No, ma'am."

"But you're not letting this go, are you?"

Noah shrugged out of his coat and draped it over her shoulders. With all of the internal armor and padding, it had to weigh a quarter what she did, but at least it would keep her warm. Wrapping her fingers around it, she hitched it up off her shoulders then burrowed into it.

" 'Fraid not. 'Cause to be honest, I'd rather face your wrath than your daughter's. I've been on the receiving end of it once and I still have scars."

"She puts up with a lot more than most before

it gets the better of her," Sabina said. Narrowing her eyes at him, she continued, "You must have tried extra hard to make her mad."

"I was young and stupid. Really, really stupid."

"So you know what's waiting for me if you call her."

"Dr. Wiley it is." Thankfully Layne had programmed the doctor's number into his phone for emergencies.

The doctor didn't even ask for an explanation before he agreed to be there in ten minutes. Not that Noah could blame the guy. Having a thing for one of the Dalton girls tended to block out rational thought.

With his bike in neutral, he rolled it the five blocks to Sabina's house and parked it on the street. The lights burned inside the house, as if she'd simply walked out in the middle of doing something. They sat in the living room where framed photos of Penelope and Ella were displayed on every surface. It was like watching the kid grow up right in front of him. He could tell approximately when Ella had gotten sick by the way Penelope's smile no longer seemed effortless. The kid, however, grinned in every shot, eyes focused and bright.

"You don't need to stay with me. I'm all right," Sabina said.

Noah leaned forward, dropping his elbows to his knees. He looked over at her and smiled.

"First Penelope. Now you. Wanting to get rid of me must be hereditary."

"I remember you. From when you were younger. Always looking for something high to jump off of and anything with enough speed to give your mama a heart attack. But you slowed down around my daughter, like maybe you'd found what you'd been chasing after all your life. Then you went and broke her heart. You don't know how lucky you were that the apothecary table never gave me a recipe to curse you for that. But if you hadn't run off the way you did, Penelope wouldn't have gone looking for someone to take your place and Ella wouldn't be here. So I guess I should thank you."

"I don't know what to say to that."

She reached over and patted his arm with a clammy hand. "That's okay. I just wanted you to know that you shouldn't let Penelope chase you off if you're looking to come home. She's been happy without you whether she'll admit it to you or not."

Of course Penelope had been happy without him. He'd be an idiot if he had thought otherwise.

Marco came in a few minutes later without knocking. His familiarity with the house and its occupant was evident.

Crouching in front of Sabina, he took her hands. "How far away are you tonight?"

"Not very," she said. "Not anymore."

"Do you want to tell me what happened?"

Sabina pulled her hands free and waved them in the air as she spoke. "Everyone's all up in arms about the festival and Penelope refuses to believe that the Kismet hot chocolate works anymore. All she sees is that Ella's still so sick. And if the magic didn't fix her future, why would it change anyone else's?"

The magic must have had more of a hold over her than they both thought if she didn't remember Ella had been cured. Why anyone would purposely put themselves through the emotional wringer like that made no damn sense to Noah. "Ella's not sick anymore," he said.

"And how was this going to fix it?" Marco asked as if Noah hadn't spoken. Somehow he managed to keep his frustration out of his voice. Or maybe this was so commonplace he didn't get frustrated with Sabina anymore. Marco stood and slipped his hands into his pants pockets.

"I thought maybe—" She turned her wide, sad eyes to Marco, the apology plain on her face. "I thought maybe Ollie would know how to change her mind. He always understood how to get through to her when she was being stubborn."

"You know Penelope will only change her mind if she wants to. We can put the truth right in front of her face, but until she's ready to see it, it will be as if it doesn't exist."

And Noah wondered what truth Penelope

119

would see if she bothered to look at him long enough.

Penelope kept her gaze on the ground a few feet ahead of her. If she didn't make eye contact with anyone, she might make it through the walk back from school with Ella without incident.

They got as far as the park.

"Fancy meeting you here," Noah said.

River snapped her head up, forehead scrunched as she narrowed her eyes at him. Her cheeks were already pink from the cold. "No, it's not. We've been waiting for them."

Anyone else in town would have stopped Penelope to plead their case for continuing the festival. But not Noah. Despite what he'd said on the cocktail napkin he'd left on her shop's window, he didn't believe in fate or the magic of the festival. Whatever he wanted from her now had nothing to do with that.

Penelope didn't know if that was better or worse.

"First rule of being a good sidekick, never reveal our secret plans to anyone. But especially not the people we hope to involve in said plans." He glanced at Penelope, his eyes bright with amusement. Then he hooked an arm around his niece's shoulders and leaned over so only a few inches separated their faces. "Rule number two, always have a backup plan. In this case, Fish, that means running off to play with Ella while I distract her mom."

Ella at least hesitated, eyes veering to Penelope for a fraction of a second before latching on to River's hand and racing away.

"You could've just said hi to us at school and avoided all of the secret planning to begin with," Penelope said, her attention on the girls instead of Noah.

"Yeah, but I didn't want it to *seem* like I was trying to get you to talk to me. You haven't exactly been happy to see me the last few times I've tried."

Did he have selective amnesia about their past or was Noah really just so arrogant that he thought she'd still be hung up on him despite how he'd left things between them? She cut her eyes back to him. He wouldn't charm her so easily this go-round. "And lying in wait at the park for us to walk by is supposed to help how?"

Noah dragged a hand through his shaggy hair, his fingers catching in places where the wind had tangled it. "Well, if Fish had played it cool, it would've seemed less like an ambush and then maybe you wouldn't mind hanging out with me while the girls played." His hand fisted at the back of his head to keep his hair in place. When he looked down at Penelope, the playfulness of a moment before had vanished and in its place was a pinched expression Penelope couldn't read.

121

"Seriously, though, I don't know how to tell Fish that I'm the reason Ella can't play with her after school."

"Why wouldn't I let the girls play together?"

"Because I'm here. Thought that part was clear."

Penelope turned away from him to find Ella and River skipping across the park hand in hand. Their laughter was just a hint of sound in the air. But it was enough to remind Penelope that nothing came above her daughter's happiness.

"It's a small town, Noah. Avoiding each other would be impossible even without River and Ella in the mix. And I really don't want to spend the next few months dreading our inevitable run-ins because life is too short to be angry and stressed out over things that I can't control."

"Which means what exactly?" he asked.

"I can't promise I'll be happy to see you, but I'll do a better job of pretending. At least when the girls are around."

Noah crossed his arms over his chest and looked down at her. A hunk of hair fell across his eyes. "That's the best I'm gonna get then, huh?"

"For now," she said, softening her voice to take some of the sting out of her words. Then she added, "See, I'm trying already."

"So, what? We just talk like we're friends?"

What was she getting herself into? Penelope shifted her weight from one leg to the other and said, "Friends know things about each other. We're practically strangers."

"Would a stranger know that the night before your eighteenth birthday you drove down to Asheville to go to the Snow Patrol concert and then had to sweet-talk the manager to let you in because you weren't technically old enough yet?" he asked.

The concert had been one of their first dates. Penelope had been up front with the bouncer at the club, pointing out her birthdate and swearing she'd be eighteen at midnight. She had even offered up her mom's number for the manager to call and confirm she wasn't lying. But in the end, she hadn't been the one to get the manager to draw a large X on each of her hands in black permanent marker and allow her to go inside.

"It wasn't so much my sweet-talking as you slipping him some money when you thought I wasn't looking," she said. Penelope still had the ticket stub tucked into one of the ring slots of her jewelry box. She couldn't bring herself to throw it away, even after Noah was gone.

"You weren't supposed to know about that," he said.

"Well, I do."

Noah smiled at her. "And you were trying to say we don't know anything about each other anymore."

"That was a long time ago, Noah. I'm not the same person I used to be."

"Neither am I." He dropped his arms and stepped closer to her. "I know I screwed up and I'm—"

"No." Penelope held up a hand, fingers stopping inches from Noah's chest. He did not get to do this now. Not when Ella's diagnosis had pushed Penelope so close to breaking already. "If you want this truce to work, don't apologize. Don't try to explain why you did what you did. I don't want to know."

"But I am sorry, Penelope." His voice was thick with the truth of it.

"I don't care," she said.

She couldn't let herself. Because letting go of her anger toward Noah would leave too much room for the heartache to take over.

12

Snow always brought people into the shop. Even with their gloved hands, scarfed necks, and thick wool coats, they still wanted to be warmer. So they'd buy a large hot chocolate and sit by the fire reading or talking with friends or they'd eat a Dragon's Breath truffle for a few hours of warmth before heading back out into the cold.

Penelope was tempted to sneak a truffle herself as another gust of wind whipped in through the opening door. But without knowing if she or her mom had made that batch, she wasn't willing to risk it. She pulled a cardigan on over her apron and held on to cups for an extra second or two after she'd added the steamed milk before scooting them across the counter.

When she hit a lull just before noon, she brewed a hot cup of lavender honey tea and started working her way through the list of inventory that needed replenishing. She held her breath when she stirred the ground peppers into the dark chocolate cocoa mix, as if just smelling it would cause her to dream of Noah again. The steady flow of customers and the slow dusting of snow had made it easier to stay focused.

But her mental slipup seemed to be enough for the universe to take notice. Noah's sister-in-law, Layne, hesitated outside the front door, looking over her shoulder as if embarrassed to be seen entering the store. Penelope wiped her hands on her apron and headed back out front just as the door swung closed. Layne shook snow off her coat and tucked a damp strand of her sandy-blond hair behind her ear. Her peacock-green corduroy pants unapologetically played up her curves as she made her way to the counter. She tossed out a few timid smiles to people as she passed the couches.

At least it's not him. With his stupid smile and stupid laugh and stupid, perfect hair.

Penelope pinched her eyes shut to block the image of Noah. Forcing a smile, she looked up and said, "Is it getting worse out there?"

"Oh, uh, not really. The snow doesn't seem to be sticking," Layne said. She tugged on her scarf so it hung loose around her neck and checked the sidewalk again. "But apparently it's enough to send everyone out for a drink of one kind or another. The bar just opened, and it's already packed."

"Yeah, I guess everyone's looking for some kind of escape today."

Layne shrugged and drummed her fingers on the counter in time to the Weepies song drifting from the speakers behind the counter. Her long

126

lashes fluttered as she looked around the room, careful not to land on anyone too long.

Penelope hooked her thumbs in the apron pockets and asked, "Is there something I can get you?"

"It smells amazing in here. I can see why my daughter likes this place so much. My husband always brings her in 'cause I thought the magic was just a gimmick, you know. Something to boost sales and give the shop an air of intrigue. And to be honest, I thought you and your mom were kooks for believing in it." Layne picked at her bottom lip with her electric-blue thumbnail. "I'm so sorry. That's not at all what I wanted to say when I came in here."

"It's okay. I'm used to weird looks for what we do here," Penelope said, trying not to let too much of her irritation leak into her voice. She looked at Layne, with her jittery fingers that tapped against her lips and their inability to keep the words in. "And the magic is real. At least for the people who believe in it. The ones that don't either chalk it up to a strange reaction to coincidence or are so closed off that the magic can't even touch them."

"God, that must be the absolute worst. Like being a Muggle in a Harry Potter world. Except I guess they wouldn't even know to be sad about it. I hope I'm not one of them." Her laugh trailed off a second after it started. She pressed her fingers to her mouth again as her eyes went wide. "Crap, what if I am? What if because this is my first time here the magic knows I'm a skeptic and I feel nothing?"

Penelope laughed. "There's only one way to find out. Well, technically we have half a dozen candies and a few hot chocolates that would do the trick. So, you get to pick your poison, so to speak."

"So to speak," Layne echoed. But she smiled at Penelope, one eyebrow lifting in amusement. The first real smile she'd given since entering the shop. "Do you have anything that can make me act like less of a crazy person around new people? I think I'd like to give that a try." Her laugh erased the last trace of skepticism.

"How about a jasmine tea caramel that will calm nerves? It's a little more subtle than the others but lasts longer. Maybe three to four hours instead of only two."

"I can probably handle that. And I'm sure I need it. Tucker, God love him, is not a good sit-around-and-do-nothing kind of guy. He's about to drive me up a wall."

Pulling three caramels from the refrigerated glass case, Penelope handed one to Layne and set the other two in a clear gift bag. "Save these for when you really need them." She waved away Layne's money. "Consider it a trade. I was supposed to call you and set up a play date with the girls. Do you think River would be up for that?"

Layne bit into her candy and closed her eyes as she chewed and swallowed. "Um, yeah, I think that would be great. We just can't do it here. River and I might never leave." She paused. "Holy wow, that was good."

"I'm glad you liked it."

"Like is an understatement. I would fight Noah to be the one who gets to bring River in if I thought she would let me. But Uncle Noah is much cooler than me, so while he's here, he gets all the attention."

"The novelty might wear off if he decided not to leave," Penelope said, letting a little snark tinge her words.

Layne either ignored the tone on purpose or missed it altogether. "It'd be nice to have him around more. Maybe not in my house all the time, but in town, in the bar. He wouldn't have to miss out on all the birthdays and holidays and weekend cookouts. And he'd see that life in Malarkey is actually pretty great and he could make it home again. Then maybe he'd want to settle down and start a family of his own."

Despite her desire for Noah to get out of town as quickly as possible, Penelope's skin warmed as she remembered the dream kiss. Part of her—a part that was bigger than she realized—wanted the chance to find out what it felt like in real life. Then the image of her mom, lost in the past and more than a little broken, flashed into her mind. If Noah hadn't blown her off after she'd given him both her heart and her body, everything would be different. If she'd had the sense not to believe the chocolates in the first place.

But she couldn't let herself forget it wasn't just her heart on the line this time.

"I'm guessing Noah doesn't know you're here trying to talk me into dating him?"

"Crap. That's not what I'm doing. I just meant some girl, any girl, not you. He would probably skip town immediately if he thought I was over here trying to find him a girl so he'd decide to move back for good. So could you maybe not mention this to him?"

"If only I had a chocolate that could let you time travel and you could erase this whole conversation." Penelope smiled.

Layne tightened her scarf, adjusting the two ends that dangled on either side of her collarbone until they were even. "Yeah, but then we wouldn't have talked and I think I might regret that. I kinda like you."

"I kinda like you too," Penelope said. She laughed when Layne hid half of her face behind her hand, the tops of her cheeks turning pink at hearing her not-quite-a-compliment repeated back.

Why did she have to be Noah's sister-in-law? Becoming friends with Layne was the exact opposite of staying away from Noah. But damn if she didn't want to.

13

Noah clenched his jaw as the craving for a cigarette ate away at his composure. He'd gone eight days without one, and the only thing that kept him from bumming one now was the promise he'd made to River on his first night back in town when she'd caught him on the back porch and yanked the lit cigarette from his hand. She'd looked him right in the eye and said, "You don't smoke anymore, okay, Uncle Noah?" He might've handled the cold-turkey shit better if he had another outlet for stress, but the universe seemed to enjoy screwing with him and offered no reprieve.

He hauled a steaming basket of pint glasses from the kitchen out to the bar. The heat nipped at his fingers as he unloaded them onto the shelf, but he barely registered it. His fingertips were all but numb after so many years handling just-from-the-washer drinkware. With his brother set up at the bar, he could probably manage to slip out for a few minutes. To go see Penelope. Check on her mom. But every time he thought they'd finally hit a lull, another group of people shuffled inside, shaking off snow and chaining him to the bar for another half hour.

"I forgot how crazy snow makes people around here," he said to Tucker. "Is it gonna be like this all day?"

Tucker shoved the blunt end of a fork wrapped in a napkin underneath the lip of his cast and jerked it back and forth on his thigh. "Why, you got somewhere better to be?"

"Maybe," he said, thinking of Penelope again. She'd removed all of the notes the town left on her shop windows, which meant she must've read the one he left for her. It didn't make up for what he'd done, but he needed her to know he wasn't as heartless as he'd seemed back then.

"Sucks to be you then."

Noah sent his brother a smug grin. "At least I can scratch an itch without the use of utensils."

"Funny," Tucker said. He tossed the towel onto the bar and pushed the fork farther in until only the tines stuck out. "The damn bone doesn't even hurt anymore. But the itching is enough to make me want to claw my own skin off."

"You might want to go outside for that. Don't want to chase off your customers." Noah beat his knuckles on the bar and rocked back on his heels, a smile tugging at one side of his mouth. "On second thought, how about a few more forks? I can probably rustle up a cleaver if you want to just lob the whole thing off and be done with it."

"I'll manage on my own, thanks. And you

can keep right on serving drinks until the snow fizzles out and all these people head home."

"Lucky me," Noah said.

He let his gaze drift outside. Thick trails of footprints traveling diagonally across the street and up and down the sidewalks kept the snow from sticking for too long. *I can always see her tomorrow.* He ran his hands through his hair, locking them on the back of his neck and blowing out a frustrated breath.

Tucker checked the door over his shoulder and then turned back to Noah with his mouth set in a serious line. "Listen, I know this isn't where you want to be, but I am grateful you're here."

"It's not so bad here. I mean, if I had my own place, my cat, and all my shit, it'd be better, but I would maybe not hate moving back."

"I could probably muster up some excitement for that. And a job, if you wanted. But Lee will kill both of us if you quit outright. He only gave you the time off because he knew you'd be dying to get back to big-city life after your stint here."

Noah had worked for Lee going on five years. Only Tucker knew Noah better. So when Lee asked if it was okay to schedule him for a few weekend shifts over the next couple of months, Noah had seen it as the lifeline it was.

"He won't kill us. But he might try to have me committed. He doesn't even expect me to make it a month before I jump ship and go home." Noah slid a pint glass under the tap and let the golden liquid run down the side to keep the head from forming too thickly. "And seeing as how I own half this damn place, I can give myself a job, thanks." He set the beer on the end of the bar and started on the Bloody Mary that went with it.

"I thought the whole point of a silent partner was to give me your money and shut the hell up," Tucker joked.

"If I'd kept my mouth shut, you'd have railroad ties attached to the walls, leaking toxic chemicals into the air for your customers to breathe in. And I'm pretty sure that without me, you'd have the most uncomfortable bar stools in the history of the world. Hell, I should give myself a raise."

"If you're serious about coming home, we'll talk about it."

"All right then." He topped the cocktail with a skewer of a green olive sandwiched between two jalapeño slices and grinned at his brother.

As the next rush hit, Noah shifted into autopilot and mulled the idea of moving back to Malarkey. He hadn't realized how much he'd missed his brother and the way bullshitting with Tucker made his worries seem less overwhelming. He could do it. Move back to Malarkey and do what he loved around people he loved.

And not give a shit if Penelope blows me off.

But even as he thought it, something twisted in his chest.

Yeah, he could do it. But he couldn't convince himself she didn't matter.

He put her out of his mind and focused on the drink orders. When Layne came in a little while later, he couldn't help but notice the way his brother shifted toward her, his eyes taking in every inch of her. The way Tucker's shoulders stiffened at Layne's wide-eyed stare, and how he kept his smile easy so his worry didn't intensify her own.

"So, I just stopped in at the Chocolate Cottage and made a complete idiot out of myself," she said. She slumped onto a stool and laid her head on the bar with a low moan. Her arms stretched across the slick wood so her hands hung off the opposite side, and she fiddled with the base of one tap. "I'm pretty sure I insulted Penelope like five times without meaning to."

"Don't worry. I'm sure you weren't any worse than Noah is around her," Tucker said. He leaned over and kissed his wife's head.

Noah slopped the oatmeal stout over the rim of the glass when he jerked to close the tap. "Whoa, how did I get dragged into that? And what makes you think I act like an idiot around her?"

"Because you always do. She's your Kryptonite, little brother. Any suaveness you might possess becomes totally incapacitated around that woman. Though it's kind of a douche move, passing that trait on to my wife."

Layne lifted her head and dragged her hair back from her pink cheeks. "I'm serious," she said before Noah could reply. "I went in to meet her since River's been asking to have Ella for a sleepover, and she's really nice and didn't kick me out when I basically called her a freak to her face. Why do you two let me out in public?"

"Practice makes perfect?" Tucker said.

"I hate you," she said. But she smiled and sat up straighter.

Noah waited a few breaths, letting the silence act as a buffer between the mention of Penelope and his curiosity about how she'd reacted to Layne. Then he asked, "So what did you talk about?" He hoped he'd sounded casual. The flash of his brother's eyes told him he hadn't.

"Aside from the stuff I'm trying to pretend did not actually come out of my mouth, mostly just the girls and whether or not the chocolates are magic," she said.

Tucker wrapped an arm around Layne's shoulders, holding her closer to him. Dropping his voice to a gruff whisper, he said, "What he means is did you talk him up?"

"Why would I do that? Shit, was I supposed to?" She whipped her doe eyes to Noah. He jerked a shoulder like it was no big deal and looked away. "Oh, my God. Is she the girl Tucker swears you never got over?"

"Ding, ding, ding," Tucker shouted.

Noah threw a damp bar towel at his brother's head. "You're an ass."

"Runs in the family. But seriously, you've got to get over her," Tucker said. "It's not healthy to let it go on this long. The commercials say to call a doctor after four hours, and you've had a hard-on for her for what, nine years?"

"It's not like I've just been letting myself rot away while I waited on her to give me another go," Noah said. He pried the caps off two light beers and flicked them into the trash. He passed the bottles across the bar to the waitress. When she walked away to deliver the order, he said, "And I'm pretty sure for the past few years you're always the one to bring her up, not me."

"It's my job as your big brother to rub your face in what you're missing."

"Yep. Ass," Noah said.

Layne shifted on the stool, pulling one leg up under her and leaning into the bar top as if trying to shield their conversation from prying ears, though the closest person sat at the far end to hear the basketball game on the television. "Not like I know her or anything, but she doesn't seem like your type," she said.

"Yeah, Noah, she is a little lacking in the T&A department," Tucker joked. With his cast propped on the stool next to him, he wasn't fast enough to avoid Layne's smack on the arm. "Hey, you've seen the girls he dates. I'm just giving him a hard time."

"When a relationship is ninety percent about the sex, whether we connect on an emotional level isn't that important." Noah tapped the side of his head. "But a girl who can mess up my head with one smile and still make me want to go home and take a long shower, that's hard to ignore."

"I don't want to know this," Layne said.

Noah smiled and pointed at his brother. "He started it."

Tucker grabbed Noah's finger and bent it back, laughing when Noah shook him loose. "With good reason. You've known for years that you don't have a shot with Penelope. Why the hell do you keep trying?"

The image of Penelope as she'd been in high school, with bright teal streaks in her dark hair and black eyeliner making her brown eyes piercing, popped into Noah's head. She'd been this odd combination of calm and focused on the inside and vibrant and full of laughter on the outside. And he'd been ridiculously attracted to both sides. His pulse spiked when he thought of how short her hair was now, making him want to kiss the exposed expanse of skin on the back of her neck.

"I don't know." But he did. He'd blown his chance with Penelope. Knew even as he was doing it that he'd probably regret it. But he did it anyway. And he'd always wondered if she'd been right about their future together. "Back in high school she was absolutely sure of who she was and what she wanted. It was impossible not to be a little in love with her for it."

"So what did you do about it?" Layne asked.

Tucker chuckled to himself and said, "Dude got out his boom box and held it over his head outside her window and went all 1980s rom-com on her."

Noah laughed and flipped him off. "Yeah, says the guy who built a life-sized TARDIS, with sound effects and all no less, to convince a girl he was worth her time. You're full of shit."

"It worked," Layne said. She laced her fingers with Tucker's on the bar.

"Damn right it worked," Tucker said, grinning at her. He scratched at his leg again with his free hand. "Too bad for Noah I got all of the getting-the-girl genes."

"At least you were smart enough to use them on the right girl," Noah said.

"Yes, I was. Meanwhile you're still pining for yours. Which, I gotta say, is pretty damn ironic since Penelope sells magical love chocolates for a living."

"It's only ironic if you ignore all the other kinds of magic she sells."

Tucker punched him on the arm. "I'm just

saying, if you want any sort of shot with her, those chocolates might be your only hope."

Shaking his head, Noah looked out the front window as if he could somehow see Penelope in her store a few blocks over. Falling in love wasn't his problem. What he really needed was a way to get Penelope to stop trying to kill him with her mind long enough to see he had changed. But if she had a recipe for forgiveness, she'd sooner stop selling chocolates altogether than give that power to him. Which meant he'd just have to get back on her good side the old-fashioned way.

14

While Penelope waited for Layne to get back to her on a good time for their girls to play together, she focused on a few things on her daughter's list that she could make happen immediately. Today they were starting with cake for breakfast and then moving on to the animal shelter in search of the perfect kitten.

"You've been bugging me to leave since six this morning. And now that it's time to go, you aren't even dressed," Penelope said as she walked into Ella's room.

"I *was* dressed. You saw me earlier. But my owl shirt didn't go with my necklace so I had to change." Ella pointed at the shirt she'd discarded on the bed. Stretched out next to it on the rumpled sheets was the compass necklace the apothecary table had given her. "Just close your eyes for a second and when you open them I'll be dressed again. Okay?"

"I'm not sure the animal shelter is the best place to wear that necklace."

"But Mama, I have to wear it. How else am I going to find the kitten that's supposed to love me?"

Penelope wanted to tell her that any kitten in that place would love her just for petting it, but the look of disappointment on Ella's face made her give in. "You're right. I would hate for you to bring home the wrong one by mistake." She lifted the necklace from the bed and the dial spun at a dizzying speed. Maybe it would lead Ella to an animal that would love her.

"That would be so sad," Ella agreed. "I only have so much time left. I can't spend it with the wrong cat." She tugged on a solid navy shirt and flung out her hand for the necklace. She slipped the long chain over her head. Against the dark fabric, the white stars of the constellation popped.

"Perfect," Penelope said, breathing through the pang in her chest at Ella's casual reference to dying.

Ella stroked a finger over it then said, "C'mon. It's cake time."

She spent the whole drive to the Orchard Street Cafe with the necklace lying faceup on her palm. Whenever Penelope asked what she was looking for, Ella said, "Nothing" in the way that meant something but she wasn't ready to share her secret with anyone else yet. So Penelope turned up the volume on the radio—one of the stations that thankfully didn't adopt the Christmas-music-twenty-four-seven philosophy—and sang along to Ingrid Michaelson.

The gravel lot at the cafe was packed. It was

usually crowded on the weekends, but since Zan had dreamed of her ex-boyfriend and told everyone she was leaving town, people were lining up almost every day in case it was their last chance to get one of the breakfast plates the cafe had been serving through three different owners. All the owners had grand plans to make the cafe's menu their own, but there was something almost magical about the dozen or so combinations of eggs and meat and potatoes and sauces that couldn't be replicated at home. And they'd ended up not changing a thing.

The first available parking spot was down a residential street two blocks over. Penelope held Ella's hand as they walked down the sidewalk. She let Ella swing their arms between them faster and faster until she tripped from the momentum. Penelope hauled her back up before she face-planted on the sidewalk.

"Whoa. I was almost Ella-roadkill," Ella said.

"I know you're excited about today, but let's maybe take it down a notch. Okay? Unless you added breaking your leg to your list when I wasn't looking."

"Maybe I did." A laugh bubbled out of her and lasted all the way up the street. It only fizzled out when she raced up the front steps of the old cottage that housed the cafe. She pulled up short, her sneakers squeaking on the wooden porch. "Mama, look!"

Just like at the Chocolate Cottage a few days before, dozens of notes covered the door to the cafe. Penelope didn't have to read them to know they all gave Zan a reason to stay. Were they still up because they had worked?

"They're love notes," Ella said. She ran her finger over note after note, underscoring the word "love."

"I see that."

Penelope gripped the brass handle, careful not to tear the paper taped beneath it. She ushered Ella inside ahead of her. They were greeted with a rush of hot air and the intoxicating scent of bacon and the hint of something sweet. Behind the counter, Zan eyed the door. She was angled away, as if she was ready to bolt out the back. Her shoulders relaxed when Penelope closed the door behind her.

Every table was occupied. Only a handful of people greeted Penelope, though they all turned to give her a once-over. Apparently word had spread about her plans for the festival. And from the hard set of their mouths and the narrowed stares they leveled at her, their initial plan to convince her she was wrong had moved into phase two: ignore her to show her what she's missing.

If that was how they wanted to act, then fine. Penelope wasn't going to stoop to their level.

"Good morning," she called to the room at large.

They all stuffed a bit of food in their mouths or sipped their steaming coffee as excuses not to respond. She rolled her eyes, though no one was watching her to see it.

"She said good morning," Ella sang and waved to a half dozen people.

The room erupted in a chorus of *hello*s and *good morning*s and a few begrudging *hey*s. No one could resist Ella's charm.

Bending down, Penelope wrapped her arms around her daughter and squeezed her. Ella's flyaway hairs ticked her cheek. "While we wait for a table, why don't you go check out the cakes and pick out the one you want?"

"Can I get a hot chocolate too?" Ella's crooked-tooth smile lit up her face.

"I think that would be a sugar overload for this early in the morning."

"You only live once, Mama," Ella said.

Where in the world had she picked up that phrase? Penelope simply shook her head.

"Okay. Milk?"

"That sounds like a better choice," Penelope said.

Ella raced over to the counter and read each sign aloud. Zan whispered something to her that made her reach for her necklace again as she stretched onto her tiptoes to get a better look at the selection of cakes sitting on pedestals of varying heights. She paced to the end of the counter and back, as if picking the right flavor was the most important decision she would make all day.

Considering cake for breakfast was a serious bucket list item, maybe it was.

Penelope breathed through the panic that threatened to implode her chest. She'd known from the moment the doctor suggested the list that it would cause her equal amounts of happiness and heartache as Ella checked each one off. But the whole point was to make Ella happy. And falling apart over a piece of cake would ruin the whole thing. She forced herself to smile in hopes of tricking her brain into feeling happy for real.

Zan stopped next to her, coffee pot in hand, and kept her back to the bulk of her patrons. "I heard about the festival. And I just wanted to say that I agree with you. I figured a lot of people aren't going to tell you that, so I wanted you to know."

"Oh, thanks," Penelope said. She glanced at Ella to make certain she was out of earshot. Today was about making her daughter happy. Telling her there might not be a festival this year—her last year—did not fit into that plan. "You and I are definitely in the minority on this one."

"Did you know I stayed here because of the festival?"

"No."

"Yeah. I came to town two days before the

147

festival last year. Ruth Anne had come up to me at a rest stop when I was looking through the maps trying to figure out where the heck I was, and she just started talking about how nice and quiet and safe Malarkey was. Almost like she knew exactly what I was looking for even if I had no clue how to find it. And I decided why not. Some small, out-of-the-way town might be good for a few days. And then at the festival, with all the talk about fate and wishing for the future you wanted, I thought 'What if they're right? What if I could stay here and make the life I've always wanted?' I mean, who wouldn't want to stay in a quirky little town?"

There were plenty of people who didn't. And Penelope was always happy to see them go. But when someone loved it in Malarkey and had to move away for reasons beyond their control—like Zan—that left a hollow feeling in her chest. "The town does have a way of charming people."

"It does. I really hate that I have to leave," Zan said.

"So the other chocolates my mom sent home with you didn't help?" Penelope scooted out of the way as three women stood up from their chairs a few feet away and shuffled into their coats and hats.

Zan shook her head. "I don't know." She switched the coffee pot to her other hand and checked over her shoulder. She waited for the

148

women to say their goodbyes and make their exit. Then she leaned closer to Penelope and said, "They made me realize that I couldn't just jump in the car instantly and go. I put every penny I had into buying this place. I can't leave until I sell it. Which is proving harder than I'd expected."

"I saw the notes outside. They're not going to make it easy on you. An outsider is your best bet. Everyone who's already in Malarkey turned Eileen down when she offered it to them in hopes that she'd change her mind and stay if she couldn't find any takers."

"Damn."

"I'm sorry. I know that's not what you want to hear, but I figured you should know what you're up against," Penelope said.

"It's okay. I kinda already knew that since no one's even asked me about it since the For Sale sign went up two weeks ago."

Penelope couldn't help the next question. "Will you be okay if your ex finds you before you can sell it?"

Zan dropped her gaze to the floor. "I'm trying to convince myself I'm not scared of him anymore. I'm not sure it's working yet, but I have hope. But if you have any chocolates that will help, I will buy every last one you've got." When she looked back up, she gave Penelope a half smile.

"We have one that will give you a few hours of confidence, but that's about it."

"Oh well. Guess I'm on my own then."

"I might not be able to help magically, but if you need anything, I'm here. Okay?"

"Thanks, Penelope." Zan squeezed her arm then got back to work.

One of the servers came to clear the vacated table with Ella in tow. While the girl stacked dirty plates and cups, Ella held up her plate with a double-sized slice of caramel cake with both hands. Her grin was definitely worth the appalled looks a few of the customers gave Penelope when she gave her daughter a thumbs-up.

Good thing what they thought of Penelope's parenting skills didn't matter.

She shrugged out of her coat and slung it on the back of the chair. Goose bumps broke out on her skin at the sudden loss of warmth. And for a second she contemplated using the hot chocolate bonbons again to turn off her ability to get cold. Somehow that felt like cheating. She rubbed her arms to chase away the chill. Another waitress set a second piece of caramel cake on the table for Penelope. "Interesting choice, kid. I expected you to go for the double chocolate," Penelope said.

"Almost. I thought maybe the necklace would help me choose," Ella said. She set the plate down and picked up her fork before she was all the way seated. "But it didn't."

"I don't think it works on things that aren't alive."

"It should. Because I love cake. I would marry it if I could. But I'm too young."

Ella handled her diagnosis with a maturity that should have been well beyond an eight-year-old. But sometimes—like right then—Ella acting her age caught Penelope completely off guard. The laugh bubbled out of her. "Yes, you're too young. That's why you can't marry cake."

Ella banged her fork on the side of the plate to get Penelope's attention. "Mama! Don't laugh at me."

"I'm sorry. But that was really cute."

"I'm always really cute."

"That you are," Penelope agreed. She forked up a bite of cake, the caramel icing dissolving on her tongue. She was constantly amazed that Ella could stay so positive despite knowing she didn't have much time left.

"He's not here," Ella announced. She chewed on her lip, as if trying to keep the disappointment from leaking out.

Penelope looked around to see what she was missing. "Who's not?"

"My kitten."

"What do you mean?"

"The one that's supposed to be mine isn't here," Ella said.

Since they were the only ones at the shelter, Brenda had let Ella take a dozen kittens into the empty ring they usually used for dogs. She'd sat cross-legged in the middle of the floor, toy mice scattered in a semicircle around her. The kittens had climbed all over her, licked her fingers with their sandpapery tongues, and purred against her cheeks. Ella had squealed in delight.

But after half an hour of play with every kitten up for adoption, she was saying she couldn't pick one? Even Penelope had found one long-haired orange kitten she could picture snuggling on the bed with her at night.

Penelope set it down in the cuddle pile the others had formed. No sense getting attached if Ella didn't want to take him home. The calico one with slightly crossed eyes zonked out in Ella's lap wouldn't have been Penelope's pick, but it wasn't her bucket list. "What about that one? He's been attached to you since the second you sat down. He looks pretty in love with you if you ask me."

"Nah. He's just asleep."

"Okay. But why don't you think he's the one?"

Ella lifted the chain so the compass dangled in front of her face. "It's not doing anything. Not even a little wiggle." She gave it a shake for good measure. The needle stayed frozen in place.

"That doesn't mean anything, Ella." Penelope reached over and cupped her hand around Ella's, obscuring the necklace from view. "We don't even know what makes the compass work."

"Yes we do. It's love."

"I know that's what the note said, but that doesn't mean it's true."

"It's magic, Mama. It only works if you believe in it. Like Tinker Bell." Ella pulled away from Penelope. The kitten in her lap let out a surprised mew and Ella soothed it with a few quick strokes between the ears.

Penelope let her hand fall to the cool cement floor. "Okay, well, maybe if you believe one of these kittens is yours, the necklace will do what you want it to."

"Even I know you can't trick magic. Because if you could, I know you would've fixed me by now."

No, you couldn't. Magic was always going to get its way.

"So, no kitten?" Penelope asked.

Ella shook her head. "No kitten. But I can keep looking, right? Since I didn't get to check it off my list."

"Of course you can. We'll keep looking as long as it takes to find the perfect one."

Penelope just hoped it would happen before they ran out of time.

15

It had taken the better part of a week, but most of the ruckus about Penelope refusing to make the hot chocolate for the festival had died down. Whether people were planning another stunt to change her mind or if they'd finally realized she wouldn't budge, she had no clue. When Megha swung by the shop half an hour before closing and insisted they go out for a drink, Penelope's first thought was that being social was practically an invitation for people to start in on her again.

Her second was that Noah might think she'd wanted to see him. But she didn't say it out loud. She couldn't give her friend the satisfaction of knowing she thought about Noah in the first place.

And she couldn't hide from the town forever.

When they met at the Rehab Bar an hour later, Penelope's eyes went straight to the bar. But instead of Noah, Layne stood behind the taps, focused on the beer she was pulling as if it might overflow if she so much as blinked. Penelope slid onto one of the few empty stools and smiled at her.

She'd only been in Rehab a handful of times since Tucker opened it four years before. Dim light shone down from headlights of old cars that were suspended from metal pipes snaking across the ceiling. Instead of art, rusted gears in various shapes and sizes hung on the walls. The exposed brick walls were scarred and scorched in places from a fire half a century before when the building was a grain and feed store. The bottom of the bar, built from half a dozen different shades of reclaimed lumber, was just as beat up as the walls, with deep grooves and pockmarks marring the surface.

"Hey, Layne," she said. "I didn't expect to see you working the bar."

"Oh, hey. What are you doing here?" Layne asked.

"Impromptu girls' night." Penelope motioned to Megha, who was too busy checking out the purple underlayer of Layne's hair to do more than wave a hello. Penelope hadn't noticed the dye when they'd met the week before, but with it pulled up into a ponytail to keep it out of Layne's face while she worked, it was hard to miss.

Layne passed the beer to a waitress and sagged into the bar, her elbows holding up most of her weight. "Lucky you. Mine's impromptu be-the-bartender night. So, what can I get you?"

"The biggest gin and tonic you can legally make me," Megha said.

"And a Jack and ginger. Normal-sized, please," Penelope said.

When Layne set down their drinks a minute later, Megha asked her, "Where's Noah?" She poked Penelope in the ribs with her elbow.

Swatting her arm away, Penelope shot her friend a death-glare. Which only made Megha more gleeful.

Thankfully the whole exchange didn't even register with Layne. "He got called back home to work for a few days. His boss needed him to take tonight's shift along with a dozen other nights over the next few months. He's going to be even more annoyed when he finds out that he missed you."

Penelope rested her elbows on the bar and leaned forward. "Then don't tell him."

"I'm sorry. What am I missing?" Megha asked. She spun on her stool to face Penelope. "You've seen him, haven't you?"

"We've run into each other a few times. Small talk, that's it."

"Right. So is this the part where you get all swoony and tell me how seriously hot Noah is and then I get to say 'I told you so'?"

"No, this is the part where you sit there and drink your damn drink instead of being all gloaty and superior," Penelope said.

"Lucky for me, I can drink and be gloaty at the same time. See?" Megha flashed her a toothy grin then tipped back her gin and tonic.

Penelope smiled right back. "That's funny. Me too." She raised her glass, angling it toward her friend in a salute. "So, any new details on this blind date your mom's trying to set you up on? Has she given you his name yet or is she still refusing to tell you anything?"

Megha tapped her nails on the glass. "Damn woman knows that my curiosity will win out over stubbornness, so I still know nothing. Not even if he's picking me up or if I'm meeting him somewhere. She said I'll find out at the appropriate time, not a second sooner."

"She's serious about this one, huh?"

"I don't know. Could be she's just messing with me for fun. You know, get my hopes up and then say 'There is no date, Megha. I just wanted to prove to you that you want to find a husband as badly as I want you to have one. Now go get one before we both die of old age.' "

Layne paused by the ice bin in front of them, two rocks glasses balanced in one hand. "Since when is twenty-seven old?" She shook her head, gave Megha an apologetic smile, and turned her attention back to scooping ice into the glasses. "Sorry, I didn't mean to butt in. Tucker never listens to me when I tell him I'm not good behind the bar."

"You're fine. I'm a hairstylist, so butting in is a natural part of my day. And it's old since my mom had already been married for six years and popped out two kids by my age. Granted, my grandparents arranged for my parents to marry so my mom doesn't know how hard it is to find the right guy. But still, she thinks I should've figured it all out by now and isn't afraid to let me know it."

"Oh, silly me," Penelope said. "I thought you enjoyed the detour-boys on the road to true love."

"Ooh, detour-boys. I like that."

"I thought you might." Penelope held up her glass and clinked it to Megha's.

Megha downed the rest of her drink like it was a shot and asked for another along with a glass of water. "Detours are fun. Dead-ends are starting to wear on me."

"You know," Layne said, a smile playing on her lips, "I've heard rumors about some hot chocolate that might help with that."

"I've offered," Penelope said.

Megha leaned an elbow onto the bar, shifting closer to Layne as if sharing a secret. "If the girl who makes it won't drink it to find her soul mate, why would I?"

"Wait. What? You haven't used it, Penelope?" Layne's finger slipped on the soda gun, spraying a bubbly stream of dark liquid onto the floor. She dropped it back into the holder and covered the mess with a bar rag.

Penelope ducked her head to avoid meeting

either of their stares, knowing the truth about her past with Noah would be written all over her face.

"If she had, do you think she'd still be single?" Megha asked.

"We're talking about your love life, not mine," Penelope said.

"If you want to get technical, we were talking about you and Noah before you changed the subject, so . . ." Megha trailed off.

Damn it. She had walked right into that one.

Layne saved her from responding by saying, "Ooh, you should both drink it. And I totally want to be there with you when you do. Something tells me we'd have a lot of fun when I'm not at work."

"Yes to the hanging-out-again part," Megha said. She plucked an ice cube from her drink and popped it in her mouth. "Maybe to the hot chocolate. I'm not that desperate yet. But you never know, my next blind date could push me right over that edge."

Penelope secretly loved how Megha was determined to find love on her own. Most people took the easy way. But Megha believed the surprise of finding yourself suddenly in love was the best part. "Luckily for you, I know you don't mean that."

"I said it *could*. Technically, that is a possibility."

"One you'd run screaming from," Penelope said.

Megha just laughed in response.

Layne tapped the counter in front of Penelope. "And for what it's worth, I would love to see you and Noah together. And not just because it would be nice to have another girl around to even things up a bit. If you stopped trying so hard to avoid him, you might actually like him."

"Not you too?" Penelope asked.

"He's my brother-in-law. I've gotta pull for him," she said.

There was nothing Penelope could say that wouldn't give them more reason to push her and Noah together. But she couldn't stay silent either. "I never said I—" Her phone lit up on the bar with an incoming call. Snatching it up, she swiped across her mom's picture to answer. "Hey, Mama, is everything okay?"

Whatever Sabina said in response was lost in the clamor of the bar.

"Hold on a second. I can't hear you." Penelope told Megha she'd be right back and went outside. When the door shut behind her, blocking the music and the wall of voices, it took a few seconds for her ears to stop ringing. "Are you still there?"

"Yes, I'm here. I'm sorry I had to pull you away from your night out with Megha."

"It's okay. What did you say a minute ago?"

160

Her mom hesitated, her breath crackling through the phone. Then she said, "Ella's not feeling well. I don't think it's anything to worry about. She's just a little feverish and sick to her stomach. But I didn't want to wait until you came home to tell you."

Penelope couldn't pinpoint what about her mom's voice sounded off, only that it did. It was too fast or too controlled or too *something*. But of course her mom was worried about Ella. That's probably all it was.

Penelope shivered, having run outside without her coat or gloves, and huddled against the front of the building as out of the wind as she could get. "Thanks. Have you called Marco? We're supposed to let him know when she has an episode."

"I will call him as soon as we hang up. Do you think he'll want to see her tonight?"

"I thought you said she wasn't that bad. If you think she needs to go to him or the hospital, I can be home in ten minutes."

"No, no. You should stay. Ella will be fine. I just wanted to be sure I knew what you normally do in these situations," Sabina said.

She was normally home and could explain to Marco in detail what Ella was experiencing. And then he'd tell her it was perfectly normal in Ella's condition and to bring her in the following day for a quick checkup. Even with as much time as Sabina spent with Ella, she didn't know the subtle differences in how the tumor affected Ella as well as Penelope did. Staying out with her friend while her daughter was sicker than usual was not an option.

"It's okay. I'll come home and call him. You know I'd just sit here and worry until I got home anyway," Penelope said.

"I promise you she's okay," Sabina said. Her voice did the weird thing again. Like there were other words that wanted to come out in place of the ones that did.

"Tell her I'm on my way." Penelope opened the bar door, grateful for the rush of noise that would drown out the nervousness of whatever her mother was not saying.

16

She'd found Ella curled up on the bathmat in only her undies with Penelope's terry-cloth robe bunched under her head as a makeshift pillow. Ella's body radiated heat when Penelope lifted her. Instead of taking her to bed, Penelope sat on the closed toilet seat cradling her while the sink filled with lukewarm water. She grabbed a washcloth from the towel rack and soaked it in the water, making as few movements as possible to keep from jostling Ella too much. Ella's eyes fluttered open as the water dribbled down her cheeks.

It had helped to bring her fever down some. The ibuprofen she'd given Ella just before tucking her into bed did the rest.

In the morning, Ella said she felt well enough to go to school. Penelope had already called Marco to make an appointment to have her checked out. She almost gave in when Ella whipped out her list and stabbed the paper with her index finger next to where she'd written she wanted to have a whole month at school without a sick day. But in the end, she had to be the responsible mom instead of the fun mom.

Ella sulked on the drive to Marco's office. Arms crossed over her chest, lips pushed out in a pout. She stared out the window so Penelope couldn't even catch her eye in the rearview mirror. Well, Ella could be angry all she wanted. It wasn't going to change the fact that her health came before completing items on her list. And staying quiet at least meant that they weren't fighting.

They didn't sit in the waiting room for two minutes before they were called back to an exam room. The paper crackled as Ella climbed onto the table like a pro and sat there, legs swinging out and heels banging back into the base. That was the only sound she made until Marco entered the room, then Ella smiled and waved like there was no other place she'd rather be.

He was like the grandfather Ella had never had, coming to their family holiday dinners and sending Ella flowers every year on her birthday. Penelope would have been happy if her mom had ever wanted to move from being just friends with him and make Marco a more permanent part of their lives. Though there had been a few months there when Ella had first gotten sick that they had seen him almost daily anyway.

Penelope sighed, thankful that his presence could pull Ella out of her bad mood.

He unwound his stethoscope from his neck and pointed the ear pieces at Ella. "So, you had a bad night, huh?"

"Most of it was okay. It was just the end that was bad," Ella said. Familiar with the routine, she paused while he listened to her heart. Then she continued, "I fell asleep in the bathroom. Right next to the toilet. That was gross."

Penelope hated that Ella was so used to being sick that the worst part of last night was sleeping on the bathroom floor. "She had a fever of a hundred and two last night and my mom said she'd been vomiting. But this morning it's like nothing was wrong. So I don't know if it's tumor related or just a stomach bug."

"Let's see if we can figure out what's going on." Marco stuck the thermometer in Ella's mouth and made a few notes on her chart while he waited. When it beeped, revealing a normal temperature, he said, "How are you feeling now, Ella? Any headaches, dizziness, feeling like you want to throw up again?"

Ella picked at the edge of the paper table liner. She made a small tear and tried to smooth it back into place. "No, none of that."

"Is it something else?"

"Nope," she said.

"Well, your mom didn't bring you to see me because you felt great. Something was wrong last night for you to be so sick. What were you doing before you started to feel bad?"

Penelope hadn't thought to ask that. Leaning forward in the chair, she was suddenly hopeful that this wasn't a result of Ella's disease worsening.

Ella shot a quick look at Penelope, a flash of nerves staining her cheeks pink. "Grams gave me some new chocolates last night and I don't think the magic worked right. That's why I was sick. I'm not getting worse or anything."

New chocolates. The two words repeated over and over in Penelope's head. What had her mother done? She stood and stroked a hand over Ella's hair. "You didn't tell me about the chocolates," she said.

"It was a secret. In case it didn't work." Ella lowered her eyes to the tear in the paper she had made another inch longer by messing with it. "Grams said you would be upset if it didn't make me better."

"I'm not upset." At least, she wasn't upset about the chocolate not working. She wouldn't have expected it to. But using the chocolates on Ella without knowing what they might do was inexcusable. "But I will be much more than upset if either of you ever does that again. Okay?"

Marco cut in, bending down so his face was level with Ella's. "Wait a minute. Ella, your grandmother might have a recipe that can cure you?" He was almost as fascinated with their chocolates as he was with Sabina. In any other town, he would have laughed off the very idea of magic as a replacement for medicine. But

166

having lived in Malarkey most of his life, it was impossible not to believe in it.

"No," Penelope said. It came out so sharp Marco moved back a step.

"She just thought it could," Ella said.

"In that case, maybe it would be a good idea to not eat anything you're not sure about, okay? Your body's already fighting pretty hard and we don't want to add more things it has to fight off if we can help it."

Ella relaxed, her hands going still beside her, when he tipped her chin up and smiled at her.

"Okay. I'll be careful. I don't want my body to die faster."

"Don't worry," Penelope said to Marco, some of her anger leaching into her voice. "I will make it very clear to my mother that this cannot happen again."

"All right. Sounds like we're all on the same page. Now before I let you go, Ella, tell me something good that's happened," he said.

She scooted to the end of the table and dropped to her feet. Reaching into her back pocket, she extracted a folded sheet of paper and waved it in the air to open it. "I've done like eight things on my list already. Haven't I, Mama?"

Penelope smiled at her, grateful their standoff was over. "Yes, you have."

Marco gave Ella a high five. "That's great. What's been the best thing so far?"

"My mom and I went ice skating. I wasn't very good at it because I kept falling down, but it didn't hurt that much. And she said as long as I didn't hit my head we could keep going around and around. So we did," she said.

"I wish I could've seen that," he said.

"Oh, no. Be glad you didn't. We're not the most graceful skaters. But it was fun," Penelope said.

Ella smoothed the paper against her stomach. Then she held it out to show him what was left. "I'm working on a couple other ones, but they're harder than I thought."

Marco gripped the paper to keep it steady. "Like what?"

"Finding a kitten and going a month without missing a single day of school. I was doing really good on the school thing until today." Ella made a little *hmpf* sound but didn't blame Penelope again. "And who knew finding one little cat would take so long?"

"I don't know what to tell you about school. You've got a bit of a mess in your head. That means you're going to miss some days."

"Or a lot of days," she said.

"Yes, or a lot of days. And there's not much any of us can do about that. But I can help you with your cat problem. I saw an article in the paper this morning about how the animal shelter has a dozen or more cats that need homes."

Ella folded the list, careful to align the creases

so she didn't make new ones. "I've tried all of them already."

Penelope met Marco's confused glance. "Don't ask."

"Well, I'm sure you'll figure it out, Ella," he said.

"I will. It's on my list, so I have to. And there are still a lot of other things on my list too so I can't die until they're all checked off."

Do you hear that, Universe? Penelope thought. Wanting to finish the list was such a small request in the grand scheme of things. Ella should be given enough time to do it.

Marco whistled. "Sounds like you've got a busy schedule ahead. Why don't you run out front and see Miss Ruby. She's got a tin of shortbread cookies at her desk. I bet if you asked nicely she'd give you a couple."

"Thanks, Dr. Marco," she said and raced out of the room.

Penelope waited until she could hear Ella and Ruby talking out front. Then she sat on the table Ella had vacated. "I'm sorry about my mom. I should've known she would try something like that. She's convinced I'm making the wrong decision."

"She believes in her magic. We can't fault her for that," he said.

He didn't get to defend her mom. Not on this one.

"We can when it hurts my kid," Penelope said. She tugged on the strip of paper on the table that Ella had ripped and tore it free. "I know you care about my mom, but you can't honestly tell me you think this was okay."

He covered her hand with his. His large, warm fingers squeezed hers. "No, of course I don't. I can try to talk to her if you want."

"Thanks for the offer, but this is something I need to make her understand on my own. She doesn't have to agree with it, but I need her to respect my decision." If she couldn't, there was no way anyone else would.

"You still haven't told anyone about Ella's condition?"

"Only a few people. I'm sure you've seen how upset they all are about the festival. What do you think they'd do if they knew that we'd stopped Ella's treatment?" she said.

"I would hope they'd understand that this is the last option any of us want. I wouldn't have recommended it if there was anything else I could do to save her." He released her hand and gave her a sad, understanding smile. "But you are probably right. People around here tend to think everyone's business is their business. They would make this even harder for both of you."

And that kind of judgment would haunt her the rest of her life.

• • •

Penelope left Ella on one of the shop's sofas with a group of regulars and ushered her mom into the back where they wouldn't make a scene. Waiting until the place was empty—or better yet, when they weren't in the shop at all—would have been a better option, but she wouldn't be able to work beside her mom all day, acting like she wasn't fuming. Her emotions were too raw for that today.

Half a dozen drawers on the apothecary table were open, just an inch or two of the insides showing. Penelope picked up a recipe card from the top of the table. *Witch hazel and dark chocolate toffee.* She'd never seen that recipe before. The toffee they sold was the nonmagical kind.

"Mama," Penelope said, the card trembling in her hand. "Is this what you used on her?"

Sabina twisted her hands together and stared at the table instead of her daughter. "It was supposed to make her better. I didn't think she'd get sick from it."

"Well, she did. I can't believe you would do that to her."

"I thought it would help."

Penelope slammed her fist down on the table, rattling its contents and making a couple of the drawers bang shut. "Help? You gave my sick daughter something you'd never tried. Something you had no idea how it would affect her. And you did it all behind my back. How is that helpful?"

"I had to do something. You weren't willing to try more aggressive treatment and I knew you'd say no to the recipe."

"Apparently for good reason. Your chocolates didn't make her better. All you managed to do was give her a really bad night and keep her out of school for the day so now she has to start that bucket list item all over again."

Sabina rubbed a hand down Penelope's arm, her fingers tightening hard when they reached her wrist. She only loosened her grip when Penelope met her eyes. "You know I wouldn't do anything to hurt her. I spent all night trying to get an antidote from the table, but it's being stubborn."

"That's because there isn't anything that can fix her. How many times do we have to have this argument before you will listen?" Penelope jerked out of her mom's grasp. She held her hands in front of her to keep her mom from touching her again.

"What good does it do us to have magical chocolates if we can't use them when we need them?" her mom asked.

"I honestly don't know, Mama." She threw the recipe card onto the table. It slid across the surface and slipped over the back edge, lost between the table and the alcove wall. Too bad the damage had already been done. "I've always thought this magic was a gift. But lately all it seems to bring is pain."

Sabina shook her head, her dark curls whipping around her shoulders. "No, no, no. You know that is not true. Our chocolates help so many people, Penelope. You do the books every month. You know how busy we are. If we were hurting people, we would have gone out of business years ago. They would have run us out of town. The only one who is second-guessing the magic is you."

"That doesn't mean I'm not right," Penelope said.

"And it doesn't mean that you are."

Ella stomped into the kitchen, hands on her hips and her best scolding look pinching her face. "We can hear you out there, you know." She stared them both down and after a few seconds she whirled around and left.

It didn't matter how many "we" was. Having anyone in town learn Ella's secret would bring the whole thing crashing down. Penelope rubbed her temples in a vain attempt to calm down. "Please just promise me you will stop trying to find something in the table to use on her."

"So I'm just supposed to watch her die?" Sabina asked.

"No, Mama, you're supposed to watch her live."

What was the point of knowing the future if they ignored all of the best parts?

"That's exactly what I'm trying to do, honey." Sabina slid one drawer shut in the apothecary table, then another. When Ella laughed at something out front, she turned toward the sound, her shoulders crumpling forward. "But there won't be anything left to watch if we sit here and do nothing to save her."

Her mom's voice was barely a whisper, but the words sliced through Penelope's chest as if she were made of marshmallow. "I'm not saying we give up hope. Believe me, I would give anything to find a way to fix her. But we can't ignore the fact that we could still lose her no matter what we do."

And if Penelope didn't keep one foot grounded in reality, she was in danger of losing herself right along with Ella.

17

Since going to see the doctor a few days before, Ella hadn't stopped asking Penelope if she could do something else on her list. Like inviting River for a sleepover or dyeing her hair. She was running out of time, Ella had said. There were so many things left to do. And she didn't want to miss out on any of them.

They'd made it a full ten hours since the last inquiry, but that was only because Ella had been asleep for most of that time. At breakfast, Penelope sipped her coffee and waited.

Halfway through her bowl of oatmeal, Ella broke. "Mama?" she asked, her voice wavering. She tapped Penelope's hand with a finger sticky from the brown sugar she crumbled up on her oatmeal. "Is it okay if I stay at the shop this afternoon instead of going to Grams's?"

The request wasn't directly about her list, but Penelope couldn't shake the feeling that was the reason behind it. "Maybe."

"Why only maybe?"

"Why do you want to be at the shop? You always complain about how bored you are there," Penelope said. She could see the gears turning in Ella's head already, trying to sneak Penelope more of the Corazón hot chocolate or one of the other charmed candies to make her more open to the idea of liking Noah.

"I want to see if there's anything new in the magic table." Ella spooned a bite of her oatmeal into her mouth as soon as the last word was out of it.

Penelope turned her coffee cup in her hands, letting the heat warm her skin. "Magic's not something to play with. If the table gives you something, it's for a reason, but you can't expect it to give you something just because you want it."

Ella dug down the front of her shirt and extracted the compass necklace from where she'd hidden it. "I know. But maybe there's something that goes with this. Something else that I might need."

"Um, no, ma'am," Penelope said.

"What?" Ella asked with a shrug and a guilty grin.

"Go right back upstairs and leave that on your dresser. It is not a toy."

"But I need to keep it with me, Mama."

"You are not going to find love on the playground." She took a sip of her coffee and eyed her daughter over the cup. Ella's shoulders slumped, making her bony shoulder blades even more pronounced. "You can wear it around the house and on special occasions outside of the house, but that's it, okay? I don't want it to get lost or broken."

"I thought you said it was already broken," Ella said.

Penelope thumped her forefinger on the top of Ella's head. "Don't push it, Ella, or I'll take it away until you're old enough to take proper care of it." As soon as the words were out, she wanted to take them back. Talking about Ella growing up like it was a real possibility was a bad habit she was still trying to break herself of. If she let herself forget what future they were headed toward, it would be that much harder on her when they reached it.

"I'm old enough now. I promise." Ella slipped the chain from around her neck and walked back up the stairs with exaggerated care.

When Ella came back down a few minutes later with her book bag straps slung over her shoulders, Penelope said, "Pull down your shirt."

Ella gripped the collar of her T-shirt with one hand and lifted her short hair off her neck with the other. "I took it off," she said. She looked up at Penelope, her eyes bright with defiance despite her acquiescence.

After school, Ella dragged a stool in front of the apothecary table and parked there for the better part of an hour. She opened every drawer on the top row before moving down to the next. When Penelope asked what she was looking for, Ella told her, "Whatever the table thinks I need," and went through them all again. Bottles of extracts rattled as she shoved their drawers back into place. Bars of dark chocolate and stems of dried lavender and rosemary scented the room when she opened their drawers, despite already knowing what was inside.

The table still hadn't given up anything by the third search.

Leaning forward, Ella laid her head on the top of the table and draped her arms over the sides in a hug. She whispered something into the wood, too quiet for Penelope to hear.

"Why don't you take a break?" Penelope suggested. "Maybe start your homework. I'm sure you have something you need to be working on."

Unlike most kids in her grade, Ella completed extra work every night to catch up on all the school she had missed.

"Maybe the table will do my math for me. I probably won't need to know how to make fractions in heaven anyway."

The logic behind Ella's words didn't make them hurt any less. Penelope pressed her knuckles to her chest to keep it from ripping open right then and there and spilling her heart onto the floor. "Thankfully, we still have some time before heaven happens. And if you try and ask the table for help, you won't even be allowed in the same room with it for a month."

Ella released the table, walked across the room, and stopped in front of Penelope, arms crossed over her chest and mouth stuck open in shock. "You'd kick me out of the kitchen?"

"You know better than to mess with magic." She didn't mention the hot chocolate incident from a few weeks before. If Ella knew it had worked, she might try it again to force Penelope to admit Noah belonged with them.

Looking between Penelope and the table, Ella's eyebrows dipped down in concentration. After a minute, she frowned, hauled her book bag from underneath the chair where she'd stashed it, and removed her wrinkled homework calendar. She smoothed it on the table in front of Penelope and said, "I just have reading to do tonight, and my book's at home."

"Well, I guess you're gonna have to find something else to do until we close that doesn't involve the apothecary table."

"Maybe I could go make sure all of the marshmallows and caramels are full."

"That sounds like an excellent idea," Penelope said.

Ella latched onto her hand and pulled her out front just as River, with Noah in tow, marched toward the counter and locked her eyes on the chocolates piled on square plates in the display case.

"You came," Ella said, her eyes going wide. She dropped Penelope's hand but didn't make a move to meet them on the other side of the counter.

"How could I turn down your invitation?" Noah said, waving a folded piece of pink construction paper. He flicked his eyes to Penelope, his mouth cocked in a smirk.

"Hi, Ella," River said.

"Hi," Ella said with slightly less enthusiasm than her greeting for Noah.

River's lips scrunched into a pout. "I gave him your note, and I didn't read it, just like I promised."

Noah tugged on River's curly hair, stretching out one thick coil and releasing it so it bounced back into place. She leaned back into him and wrapped her arms behind her around his waist. "I figure between the three of us, we can convince your mom to let me take you both out," he said.

Ella shot a look at Penelope and said, "Yeah, we can." She hooked her fingers around two mug handles and darted out from behind the counter. "Hey, River, do you want some hot chocolate?"

"As long as it's not the spicy stuff. My dad says I can't drink that one because the peppers are so hot they'll burn a hole in my stomach." She released her hold on Noah and raced Ella into the pantry.

"I'm not allowed to drink that one either. But not because it's hot. It's one of the magic ones so I'm not even supposed to touch it. Sometimes I do anyway."

Though the last words were whispered, they carried back to Penelope.

"A word of advice," she said to Noah. "Don't eat or drink anything she gives you in here."

"Why not?"

Across the room, glass clanked as the girls filled their cups with powder and, from the sound of it, enough mix-ins to make the hot chocolate more of a meal than a drink. They took turns checking over their shoulders to ensure Penelope and Noah weren't coming to stop them.

"She's tricky, that one. Ella will slip you one of the charmed chocolates and you won't know what hit you until you're professing your love to the horse that leads the carriage rides around the square." Penelope dug her nails into the crook of her arm to keep her face straight.

Noah rocked back on his heels and jammed his hands in his pockets. "You can't really do that, can you? Make people fall in love? With other people or horses?" A hint of apprehension cut the humor in his husky voice.

"I hope for your sake you don't ever find out."

Ella looked at them, a giant chocolate-dipped

marshmallow poised to drop in her mug. "Ooh, River and I could look for a recipe that makes people fall in love. Then I could use it on my mom."

"You should probably rethink that plan, kid," Penelope called to Ella. She twisted the knob on the espresso machine and dipped the wand into a pitcher of milk for the girls' drinks. Testing the bottom of the metal with her little finger, she let it heat up but shut the steam off before the milk got too hot for them to drink.

When Ella stopped in front of the counter, she said, "But I don't want you to be all alone when—" She slapped a hand over her mouth to keep the last few words in.

Penelope forced her shoulders to relax, pretending her daughter hadn't almost just let slip that she was dying. Thankfully neither Noah nor River seemed to notice. Or if they did, they kept their questions to themselves. She closed her eyes for a second. It was all too easy to imagine how her life without Ella would be just as dark. When she looked at her daughter again, she kept her voice as light as the lump in her throat would allow. "I know. But that's not something you need to worry about. I promise I'll be okay."

"No, you won't. You'll be like Grams and have to eat chocolates to be happy," Ella said. She jammed her cup onto the counter with enough force to send a puff of chocolate powder shooting into the air above it. "But if you had someone to love you, you would be happy all on your own."

It was so close to what she'd said to her own mom that Penelope couldn't argue with her. She filled both girls' cups without a reply.

"I've gotta say, Ella, you do make a pretty good argument for your mom falling in love," Noah said.

The cluster of high school girls on the couches turned as his words rang out around the room. Like just the mention of love in the shop would make something magical happen. Only the one who didn't believe in magic, but put up with studying in the shop a few times a week because her friends overruled her, continued to read her textbook.

Ella reached toward her chest and then let her hand drop. She flashed a toothy smile before turning away. "I know. And I'm working on it," she said, which sent her and River into a fit of giggles next to her. Then they ran off to gather spoons and napkins and claim their spots on the floor by the front window.

The girls on the couch eyed Noah and giggled too. Penelope let out an annoyed breath.

"You really have to stop encouraging her," she said.

Noah moved one of the stools from the bar on the right side of the room and made a spot for himself at the counter. "But she's the only Dalton girl who seems to enjoy it." He picked up a wrapped caramel and twirled it by one end. The cellophane crackled with each half turn.

Penelope pinched the candy between thumb and forefinger to stop it. "Ella's too young to know better yet."

"Her father must've been a real piece of work if he made you think all guys are jerks."

"It's hard to get over someone telling you they don't love you and see no future with you." She kept her voice even, almost flippant in case he recognized the words as his own. Though of course he wouldn't. Since he'd been back, he'd been nothing but charming and friendly to her, as if he'd forgotten the way things had ended between them.

But he flinched. And a stupid pinprick of hope that he regretted how he'd treated her poked through her defenses.

"How did Ella take him leaving?" Noah asked.

"Brilliantly. Considering it was a long time ago."

"That's definitely his loss. She's such a sweet kid. And if he's going to be an asshole about it, he doesn't deserve her."

Penelope propped her elbows on the counter and leaned closer to him, her forearms stretching between them. "It is his loss. And sometimes I really hate that he'll never know what he's missing. But then I remind myself that she doesn't care that he's not around so I shouldn't either."

"Sounds like she wants someone around for you, though, even if it's not because she wants to have a dad," Noah said. He covered her hands with his and rubbed his thumb back and forth over her fingers.

She shivered at the unexpected touch. "My mother's brainwashed her with all her talk about magic and true love. But the future isn't always what we want it to be." Noah should have known that better than most.

"Yeah, but that's one of the risks of knowing what's in store for your life, isn't it? I mean, when it's unknown, the future can be as hopeful as you want it to be. But once you know, that's it. No going back. You've just got to learn to live with it."

"You say that like it's so easy to move on when you're faced with a future you don't want. Knowing there might not be anything you can do to stop it from coming true." Penelope realized her hand was still in his and pulled away.

Noah gave a short, mirthless laugh. "I'm pretty sure you've found a way around it." He leaned back and studied her, his eyes sharp and accusing.

All she could do was stare at him. It was the first time he'd come close to talking about her long-ago confession that they were meant to be together. That he was her fate. He'd practically run away then, as fast and as far as he could, wanting nothing to do with the future she'd dreamed of for them.

They watched each other for a moment, neither acknowledging what he'd said.

He dropped his arms to his knees again and picked at the edge of the counter with his thumb. "What about the people on the other side of the relationships your chocolates mess with? Does the magic take what they want into consideration?"

Penelope had no clue how to answer that. She didn't make the magic or the rules. She just followed them. She took a deep, steadying breath. Over his shoulder, the girls dipped plastic spoons in their drinks and fished out long strings of melty caramel and fat, gooey marshmallows. Their whispers slunk off into the corners of the room to hide.

"I get recipes that are very specific for how to make the magic work. But exactly what that magic will do? It's not always as cut-and-dried. The magic's not good or bad. It just is. So it must take both people into account," she said.

"So what happens when one of those people decides to ignore the future? Does the other person not have a say in it? Or do they need to use the magic too to make it work?"

Raising an eyebrow at his implication that she was the one now ignoring the magic, she said, "If someone chooses to ignore it, she would have her reasons and he should respect that."

Noah scooted an inch closer. His fingers toyed with the tips of hers and he looked up at her from under thick lashes. "What if he's not a respectful kind of guy?" The playfulness edged back into his voice, curving the corners of his mouth up.

"Then maybe she's right to keep her distance."

"Maybe he's gonna have to change her mind," he said.

God, why couldn't Noah make this easy?

Penelope curled her index finger around his and shook to ensure she had his full attention. "Okay, but you seriously have to stop telling Ella you'll take her to dinner. She doesn't know you're joking. She hasn't had a lot of men in her life and I don't want her to think you're anything but her friend's uncle who's just here for a few months, okay?"

Noah's mouth dropped open. "Wow, I knew you weren't my biggest fan or anything, but are you trying to run me out of town already?"

"No!" Ella's voice was so high it sounded like a yelp. She jumped up from the floor, where she and River had been inching slowly closer, unnoticed. She pressed her small body against his stool but kept her pleading eyes on Penelope. "Don't make him leave. Please, Mama, he'll stay if you tell him you want him to."

Penelope skirted the counter and bent down

so her face was level with Ella's. "Calm down, sweetie. We talked about this, remember?"

Noah looked at Penelope over Ella's trembling head. "Sorry. I didn't mean to freak her out," he whispered. His eyes asked the question he hadn't said aloud. *Why does she care if I stay?*

"It's not you," Penelope assured him, though it had everything to do with him. "It's been a weird couple of days. But she'll be fine." Putting her hands on Ella's shoulders, she pulled her daughter a few steps away from him.

Ella struggled against her hold and managed to twist around. "You're supposed to be here. With us. See?" She pulled something from the collar of her shirt and thrust it toward him. The compass sat faceup on her palm, the dial spinning madly around and around. It snapped to a stop so it pointed one end at Ella and Penelope and the other at Noah. When Penelope reached for it, Ella jerked her arm back, closing her fingers to hide it from view. "Wait!"

"Ella," she warned, stretching out the syllables. She waited for her daughter to meet her eyes before continuing, "I thought I told you to leave that at home this morning."

"But it's doing it for him too, just like I knew it would. This proves he's supposed to stay."

The wood creaked when Noah shifted on the stool. River slipped her hand into his. A smear of chocolate had dried into a crust above her top lip.

"I'm not sure if that's good or bad. Or if I even understand it," he said. He ran his free hand through his hair and leveled his gaze on Ella.

"It's good," Ella told him. She beamed at him and added, "Really, really good. You're finally here. That's better than cake for breakfast."

Noah returned the smile, the resemblance between the two unmistakable. It was easier to ignore the traits Ella got from him when he wasn't around. But side by side, Penelope wondered how long it would be before other people started noticing, comparing. If she was lucky, Noah would be gone before that happened.

But when had she been lucky where he was concerned?

"It's hard to argue with that," he said.

Penelope nudged Ella another step back. "This is what I was talking about, Noah. Saying things like that, encouraging her infatuation with you, doesn't help."

"I'll work on it, okay?" Noah said. "As long as you work on giving me a chance."

"You're not really in a position to bargain with me. My kid, my rules."

"Point taken." He straightened on the stool, pulling his shoulders back and nodding at her.

Ella tipped her head up to look at Penelope. Her long lashes fluttered when she inhaled a deep breath. "Do I get a say?"

"Nope," Penelope said. She cupped Ella's face

to keep her from pulling away. "And unless you want me to take the necklace away right now, you need to go put it in your bag without arguing. Got it?"

When Penelope released her, Ella tugged the chain from around her neck and glanced at Noah again. She didn't smile. She just studied him a moment then turned away. Her footsteps were sluggish as she walked to her backpack and zipped the necklace inside.

How was Penelope supposed to keep Noah safely on the periphery of their lives when Ella was so intent on making him an integral part?

18

Noah thought that his nicotine cravings would've calmed down after a few weeks of abstinence, but walking through the cloud of smoke from some of the waitstaff and kitchen guys in the parking lot on his break left an ache in the back of his throat. He sped up to get past it and hooked a right onto Hawthorne Street. Walking a six-block loop through downtown had become a ritual. As much to calm his jittery nerves as to clear his head.

When anyone asked him why he left town in the first place, he always said small-town life was akin to living in an ant farm. Same view. Same people. Same boring life day in and day out. But the longer he stayed in Malarkey—and the more he allowed himself to be a part of life there—he had to admit it felt really damn good knowing the people in the stories his customers shared while they knocked back a few beers at the end of the night. He liked being someplace where he was more than just the bartender people unloaded their problems on. Where he could feel like part of his family again.

Where he could maybe do something about the real reason he'd stayed away so long.

Rounding the corner onto Park Street, Noah instinctively sought out the Chocolate Cottage amid the other shops. The streetlights caught on the gold lettering on the windows, making it hard to miss. It wasn't a coincidence his nightly walks took him past Penelope's chocolate shop. The chocolates had once told her that Noah would be her true love. And at eighteen, that had scared the shit out of him. Still did, if he was being brutally honest, which was how he preferred to do things these days. But somewhere in the middle of all of the fear was this tiny glint of hope that she had been right.

He still hadn't figured out what the hell to do about that yet. But since Tucker had a month or more before his cast would come off, Noah had plenty of time to decide if he wanted to try and win her back.

A light burned in the back of the chocolate shop. Voices that didn't belong to Penelope or her mom carried out the cracked front door. Noah stopped when he reached it and flicked the broken door handle with his finger. Swearing, he pushed inside as quietly as he could. He shouldn't have bothered with being stealthy. The two idiot teens who had broken in were too busy ransacking a table at the back of the kitchen area to even notice him.

"Finding anything good in there?" Noah asked.

The boys shot away from the table as if it had suddenly burst into flames. The one with shaggy blond hair and a Death Cab tee tripped over an empty drawer they'd thrown on the floor during their search and almost went down on his ass. His friend's death grip on his hoodie was the only thing that saved him.

This was going to be too easy. Noah almost felt sorry for them. But then he thought of Penelope coming into work in the morning and finding the place trashed, and he didn't mind what he was about to do so much. Somebody had to teach them a lesson.

And if he could have a little fun while doing it, all the better.

"Don't let me stop you. I've been wondering how that table worked since I was your age. I grew up with the girl who owns it. Always figured she'd find a way to hex me if I did what you two are doing, though."

Sad thing was, he was telling the truth. Discovering the secrets behind the Daltons' magic had never been worth the risk of losing Penelope's trust. But then he'd managed to do that anyway.

"We're just looking," one of them said. The ass-saver, not the ass-save-ee.

"Yeah, Penelope wouldn't really curse us for that. Would she?" the second one said.

Noah scratched his chin to keep from laughing

at them. "Depends on what you were hoping to find."

"We were looking for the fate-changing hot chocolate recipe. There're these girls at school who would do pretty much anything to get their hands on it. So we kinda told them we could get it."

"It's not even about the girls. If we had the magic, then we'd still be able to change things. Make our futures whatever we wanted. And no one would be able to stop us from using it just because they felt like it." The kid pointed an accusing finger at the table. "But there's nothing here. Like literally nothing. Every drawer is effing empty."

Either those two had piss-poor luck or the table was capable of more magic than any of them knew. And if messing with them wasn't so much fun, Noah might have shared his theories. "Maybe she knew you were coming and cleaned it out ahead of time."

"You mean she's psychic too?"

"Wouldn't put it past her," Noah said. Some of the chocolates did show the future, after all. And suddenly the idea that Penelope was psychic didn't seem as far-fetched. "What are your names?"

"Justin," ass-saver said, biting off the word so it was all sharp edges.

"Patrick," the other one added. He rubbed the

back of his neck and flicked his eyes from Noah to his friend. "Dude, we've gotta get out of here before she finds us."

"Sorry, guys, but the only place you're going now is back to my bar with me so I can call your parents," Noah said.

He inwardly cringed. Calling their parents? God, what had gotten into him? He sounded like such a prick. Teenage Noah would be so embarrassed for turning into Current Noah.

"Are you serious?" Justin asked.

Patrick bent down, gathered three of the farthest-flung drawers, and shoved them back into their holes in the table. He tried to fit one of them into four different slots before he found one the right size. "Listen, we'll put it all back the way we found it and no one besides the three of us has to know."

Noah considered it. He could send the boys on their way then see if he had any better luck getting answers out of the table. Answers that could tell him if the future Penelope had once seen with him was even still a possibility. But if he went behind her back like that, he would shred the little bit of trust they'd started to rebuild. "I think she might know something's up when she sees how you mangled her doorknob."

"I told you we should've just tried to pick it."

"Right. 'Cause that's not a skill you have to learn or anything."

"Next time," Noah said, hoping they weren't stupid enough to actually try again. "Now get all this cleaned up. And don't even think about running because I've got pictures of you both on my phone and I'll call the cops instead of your parents."

But what he didn't have on his phone was Penelope's number so he could give her a heads-up before she got to work in the morning. This was Malarkey, though. One of his customers was bound to know her number or, at the very least, where she lived now.

Penelope had put Ella to bed hours before and had talked herself out of checking on her a good dozen times. Ella's headache had been minor in comparison to some she'd had, but that was little consolation. The fact that it had been there at all was more effective at keeping Penelope awake than a strong hit of caffeine.

Giving up on sleep, she stopped at Ella's open door long enough to be certain her daughter was okay. One leg dangled off the side of the bed, but she slept soundlessly. Penelope walked downstairs, careful to keep her footfalls as soft as possible. In the kitchen she made a cup of tea and poured a generous finger of bourbon into it. Then she added one ice cube to dull the bite a bit. She took a long sip. The combination of hot water and alcohol lit a trail of fire through her chest. It was almost strong enough to burn up the helplessness festering inside.

She carried her drink into the living room and settled in the corner of the couch. The stereo came to life with the push of a button. Her favorite Rosi Golan album had been disk four in the CD changer for a few years. She listened to it often enough there was no reason to swap it out for anything else. When the first chords of "Think of Me" played low enough that it wouldn't disturb Ella upstairs, the knots in her shoulders loosened. Maybe by the end of the album she'd be able to sleep.

A few seconds into the third song, someone knocked on her door. Penelope jolted, sending tea sloshing over the side of the cup onto her hand. She set the mug on a stack of Christmas toy catalogs that had come in the mail and wiped her wet hand on her pajama pants. She peeked out one of the windows flanking the door. There was definitely someone on her porch, but in the darkness she could only make out the shape of the hulking mass, no features to clue her in as to who it was. She hesitated. The door was unlocked, like most of the homes in Malarkey. And the temptation to bolt the door made her fingers twitch. Which was ridiculous. No one in town would hurt her, even if they were upset about the festival. They'd leave more notes or possibly start a petition to make her change her mind. But scare tactics and violence weren't Malarkey's style.

"Whoever's outside is harmless," she whispered to herself. She eyed the table lamp a few feet away just in case. It was a tall, ceramic cylinder in a shade of green so pale it almost looked white, and just wide enough for her fingers not to touch when wrapped around it. She could sacrifice it if she had to.

She cracked the door open and the light from the lamp rushed out, pausing on Noah in his brown leather jacket and dark-wash jeans before getting sucked up by the night.

"Noah?" Penelope sagged against the door, blocking the slim opening. She kept one hand on the knob, the other braced against the jamb. "How do you even know where I live?"

One side of his mouth quirked up in amusement while the rest of his features remained serious, hardened. Whatever he'd come for, it wasn't a social call. "Seriously? That's what you're starting with? Not 'Hey, Noah. It's like eleven thirty on a Tuesday night. And I know you should be at work instead of standing oh-so-patiently on my doorstep while I debate letting you in, so something must be wrong.' " He pitched his voice higher on the last few words.

"I don't sound like that," she said.

He hung his head so a hunk of hair fell across his face. "That's not the point."

"Okay. So what's wrong?"

"I caught some kids breaking into your shop."

Unlike her house, the shop she did lock. She'd considered an alarm system too, but that would have required calling a company from out of town to come and install it and it had never seemed worth the effort.

Penelope managed to talk past the lump of worry in her throat. "Into *my* shop?"

"Well, it would be pretty pointless for me to come all the way over here to tell you that they broke into someone else's shop." Noah stepped forward, crowding her.

"Damn it," she whispered. She pressed a fist to her chest, her heart slapping frantically back at it. The Chocolate Cottage was more than just her job. But what if someone had decided to take it from her as retribution for her refusing to help with the festival? Her hand fell away from the door, and she used the one still clutching the doorjamb to keep her steady. "Did they damage anything? Take anything?"

"Other than the doorknob, I think everything is okay. I did a quick sweep of the place to make sure before I hauled them back to the bar to wait for their parents to come get their sorry asses. I think they were looking for something in that table with all the drawers. A bunch of them were already pulled out and tossed on the floor when they came up empty."

"The drawers were empty?" Her first instinct was to run upstairs, scoop Ella out of bed, and drive over there to make sure the table was safe. That they hadn't actually found a recipe in one of the drawers. Though even if they had, they wouldn't have been able to read it. The table's fail-safe against thieves and overly eager patrons would ensure that. But they could have found ingredients or simply eaten some of the chocolates already in the display case, hoping that would help them find whatever it was they wanted in the first place.

"Yeah, they were. But the way you just said that makes me think they weren't supposed to be."

Relief flooded her, and for the first time she noticed the frigid night air seeping through her thin pajama pants. Cinching her overlong cardigan tighter around her waist, she said, "The table they were messing with is the one that gives us all of our recipes. It probably hid everything that's inside to keep them from getting their hands on anything."

He gave her that half smile again. The not-quite-teasing, not-quite-serious one. How was she ever supposed to tell if he meant what he was saying when he used that smile?

"You say that like it's a living thing. Not something that was once a living tree but is now very much a hunk of dead wood," he said.

"It's a magic-producing table, Noah. It's not exactly normal." Penelope hugged the door closer again to keep the heat inside. Noah must have been cold too, but she couldn't bring herself to invite him in. While she was grateful he'd told her about the break-in so quickly, the scales were still tipped heavily on the jerk-who-broke-her-heart side of things. "I wasn't kidding, you know. How did you know where I live?"

"You really have to ask that in a place as tight-knit as Malarkey? There were at least five customers at the bar who could've given me directions."

Right. Of course he'd had to ask someone. Just because she'd been plagued with thoughts of him for the past few weeks didn't mean he'd been checking up on her since he came back to town. "And what about the kids in my store? How did you know they were there?"

He cupped his hands in front of his mouth and huffed hot breath onto them. "Sometimes I go for walks on my breaks. Nicotine withdrawal makes me a little antsy so the cold air and the constant movement keep me thinking about other things. Your shop is on my normal loop. They weren't exactly smart about breaking in. Busted door handle. Lights on in the back. Talking at a normal volume. Wasn't hard to spot them."

"Lucky for me then."

"I didn't call Martin over at the station yet.

Wasn't sure if you'd want to involve the cops or just handle things on your own."

The less attention this whole thing got, the better it would be for everyone. She sighed and said, "Hopefully having their parents called will be enough to keep them from doing something like this again."

"Let's hope. If not, I've got their names and I snapped a few photos of them before I let them know I was there just in case they managed to get by me."

"You've had this happen before?"

He let out a quiet laugh. "I've dealt with my share of underagers doing stupid shit. They're a lot more cooperative if you've got proof. And usually they don't do it again. At least not to me. Which in this case means not to you either."

"Thanks, Noah," she said. She turned as Ella's bare feet stomped down the stairs. "Hey, sweetie, what are you doing out of bed?"

Ella slid on the rug at the bottom of the steps and grabbed on to Penelope's waist to stop herself. Her eyes brimmed with excitement. "I woke up because I heard this little *scritching* sound by my bed." She scratched her fingers in the air for emphasis. "At first I thought it was a spider or something and I was too scared to even move. But when I turned on my light, I saw it was my necklace! It was going crazy, Mama. And I thought maybe there was a homeless kitty outside or something and I raced down here so I didn't miss my chance to get him."

A kitten would be so much better than the reason that popped into Penelope's head. At least the kitten was something they both wanted. If the necklace was reacting to Noah's presence, then she would have to admit that he had a place in their daughter's life. Whether Penelope wanted him there or not.

"Sorry, kid. No stray cats out here," Noah said before Penelope could wrap her brain around a response.

Ella's head snapped up, her smile even wider than a moment before. "Noah!" She raced to the door and threw it open to greet him properly.

"Ella!" he said back with the same amount of enthusiasm.

Penelope followed her daughter, praying that Ella didn't connect the necklace to Noah. It would've been a leap, but Ella was her grandmother's granddaughter and things like coincidence didn't exist in their worlds.

"Is he spending the night?" Ella asked.

Where did she get that idea from?

Penelope crossed her arms over Ella's chest and hauled her back so Ella was snug against her body. Looking down at her daughter, she asked, "When has a man ever spent the night in our house?"

"Never," Ella said, a hint of sadness in

her voice. "I thought maybe Noah would be different."

Noah stretched out his hand for a high five. Ella obliged. "Somebody's got to be first."

"Sorry to burst your bubble, kid. He's going back to work and you're going back to bed." Penelope shot Noah a challenging look. He stuck his hands in his pockets and kept his mouth shut.

"But I'm not tired," Ella said.

"You will be in the morning. Do you want to miss another day of school because you're too sleepy to get out of bed?" Penelope asked.

"No."

"Okay, then. Let's go." She released Ella and turned her toward the stairs. To Noah she said, "Thanks again for the heads-up. I'll let you know if I need those names."

He studied her for a moment, his eyes lingering on her lips as if he was thinking about what might have happened if she had invited him in for the night. "See you later, Penelope. Bye, Ella." He raised his voice for the last part and grinned when she turned around and told him to sleep well.

Penelope shut the door and turned the lock.

As if something that simple could keep him out of her life.

19

Penelope had resisted hustling Ella into the car the night before to go check on the shop. There was no reason to upset Ella with the news and risk the stress of it causing her headache to come back. And Penelope couldn't have fixed the door at midnight anyway. But she'd woken up every hour from vivid dreams of the table emitting thick black smoke that swallowed up her customers and her chocolates erasing people's futures so their bodies froze in place—mid-step, mid-sentence, mid-life.

Logically she knew the dreams were nothing more than her subconscious feeding off her anxiety, but she dropped Ella off at school a good twenty minutes earlier than normal and headed straight into work just to be sure everything was okay. When she got there, Noah was crouched on the sidewalk in front of her shop door. His leather jacket was tossed to the side, the sleeves of his Henley shirt shoved up to his elbows while he screwed in a new door handle.

"You fixed my door," Penelope said, not entirely sure she was happy about it. The handle was too shiny, too unused, compared to the battered old door. Its newness was impossible to miss. She gave it less than an hour before the first person asked her what happened.

"Oh, hey." He rocked back on his heels and braced a hand on the wall to keep himself steady when he looked up at her. He flashed his get-anything-he-wants smile. "I got Clover to open up the hardware store a little early. Didn't want you to have to worry about this on top of everything else."

It was hard to believe him when he said it with that smile. And when she didn't have a clue what he wanted in return. She jingled her keys in the palm of her hand. "You didn't have to do this."

"I know."

"Then why did you?"

Noah shrugged. "To be nice?"

His mouth started tugging into a smile again. She looked away. Whatever he was trying to do, it wouldn't work. She wouldn't let it. But he was definitely making it difficult.

Penelope crossed her arms over her chest and pushed for an answer. "Yeah, but why are you being nice to me?"

"No ulterior motives. It was something I could easily do and I figured it would save you some hassle," he said.

"I'll pay you back for the parts," she said.

"Receipt's already on the counter inside."

"Good." Okay, so maybe this was just a nice

gesture to help her out. She wouldn't have thought twice if anyone else in town had stopped by to help her. She should be happy he was there, accept his help, and be grateful she wasn't out there in her skirt trying to install a new door handle. "Thanks, Noah."

He dropped one knee to the ground and splayed a wide hand on the door, pushing it open so she could go inside. "I'm almost finished. I'll come in and see you before I go."

Penelope skirted around him, careful not to let her bare calf skim his arm as she passed. She could talk her mind into lumping Noah in with everyone else, but her body refused to comply. Just one touch, no matter how innocent, sparked memories of the summer when they couldn't keep their hands off of each other. If she wasn't careful, those long-buried feelings could catch fire and burn her up from the inside out.

Once inside the shop, she didn't even stop to set down her purse. She went directly to the table and opened the first drawer her fingers touched. It slid open without any resistance. Tin canisters of ground hot peppers rattled against each other. The next one she opened revealed still-wrapped bars of 70 percent dark chocolate and a cluster of cinnamon sticks tied together with twine.

Noah had said the table was empty when the would-be thieves went through it. But there everything was. Just like always.

"Thank you," she whispered to the table. She rubbed her hand along the top as if to tell it that it had done a good job. She didn't want to think about what might have happened if those boys had gotten a recipe out of it.

Penelope backtracked through the kitchen, doing a cursory check of the rest of the shop to make sure nothing else had been disturbed. As far as she could tell, they'd gotten away with nothing. Even the display case was still fully stocked. Which meant the boys hadn't just been after magic. They'd gone straight for the source. She turned to watch Noah as he collected his jacket and tools, grateful that he'd been there to stop them.

When he came inside, he said, "It came with one key." He held it out to her, pinching the skinny end between forefinger and thumb. "I can run it over and have Clover make a copy for your mom if you need me to. I don't have to be at work until noon."

"I think I can manage that. But thanks. Really." She slipped it from his grip. Her fingers skimmed over the tips of his of their own volition. Snatching her hand back, she worked the key onto her key ring so she didn't misplace it. And so she didn't have to look at Noah and see the smile she was sure had crept onto his face at the sudden contact. "How did things go with the parents last night?"

He drummed his knuckles on the counter. "Honestly, they were more relieved that I hadn't caught their kids drinking underage."

"Sure. Why be worried about a potential felony as long as the boys aren't getting drunk too?" It wouldn't have been surprising if most of the town thought the same way. They were upset enough about the festival to think they should have as much claim on the magic as she did.

"Whoa. Didn't mean to hit a nerve."

She looped the key ring onto her index finger and bounced the keys a few times before dropping them on the counter. "Do you ever mean to or are you just exceptionally good at it with me?"

"A little bit of both, actually." Noah grinned at her, and her anger receded enough for her to laugh. "But seriously, if you want to make sure they all understand it's a bigger deal than they're making it out to be, I can—" He broke off as someone entered the shop. Staring over her shoulder, he added, "Never mind."

Penelope turned, expecting to find her mom since the Chocolate Cottage didn't open for another hour, and instead found herself being rushed by the Avery sisters. Nina and Heather. They weren't twins, but some days they looked so much alike it was hard to tell them apart. Today was one of those days. With their near-identical blue eyes puffy and shot through with streaks of red and matching looks of desperation that pulled their makeup-free faces taut, they even moved in unison. They pushed in close to Penelope, edging Noah out of the way. Nina's hand clutched at Penelope's left arm to hold her in place while Heather followed suit on the right. Their fingers dug in hard enough to bruise.

"What are you doing?" Penelope managed to free one arm, which she held in front of her palm out to keep them from crowding in again.

"We need to talk to you," Nina said.

Heather clasped her hands together and pressed them to her chest. "You have to help our sons." She was a few seconds slower than her sister so her plea, softer and less demanding, was all but lost.

But Penelope heard the last word. And the nervous dancing of her stomach meant that their sons had managed to slip something past Noah last night after all. She shifted an inch or two to see his face unobstructed by the two women. He scrubbed a hand over his stubbly jaw then swore under his breath.

When Noah looked up a moment later and found her watching him, he asked, "Want me to stay?"

"It's probably better if you don't," she said.

"Definitely better," Nina said, her voice a hoarse whisper. She gripped her sister's hand at her side, their knuckles going instantly white from the pressure, and didn't bother looking at him when she added, "Unless you've got some magical abilities you've been keeping to yourself all this time and can undo whatever is wrong with our sons."

"Nope. Whatever they did, they did to themselves. Nothing I can do to help that. I'll be around if you need me, Penelope."

She nodded. He turned back once before he reached the door, but Nina and Heather were already talking again, their words running together and over each other in a frenzy of worry, and Penelope gave them her full attention.

"Okay, slow down. Can just one of you tell me what happened?" Penelope asked.

Nina released Heather's hand and slapped her fingers against the counter to get the blood flowing again. "Well, as I'm sure Noah told you, he found Justin and Patrick in here last night. We don't know exactly what they were looking for or what they might have found. Just that they're not themselves this morning and it's because of something they got here."

Something they *stole*. But correcting Nina's word choice wouldn't change whatever had happened. So instead, Penelope asked, "What did they say when you asked them?"

"They don't remember anything," Nina said.

"That's convenient," Penelope said. They were thieves *and* liars.

Heather wiped a tear from her cheek and opened

211

her eyes wide to keep more from escaping. "She doesn't just mean about last night. They don't know who they are. They can't even remember their own names. It's like their whole lives have been erased."

Her dreams from the night before rushed back to her in all-too-vivid snapshots. The magic out of control. People getting hurt, losing hope, blaming Penelope. If what Nina and Heather were saying was true, her dreams hadn't been that far off from what was actually happening to the boys.

But it wasn't possible. Even if they'd found a recipe, they shouldn't have been able to read it. The magic's defenses would have made sure of that. This had to be something else. But what, she had no clue.

Penelope gripped the key ring she'd set on the counter so the metal teeth of the keys bit into the soft skin of her palms. It wasn't hard enough to break skin, but the sudden jolt of pain helped to clear her mind. "They must've eaten something while they were here, but I don't know what would cause amnesia. We don't have any chocolates that do that."

"I don't care what it was. I just want you to fix it. Please." Nina's voice cracked, and she avoided meeting Penelope's eyes.

"All of the magic wears off eventually," Penelope said.

She led them to one of the sofas in the middle of the room. She took the leather armchair across from them. Heather perched on the edge of the couch with her hands folded between her bouncing knees while Nina leaned against the armrest for support. They both kept their eyes locked on Penelope.

"It's been almost twelve hours. Isn't that more than enough time?" Heather said.

"It depends on how many they ate. What they ate. The magic compounds the more you ingest, so it could be with them awhile yet."

Nina pressed her fingers to her mouth, but the words came out anyway. "Oh, God. What if it's permanent?"

Penelope refused to let that even be a possibility. "It won't be," she said. It couldn't be. Even the heightened effects when Sabina consumed the chocolates she made didn't last forever. "Noah said they didn't get anything from the table. So whatever they ate was made by either me or my mom. And I promise it's all safe. Whatever is happening with them will fade and their memories will come back."

Heather squeezed her sister's arm. "They made something," she said. "Last night after we picked them up. I thought they'd gone to bed but a few hours later I found them in the kitchen baking. I didn't think anything of it, but what if that's what caused it and

213

I just let them do it without even knowing?"

"They were brownies, I think. I found a couple of them wrapped up in a napkin in Patrick's hoodie this morning," Nina added. She leaned forward so she was shoulder to shoulder with her sister. A united front.

Noah had been right. These women didn't seem to care that their kids had broken into her shop and intended to steal from her. That thought temporarily overruled her empathy for the boys. Penelope pointed a finger at each of them in turn. "Let me get this straight. Your sons committed a crime and you just let them go on with their regularly scheduled evening?"

She didn't need to ask why the boys were allowed to be out that late on a school night. There usually wasn't much trouble for kids to get into in Malarkey.

"No, we talked to them and made them promise to never do anything like that again. And they were supposed to come to see you first thing this morning and apologize in person. Then when Justin woke up, his memories were gone."

"Patrick too. When we realized it was happening to both of them, we knew it had to be because of what they did here," Heather said. She glanced at Nina, who nodded her agreement.

"You have to help them, Penelope," Nina said. Not even a *please*.

She'd stopped expecting an apology about

a minute into the conversation. But Nina and Heather demanding she fix the consequences of what their kids had done was so far over the line.

She curled her fingers around the curved wooden handle of the chair and leaned toward them. "I don't *have* to do anything. They broke into my business and tried to steal from me. The only reason they didn't succeed is because they got caught." She managed to keep her voice steady despite the surge of anger running through her.

Nina's face paled as Penelope's words sunk in. "So you're just going to let them stay cursed?" she asked.

"No, I'm not. I promise you, I know how hard it is when there's something wrong with your kid that you can't fix. I'm not going to let them suffer just because I'm angry about what they did. But I need them to come into the shop and talk to me before I can do anything to help them."

"They're sorry, Penelope." A flush crept over Nina's cheeks as if finally saying the words made her realize she should have started with them. "We'll make them tell you every day for the rest of their lives if that's what it takes. But please just do whatever you can first."

Heather bobbed her head up and down, instinctively agreeing with her sister. "We will. We swear they'll apologize as many times as you want them to."

"I'm not looking for an apology," Penelope said. Though that would be nice, considering what they'd done. She sat back, dropping her hands into her lap. "I need them to bring in the recipe they used for the brownies. And then I need them to try and find an antidote in the table."

"Why can't you look for it without them?"

Penelope fought the urge to yell at them both. They were scared and defensive. Just like any mother in their position would be. God knows she'd been there more often than not in the past year. She met their eyes and gave them the truth. "Because the contents of the table are exactly the way I left them yesterday despite your boys finding nothing but empty drawers, save for the one recipe that's causing this whole mess. I'm guessing the magic is trying to teach them a lesson. And it won't give them back their memories until they have learned it."

"If I didn't know what you've been through with your daughter, I'm not sure I'd believe that the magic could be responsible for this on its own. But I honestly can't imagine you'd hurt someone else's child just to make a point," Nina said, the fight in her dissipating.

"I wouldn't. Not ever," Penelope said.

Heather stood and pulled her sister to her feet as well. "We'll bring them. And if you have any

216

sway over the magic, please do whatever you can to help them."

Penelope stayed in the chair long after they'd gone, trying to convince herself the good the table does with its magic was worth all the bad it seemed to be doling out lately.

The rest of the day was a constant stream of questions and accusations and pleas to make the boys better. As if Penelope had wiped their memories personally. As if they had been innocent bystanders in this whole thing.

Ruth Anne was the first one in after Nina and Heather went home to check on their sons. "Oh, Penelope honey, it's just awful what happened to those boys. When I heard what they did, I was ready to march over to their houses and box their ears good. But then to find out they can't even remember their own names. Well, that just broke my heart."

"I didn't do it to them," Penelope had said, unable to quell the defensive tone in her voice.

"Oh, I know that. Everybody knows that. Don't you worry." Ruth Anne patted her on the shoulder and scuttled out as quickly as she came in.

But Penelope was worried. There was no guarantee she could reverse the magic that had stolen their memories. She had to hope the table would take a cue from her and forgive them.

Otherwise, well, she didn't want to think of that possibility yet.

She tried to remain calm, objective, when reassuring everyone she would do whatever she could to help get the boys back to normal. And she succeeded rather well until the mayor came in. Henry strode right past the two women standing in line, his shoulders hunching in his wool coat and his thick fingers thumping on the counter as he waited his turn to talk at her. Because, like with everyone else that day, it wasn't going to be a conversation.

No one wanted to hear her side.

They only wanted her magic. And they wanted it to work the way they expected it to.

"Save your breath, Henry," she said before he could speak. She didn't let her eyes stray from the pot of water she was filling to steep peppermint tea. The less worried she pretended to be, the more it would calm others down. At least that was the hope. "I promise you that my mom and I are trying to fix it."

He leaned toward her, angling his back to the women whose tea she prepared. "People are scared, Penelope. And I need to make sure something like this doesn't happen again."

"Well, if you can keep idiot kids from breaking into my business, I think we'd have a better shot at it."

"I thought the magic had some sort of self-defense mechanism to keep this kind of thing from happening."

Penelope handed off two steaming cups of tea and a plate of toffee to the women behind Henry. They'd done a poor job of pretending not to eavesdrop and took their time settling on a table so they didn't miss what Penelope said in response. She smiled at them and resisted waving as they finally sat down in the chairs closest to the counter. "Nothing's foolproof, Henry. If someone wants something badly enough, they'll find a way to get it."

Well, almost anything. The line seemed to be drawn somewhere before curing inoperable brain tumors.

Thinking about Ella reminded her of the matching looks of hopelessness on the Avery sisters' faces that morning. Penelope didn't have a clue how to reverse the table's magic, but she had to believe she'd find a way.

"Some people are calling for an ad hoc town meeting," he said. "To figure out what to do about this situation and the festival."

"What good is that going to do? I mean, if someone thinks they know how to fix this, by all means, tell them to speak up," she said. "But if they're looking for a venue to all gang up on me at once so they don't have to come in here one at a time and tell me how this is all my fault, you can forget it."

He flapped the two halves of his unbuttoned coat against the warmth of the shop. "No one is blaming you."

"Maybe not yet. But they will if Justin and Patrick don't get their memories back."

No one would point out that the boys had stolen the magic. That they'd done this to themselves. That detail would be glossed over in favor of the fact that Penelope refused to let her magic be a part of the festival.

And they would never let her forget it.

20

For three nights in a row, the doorbell woke Penelope and Ella with five rapid rings that tore through the silence of the house. Each time, Ella launched out of bed, Noah's name trailing after her as she booked it downstairs to the front door. Penelope, who hadn't so much been asleep as she was simply lying in bed with her eyes closed as her mind conjured up a dozen different scenarios for how to reverse the table's magic, followed a few paces behind. Each time she had to threaten to take away Ella's necklace to keep her daughter from flinging the door wide in her haste to see if Noah was outside.

And each time, the porch was empty when Penelope flicked on the light and peered out the window. Save for a dozen pieces of paper, fighting against the cold wind, that had been tied to the branches of the magnolia tree in the yard.

Every one of the notes said the same thing. *We're sorry.*

Penelope left the Closed sign up on the front door of the Chocolate Cottage and locked the door for good measure. The Avery sisters had been waiting on the sidewalk with their sons when Penelope arrived at work, just like she'd requested every morning since Justin and Patrick lost their memories. Her mom had joined them a few minutes later, her curly hair still wet and hanging, with considerably less volume than normal, down her back. Sabina's eyes were bright and glassy when she apologized for being late. Her smile a touch too wide to be natural.

Her mom must have eaten one of the Bittersweet truffles the night before so Penelope wouldn't find out. The effects of the chocolate had diminished some but were still messing with Sabina's head. Lucky for her, Penelope could only focus on one magical crisis at the moment.

They'd had two sessions with Justin and Patrick already with no luck. The table was being stubborn. Or maybe the boys were. But whichever was at fault, it resulted in them remaining "cursed" as their moms had told anyone who would listen over the past few days.

During the first attempt to reverse the magic, Penelope had suggested remaking the brownies that had caused their problem in the first place, but using ingredients from the table that could hopefully counteract the bad magic. Nina didn't even let her finish the sentence before vetoing it. She grabbed the boys, shot a death-look at her sister, and left before Penelope or Sabina could stop them.

When they arrived for the second try, Nina seethed silently while the boys ate chocolate after chocolate that Sabina fed them.

After the fourth one, Patrick turned to Penelope, dark chocolate smudged on his top lip, and asked, "Did you get our notes?"

"I did," Penelope said. They meant well, so she tried not to be too annoyed about being woken up at 1:00 a.m. Though she still couldn't understand why their moms let them out of their houses so late at night after everything that had happened. "You found your way to my house. Does that mean some memories are starting to come back?"

"No, nothing yet. Our moms had to draw us a map."

Justin glared at his mom and aunt. The lack of recognition did nothing to soften his look of annoyance. Even though he couldn't remember who he was, some habits were too ingrained to lose. "They won't let us drive until we get our memories back so we had to ride bikes over there. They won't really let us do anything."

Sabina clucked her tongue. "And what do you think you should be allowed to do with no idea of who you are or what you might be capable of?" She looked up at them, as they both towered over her tiny frame, and scrutinized them. They were smart enough to look contrite.

"We don't know what else to do, ma'am."

Patrick's attempts to make up for his cousin's attitude seemed just as natural. "They said we needed to apologize and something about a table that really didn't make much sense, so we figured we'd go for the first one and see where that got us."

If they didn't remember the apothecary table held magic, it would be much harder to prove they were sorry for what they'd done. If they were truly sorry at all.

So for attempt three, they all crowded into the kitchen and took turns opening random drawers in the apothecary table. It wasn't the most scientific method, but Penelope had run out of ideas.

"What if this doesn't work either?" Justin asked after a string of empty drawers.

"Then we come up with something else," Patrick said.

"No," Penelope said. Four sets of eyes—the moms' blue and the boys' brown—fixed on her. Before they could yell—or worse, walk out again—she clarified, "This has to work. It's how you found the recipe to begin with."

Sabina, who had sat in a chair beside the table without saying one word since they began, finally piped up. "If you believe it will work, then it will work. If not, then you may as well go home now and start your lives over."

Heather's fingers paused on a pearl knob.

Closing her eyes, she moved her lips in a silent plea. Patrick nudged her hand away.

"I got this, Mom. I think it has to be one of us anyway," he said. When he opened the next drawer, the one that usually held the dark chocolate, a piece of paper waited for him. He held it out for them all to read.

"It's just gibberish," Nina said. She tried to pluck it from her nephew's hand, but he curled his fingers up to protect it.

"Not to me," Penelope said. She knew exactly what it would take to fix them now.

Penelope didn't have the right equipment at the shop to make the spicy rosemary brownies the recipe would yield. And while the table had given her a few of the key ingredients—like ground cayenne pepper, fresh rosemary, and dark cocoa powder—she was on her own for the more basic things like eggs and flour. All of which meant she couldn't cure the boys that very instant. Much to the Avery sisters' displeasure.

But they didn't dare argue with her. Not when she held their sons' futures—and technically their pasts too—in her hands.

By the time they arrived at Penelope's house after lunch, the brownies had been cooling on the counter for less than five minutes. The not-quite-set middle still jiggled slightly as she tested the pan.

"They're almost ready," she said when Heather and Nina crowded her at the island. "Feel free to sit."

No one moved. They all eyed the brownies, but with varying states of hope lighting their expressions.

Patrick picked up the recipe by the edges and examined the foreign words. "Do you think it'll work?"

"There's no reason it shouldn't." And there were so many reasons why it couldn't fail. Penelope focused on the positives—on Patrick and Justin regaining their memories, on the magic working when she really needed it to, on the town seeing that she was still a team player.

"That's not an answer," Justin said, rapping his knuckles on the stone countertop.

She picked up a sprig of rosemary and tore off leaves to sprinkle over the top of the brownies. "I wish I could promise that this will fix everything, but I can't. There's never a guarantee that the magic will work."

"But you think it will?" Heather asked. She turned her penetrating gaze to Penelope.

"I do," Penelope said.

Nina picked up the table knife and handed it to Penelope. "Then let's find out."

Penelope cut the still-warm brownies into nine large squares. The dark, decadent scent intensified as she extracted two pieces and scattered rosemary and sea salt on top as the recipe instructed.

Handing each boy a plate, she said, "Dig in."

Nothing happened for the first few bites.

The boys side-eyed each other, polished off their respective brownies, and went for round two. Halfway through the second square, Patrick paused. The chunk of chocolate trembled in the air an inch from his mouth.

"I told you it was a bad idea," he said.

Mouth full, Justin mumbled, "Then why'd you go along with it? It's not like I forced you."

No wonder it wasn't working. If Patrick and Justin didn't believe it would, why would the magic help them? Penelope hugged her arms across her chest and sent a silent plea out to the universe.

Please don't give up on them.

Patrick licked a rosemary leaf from his top lip. "I did it because it would have been a jerk move to make you deal with the consequences on your own. But I'm done with your crazy ideas. The next time you try and talk me into something, all I'm going to say is 'Hey, remember that time we lost our memories for a week?' "

"And I'll say, 'Hey, remember that time we got our memories back?' And then you'll have to come up with a better reason for nixing my ideas." Justin grinned at his cousin like the whole thing was one big joke.

Patrick dropped his head, shaking it, but when he looked up, he was smiling too.

The tightness in Penelope's throat eased. "Wait. Are you saying it worked? You remember?"

"Yeah. Feels like everything's back to normal," Patrick said.

"Do you remember breaking your arm when you were five and Justin convinced you to try and fly off the roof of the house?" his mother asked.

Justin wiped his fingers on the thighs of his jeans, transferring smudges of chocolate to the dark fabric. "Hey, I was gonna jump too, Aunt Heather. You and Mom just came outside before I could."

"One of these days you two are not going to be so lucky," Nina said.

"But today is not that day," Justin said, grinning.

Then the sisters started talking at once, their words stumbling over each other. Penelope couldn't make out what either one had said. But then they were hugging her at the same time, their arms tangling around her shoulders and their cheeks pressed to both of hers, locking her between them.

The crush of bodies would have been suffocating without the rush of relief buoying her from the inside.

This time, the magic had worked just the way it was supposed to.

21

The people of Malarkey were done waiting. Despite Penelope returning the boys' memories, Henry called for a town meeting. Now the only objective was settling the issue of the Festival of Fate once and for all.

Town meetings typically brought out a hundred or so residents. About a third of those treated it like a social occasion, only there to gossip while the municipal business happened around them. The rest wanted a say in what went on in town.

That night, the meeting room they usually used had been filled within ten minutes and they had to move the meeting to the recreational room, where Jada Lin taught yoga on Saturday mornings and Frank Rollins held free paint-by-number classes two nights a week. They unloaded folding chairs from the storage closet and set up row after row after row across the basketball court.

No one had bothered to turn on the heat, and the air crackled with static electricity as people removed their hats and gloves and got shocked when their skin made contact with the chairs. Half a dozen different perfumes mingled as the group continued to grow and overpowered the scent of coffee that had been left on the burner too long.

Penelope stood alone off to one side of the room. Ruth Anne and a few others had stopped by long enough to greet her and ask how she was doing, but no one wanted to be seen with her for any longer than that. If the meeting went their way, they'd all act like they hadn't been avoiding her for days. And if things tipped in her favor, well, they might all never talk to her again.

Either way it felt like losing.

She smiled as people passed, tried to look like this was any other town meeting. Like the outcome didn't affect her personally.

"They're still doing these things?" Noah asked, his face poking over her shoulder.

Penelope jumped, jamming her shoulder into his chin to encourage him to give her a little more room. When he stepped around to face her, she said, "I can promise you it's not nearly as entertaining as when we were younger and made up drinking games to go along with it."

"That's only 'cause you grew up and got all responsible and shit." He flashed the inside of his coat where he had stashed a silver flask in the pocket.

"This coming from the guy who took it upon himself to fix my door handle the other day?"

His lips parted, sliding into an easy grin.

"That wasn't being responsible. That was being chivalrous. Big difference."

Penelope laughed, and for the first time since she'd arrived at the town hall she forgot to be worried. If he didn't stop finding ways to slip through her defenses, she might be done for. A small voice inside her head asked if that would be the worst thing to happen. *Yes,* she silently answered, her conviction wavering more than she would have liked.

"So, where's the kid?"

"She's with my mom." Though it had taken a lot of convincing to get her to stay. Ella usually slept through the town meetings, her head on Penelope's lap and her legs curled up on Sabina's, but she'd wanted to be there tonight in case Noah showed up. Penelope had promised her there was no chance of that happening. Why would he go? He didn't live in town, so what happened there shouldn't have mattered to him.

Yet there he was.

"Not sick again, is she?"

And just like that her anxiety returned. He sounded genuinely concerned about Ella's health and Penelope couldn't bring herself to lie to him about it. So she did the only thing she could when it came to him. She avoided it. "Do you even know what this meeting is about?"

Noah shrugged. "Town stuff."

"Town stuff that involves pretty much everyone

here being on one side and me on the other. That's not exactly something I want my kid to have a front-row seat for."

"So, it's the big Festival of Fate showdown tonight, huh? I kinda like the festival, but I'll sit on your side if you want. Make everyone think they haven't won yet." Even as he said it, he scanned the room to see what she was up against.

Not wanting to know how many more people had come out for this, she kept her eyes locked on him. "As sweet as that offer is," and it was actually kind of sweet, "that's not necessary. I know it's a long shot. But with recent events I think I'll find a few more people who agree that a little less magic around here might be a good idea."

"All right, all right," Henry shouted to get the room's attention. His voice boomed without the need of a microphone. "Everybody find a seat."

Noah buried his hands in his coat pockets and rocked back on his heels. "Okay, well, I'm here if you change your mind." Instead of sitting, he leaned against the wall next to the emergency exit. He rested a hand on the push-bar as if he was just waiting for her signal to turn the place into a chaotic rush of bodies scrambling for safety.

She smiled at him and took a seat in the second row. Without her mom and Ella, the chairs next to her remained empty. Would her mom even come to these meetings after Ella was gone? Was this what her future looked like? The thought made her shiver. She peeled off her coat anyway and piled it on the seat next to her.

"We can't start yet. Sabina's not here," someone called.

Penelope looked around but couldn't tell who had said it. Everyone looked guilty, shifting side to side in the folding chairs and cutting quick glances in her direction without making eye contact. Their whispers crackled in the air like a live wire sparking against asphalt. Ruth Anne waved her hands as she continued her conversation with Delilah Jacobs as if Henry hadn't spoken. Zan managed a half smile when she saw Penelope, almost as if she was embarrassed to be there. A half dozen people swarmed the Avery sisters, their voices louder than most as they gave updates on the boys' status.

Thanks to Penelope and her mom, they were back to their normal selves. One of the first things Justin had asked her after his memories were restored was if she had changed her mind about the festival. The hint of arrogance in his tone made her wish, for just a second, that she'd left him memoryless. But that night, Patrick had filled her magnolia tree with thank-you notes. And instead of ringing the doorbell, he'd let her sleep through the night and wake up to discover his appreciation on her own. She left them hanging in her yard the whole day.

Marco sat behind Penelope and squeezed her shoulder. At least she had one supporter. Two, if she counted Noah. And she wasn't sure she wanted to do that yet.

"Can't we give Sabina a few more minutes?" someone on the far side asked.

"She's not going to make it tonight," Penelope said. She stopped short of apologizing.

"But she should have a say in this," Delilah said, her high-pitched voice unmistakable even in this crowd.

Andy Mills turned in his chair so he could be better seen by the majority of the room. "I can't believe Sabina would miss this meeting. She loves the Festival of Fate. Even more than the rest of us do."

"She also loves her daughter," Noah said. He didn't bother looking up as he spoke, but he still managed to capture everyone's attention. "And she probably doesn't want to listen to what y'all are going to be saying about her tonight. If it were me, I'd tell y'all where you could stick it. But Mrs. Dalton's way classier than I am, so I guess I can't blame her for staying away from all this."

Sometimes Noah made it really difficult to not like him. Penelope took a deep breath, letting his words bolster her. "Honestly, my mom just doesn't want to have to take sides. So she's not."

Henry hung his coat on the back of a chair facing the group, then sat. Looking first to Penelope then out to the rest of the room, he said, "Well, we can't blame Sabina for that, now can we?"

A few murmurs of "no" rose from the group.

"All right then. Let's get started." Henry removed a stack of paper from a folder beside his chair. "And please remember to keep your comments focused on the topic at hand and not make any personal attacks. That's not what we're here for tonight."

"No one here has it out for Penelope," Delilah said. "We just want a chance to be heard, that's all."

"And you will," he said.

Penelope listened as he ran through an overview of the agenda, which consisted of the welcome he was currently giving and a discussion of the future of the Festival of Fate. With the larger-than-expected turnout, he anticipated they would take the whole hour, so he made the executive decision as mayor to hold the remaining discussion points until the regularly scheduled meeting next month. No one argued.

"Based on the dozens of calls and letters dropped off at my office and even a few of you who've stopped me in line at the grocery store, you've all got good reasons to want to have the

Festival of Fate go on like always. I'm not going to repeat everything you've told me tonight." The crowd whispered and grumbled and shouted their displeasure. Henry quieted them with a quick wave of his hands and a few seconds of staring them into submission. "Don't worry. I'll run through the highlights."

Penelope curled her fingers around the edge of her seat.

"For one, the festival is tradition. The bonfire and camaraderie of the whole town being together as the year comes to a close. It's a part of who we are as individuals and as a town. For two, the festival is our chance to change things. Make our lives and our town better. And for three, the magic has never let us down in the past. Every single one of us has asked for the future we wanted and received it.

"Now, we can have the festival without the magic Sabina and Penelope bring us every year. We can gather in the park and throw our wishes into the fire like nothing's changed. But we all know the magic's the entire reason for the festival. Without it, there isn't much point."

And, no surprise, the whole room agreed.

Penelope had to admit the festival itself wasn't a bad idea. She just couldn't see anyone agreeing to hold it without the Kismet hot chocolate they all believed in so fiercely.

When Henry opened the meeting up to ques-

236

tions, Andy was the first to throw one out. "So, are you going to shut down the Chocolate Cottage too? Because from where we're sitting, the magic you sell there is a heck of a lot worse than people asking the universe for a specific future."

"It probably is," Penelope conceded. "But that's only because those chocolates actually work. We all just assume the Kismet hot chocolate we drink at the festival works because we want it to, but we don't have any proof that we can actually change our fate. It's nice to believe in until you need it to work. Then it just feels like a big slap in the face."

"How can you say that after we all made extra wishes for Ella's future last year? And now look at her. She's doing so well, going to school full-time and making friends. If that's not a miracle, I don't know what is," Ruth Anne said.

It was a lie. A horrible, heartbreaking lie.

Maybe they'd understand why holding a festival to celebrate the future was such a bad idea if she told them the truth.

"She's not," Penelope said. Her voice was so soft no one even heard her. She cleared her throat and tried again. "Ella's not better. She won't get better. The only miracle now is that she's doing as well as she is."

That shut everyone up. For a few seconds, the only sound in the whole room was their collective intake of breath. Then they all broke out in questions at once.

"What are you taking about?"

"I saw her yesterday. She looked fine."

"Is she still in treatment?"

"Why didn't you tell us?"

"That sweet little girl has been through so much already."

Each word hit the mark, leaving a scar as a souvenir on her heart.

Now that one truth was out there, she had no reason to keep holding on to the other. Gathering up her coat and purse in shaking hands, she looked at the roomful of people who had trusted her, believed in the magic her family had promised them.

"The Kismet hot chocolate doesn't work. It can't help you change the future. All it can do is give you false hope that there's a way around the inevitable. And that's not fair to any of us. So you can still have the festival. You can wish and you can hope for the futures you want. But magic's not going to make any difference in how things turn out."

Noah shoved open the emergency exit for her, and she stumbled past him. She felt his warm fingers on her arm. Then she felt nothing but the cold as she fled.

22

Sabina worked at the shop on her own the following day, allowing Penelope one day's reprieve. But Penelope couldn't avoid people forever. She wasn't ready to answer the barrage of questions about Ella or the Kismet hot chocolate yet, but she'd brought it on herself when she'd told most of the town about Ella, and there was no way to take it back now.

Her front porch was littered with notes from her neighbors, offering love and sympathy and wishes for a miraculous recovery. The front of the Chocolate Cottage contained at least as many letters, if not more.

"You've only made them more determined to have the festival," her mother said.

"Even knowing the hot chocolate doesn't work?"

"It's not always about the end result, Penelope. Sometimes people just want to have a little hope."

Well, they could keep their hope. It hadn't done Penelope any bit of good anyway.

The one person Penelope hadn't been able to ignore was River. When she'd invited Ella over after school one day, all Ella had to do was point at the item on her list where she'd added *Get a best frend* and Penelope caved. The Gregorys' door opened to a squeal of delight so high-pitched Penelope half-expected the neighborhood dogs to start howling. Before she got a good look at the creature it came from, a small hand whipped out, grabbed Ella, and disappeared down the hall.

Layne took her daughter's place at the door and tugged on her ponytail to tighten it. "I think she's part Nazgûl. Nothing else explains that sound." Her laugh stuttered for a second before dropping out altogether.

Penelope tried to place the thing Layne named, but couldn't get closer than knowing it was from some classic fantasy or science fiction story. "So that's normal?" she asked, smiling to ease the awkwardness.

"Only when she's really excited. But she's an eight-year-old girl, so yeah, pretty much all the time." Layne's loose-fitting tee billowed behind her as the wind rushed in the closing door.

Penelope tripped over a duffel bag that lay open at the base of a bench in the entryway. She caught herself on the wall as Layne stooped to shove it under the bench. Scuffed pointe shoes and a pale pink leotard spilled out onto the floor. Layne's face flushed when she stood and apologized, her gaze locking on the hooks above the bench that overflowed with puffy jackets and vests, a thicket of scarves, and three motorcycle helmets.

"Ella's excitement comes out of her as uncontrollable giggling. Like so much so that she almost hyperventilates," Penelope said. She followed Layne down the hall and into a bright kitchen with so many small appliances on the counters there was no work space. "The first time, I thought she was gonna pass out. I called the doctor to make sure she would be okay."

"The first time River made that sound I thought she'd busted my eardrums. I had Tucker check to make sure they weren't bleeding. Then I briefly contemplated getting her a muzzle but figured that would be frowned upon."

"Yeah, I'm not sure that would go over well, and I applaud your restraint. That might be the most intense sound I've ever heard."

"I know. If she wasn't so damn happy when she does it I'd have tried to make her stop by now. But—"

"Seeing your kid happy is the best thing in the world," Penelope finished for her.

Layne stopped at the refrigerator and motioned Penelope toward the high-top bistro table on the other side of the room. Her shoulders relaxed and her smile came quicker than it had before. "Do you want something to drink? I've got water, sweet tea, hot tea, wine."

Penelope set her clutch wallet and keys on

the table and used the footrest on the chair for balance as she pushed up into it. "Water's fine."

Layne filled two cups and carried them to the table. One looked like a blue British police box and the other was white with round black glasses and a lightning bolt over one side.

"Sorry about the plastic. We're not real fancy around here. But we could probably win a Guinness world record for having the largest collection of geek cups."

"Will you hate me if I don't know what most of them are?" Penelope asked, picking up the blue cup.

"Oh, no. I've come to terms with the fact that I'm nerdy and I don't hold it against anyone." Layne traced the lightning bolt on the other cup. "But you might not want to tell me when you don't understand a reference because then I'll probably try to convince you to give it a try. And by convince, I mean push it on you until you cave just to make me shut up."

"Duly noted."

The girls' voices carried to them from somewhere deeper in the house. Whatever they said was drowned out by bubbling laughter and stomping feet as they danced to a Taylor Swift song. Penelope watched the doorway, worrying something would break and praying it wouldn't be a bone. When the girls started laughing again,

Penelope and Layne shrugged at each other and laughed in time with their daughters.

"I wasn't at the town meeting, but Noah filled us in on what happened," Layne said. She wrapped her hands around the water cup and drummed her short nails against it in an uneven rhythm. "How are you doing? How's Ella? I just can't even imagine."

Had Penelope really thought she could avoid talking about it?

Her stomach pretzeled into a knot. "It's pretty much the worst," she said. Now that the truth was out, her lips couldn't form a lie. Instead of meeting the sympathetic look she knew Layne was giving her, she stared at the photographs of River on the wall that looked as if someone had gone by and knocked them all askew on purpose. "But it helps that Ella got to pretend to be normal for a little while. And having a friend like River has made her so happy. So there are still some good times."

"You don't have to do that, you know."

"Do what?"

"Give a rehearsed response. If you're doing it just to spare me the gory details, don't." Layne jerked her hands up as if to physically stop Penelope from running away. She knocked her cup, and water sloshed out onto the table. "You're already dealing with so much on your own, and doing it with so much more composure and an impressive lack of cussing than I ever could, the least I can do is be here to listen if that's what you need."

Grabbing a napkin from the holder, Penelope spread it out to sop up the water and said, "If I let my guard down, I won't be able to put it back up again. And then I won't make it through this. So please don't take it personally. I can't tell you how much I appreciate the offer."

Layne didn't even try to smile. And that meant more than Penelope could ever say.

"Okay. Yeah. That makes total sense. But if you—"

Shoes slapped the floor as the girls ran down the hall, drowning out the rest of the sentence. They both looked toward the kitchen entrance as two delighted faces poked around the corner and started talking at the same time in words so fast and crammed together they were unintelligible.

Ella took a breath and glanced at River for confirmation that she could share whatever news they had. Then she said, "Mama! Noah's home! C'mon, let's go see him!" She waved her hand so violently that Penelope thought her wrist might snap.

Penelope curled her fingers around the chair handles, forcing her breath to stay calm and even despite the spike in her pulse at the thought of seeing him. She couldn't trust herself not to blurt out the one secret she had left if he showed concern for Ella's health. "You can go see him without me, I think," she said.

"Okay. We'll be right back." Ella raced out of the room, repeating his name at a near-yell.

Layne swiveled her chair side to side, letting her eyes roam from Penelope to the door every few seconds as if she could see the tension pulsing off Penelope like neon lights.

Noah walked into view with Ella and River each holding one of his hands. He lifted the one attached to Ella and pointed at Penelope, his smile faltering when his eyes locked on her. "Well, this is a nice surprise. Four of my favorite girls waiting for me to get home. Now, which one of you is making my supper?" Despite the playfulness in his voice, he wasn't about to let Penelope off as easily as Layne had.

She looked away.

"We will," River said.

"Yeah, we will," Ella echoed.

As much as she wanted to let the girls distract him, Penelope's conscience wouldn't let her. "Oh, no. Don't let that one near your kitchen unless you want to bring in the hazmat guys after," she said, pointing at Ella.

"Hey," Ella said, rolling her lips into a pout.

"You know me," Noah said. "It's not fun if there's nothing at stake."

The girls tugged him into the kitchen and deposited him by the table. He held on to his smile when they told him to have a seat and decide what he wanted to eat while they got ready. He slipped into the chair next to Penelope, letting his hand graze the side of her knee for a fraction of a second then pulled away when her body went rigid.

Any amount of comfort on his part was too much when she was keeping the fact that Ella was his daughter from him.

Tucker hobbled into the kitchen, his crutches thumping against the tile floor with each step. "I love that you get the personal escort to the kitchen while the guy on crutches has to fend for himself," he said to his brother.

Layne paused to kiss him on her way to ensure the girls didn't turn the kitchen into a disaster area. Penelope almost followed but that would have been like a big flashing sign that she was avoiding Noah. So she stayed put.

"I can't help it if I'm everyone's favorite," Noah said.

"I wouldn't be so sure about that. Penelope there looks ready to jump out of her skin if you get much closer."

Penelope couldn't even tell Tucker he was wrong. Though it wasn't for any reason he might have expected.

"That was a joke," he said when she remained quiet.

Noah's expression hardened. His voice followed suit when he said, "Obviously not a very good one." Then he turned back to Penelope, tipping his head so his mouth was close to her ear. "You okay?"

She made her lips form a smile. "I'm fine, Noah."

"I didn't mean just with my brother being a jerk. Are you okay after everything the other night? Everything with Ella?"

The sincere worry in his voice only added to her guilt. She had to get away from it—from him—before it consumed her.

"Not even close. And this isn't helping," Penelope said. Pushing back from the table, she prayed her voice would hold out against her emotions. "Actually, we need to get going. Ella, c'mon, sweetie."

The girls dropped to their knees and scuttled across the floor to her. "Please," they said in unison. "Five more minutes?"

"Nope, sorry. We need to get home." Penelope held out her hand to tug Ella to her feet. "Say goodbye."

Ella ducked under the crutch Tucker had yet to drop and wrapped her arms around Noah's waist. "Bye," she whispered.

Noah rubbed his hand on Ella's back, holding her close for a second longer. He caught Penelope's eyes over the top of Ella's head and opened his mouth to say something, but ended up shaking his head and looking away.

And somehow that made her feel even worse.

23

Now that the whole town knew the truth about how sick Ella was, Penelope didn't have a good reason to keep putting off a few of Ella's bucket list items. The one that had been on every variation of the list was to dye her hair. Technically the school had a policy against unnatural hair color, but she couldn't see anyone in the administration punishing a dying girl for it.

Let them try, she thought.

"You know this is just going to keep everybody talking, right?" Megha asked as she plopped a tote bag full of hair-dyeing supplies on the kitchen table.

"I don't much care at this point," Penelope said.

"Good. So, does she know yet?"

"Nope. I thought you'd want to see her reaction."

"Her smile is going to be epic. Thanks for waiting."

This surprise was the only thing that had gotten Penelope through the day without screaming at all of the premature condolences people went out of their way to give her. They meant well, she knew that, but did they have to act as if Ella was already gone?

She leaned against the counter, mustering every ounce of happiness she could. "You're doing all the work so you definitely deserve all her excitement."

Megha settled in beside her and dropped her head to Penelope's shoulder. "I don't know how you're keeping it together so well."

"As long as she's still here, it's a good day," Penelope said.

"Damn right it is. Now let's get her down here and liven things up."

They both called for Ella at the same time. When Ella skidded into the room looking as healthy as any normal eight-year old, they smiled as big as she did.

Megha snagged Ella around the waist, bending down so their faces aligned. "Guess what we're doing tonight?"

"Eating dinner and drinking wine," Ella said.

"That *does* sound like a normal night," Megha agreed with a laugh.

"We don't always drink wine," Penelope said, but she failed to keep a straight face.

"I know." Ella tugged against Megha's hold. "So, what are we doing then?"

Spinning Ella out to arm's length and then around to face her, Megha said, "We, my sweet girl, are going to knock a big life to-do item off of your list."

"Are we gonna dye my hair?"

"As long as you still want to," Penelope said. She walked over to Megha's bag and peered inside. It looked like Megha had brought half her supplies over. Tubes of color and mixing bowls and brushes and black towels that wouldn't show the excess dye filled the bag.

Ella danced around the kitchen. "Yes! Yes! Yes!"

"Well, the only question now, kid, is what color?" Megha asked.

"I can really have any color I want?" Ella came back to stand beside Megha, bouncing on her toes as the excitement refused to let her go.

"Pretty much. I brought the basic colors I thought you might want, like pink and blue and purple. Or you could be like your mom when she was in high school and go teal."

Flashing a huge grin, Ella said, "I want purple. Like River's mom."

Penelope would put good money on Layne allowing River to dye her hair too. Not during the school year, but she imagined summers at the Gregory house were full of wild-colored hair and even more laughter. Ella would have fit right in. The fact that Ella was half-Gregory would have only made the fit that much better. Penelope's stomach lurched at the thought.

"Noah's sister-in-law?" Megha asked.

"That's the one."

Ella tugged on Megha's arm, her expression

melting into the dreamy smile and starry eyes she got anytime she talked about Noah. "Megha, are you friends with Noah too?" she asked. Even her voice turned sugary sweet.

"You and Noah are on a first-name basis?" Megha asked and shot a curious look at Penelope. Her sculpted eyebrows drew together as she searched for a sign of some secret relationship with Noah that Penelope had been keeping from her.

"Yeah. He's my mom's friend. But not like you are. He doesn't come over for dinner. Or spend the night."

Penelope threw her hands up to keep the conversation from veering off course. "Before you ask, there is nothing going on. She's talking about the night he came over to tell me about the boys who got into the shop. That's it. So don't get all excited."

Megha rolled her eyes as if she knew better than to believe that. "Yes, Ella, I know him. But apparently not as well as your mom." She pushed back from the table and used Ella's head as a makeshift bongo.

Ella squirmed away from her, giggling. "What do you know about him?"

"Let's work on your hair while we gossip. That way you get the full salon experience."

The night was supposed to be about Ella getting something she wanted. Adding Noah into the mix—even tangentially—was asking for trouble. Ella was smart enough to know that if she put something on her bucket list, Penelope would eventually give in. What the hell would she do if Ella decided Noah belonged on her list?

"Maybe this was a bad idea," she muttered.

"Too late now," Megha said with a hint of laughter in her voice.

Admitting defeat, Penelope hauled Megha's bag over to the island and started unpacking it. She lined up each item on the edge of the counter so Megha would be able to reach them from where she had set up the other stool between the island and the sink. If the vibrant shade of violet on the tube of dye was the actual color, Ella's hair was going to be visible from space. And Ella was going to love it. No question.

Megha snapped a black cape around Ella's neck to keep the dye from staining anything. Ella twirled in a circle so the cape billowed out around her like a fancy party dress. Then she climbed onto the stool, folding her arms beneath the fabric, and shook her hair back from her face.

"Do you think Noah likes purple?" she asked.

"You'll have to ask him that the next time you see him," Megha said.

Ella kept up a steady stream of questions about Noah as Megha mixed the coloring, sectioned off small hunks of Ella's hair with clips and foil sheets, and applied the bright purple paste with long, even strokes. *What was he like when you were kids? What's his favorite kind of chocolate? What's his favorite song? Does he like cats? Why isn't he married? Was he ever my mom's boyfriend? Did you want him to be your boyfriend? Why doesn't he live in Malarkey? Will he stay if we ask him to?*

Megha and Penelope both answered "I don't know" and "Maybe" and "You'll have to ask him" so many times that finally Ella grumbled that she'd just ask River at school. But it was hard to take her annoyance seriously when her scalp was covered in strips of foil that fluttered every time she shook her head in disappointment at their answers.

After Megha used a flatiron to heat-seal the color and then let it set for twenty minutes, she scooted a bar stool over to the sink and patted the seat for Ella to hop up again. While Ella got situated with a rolled towel between her neck and the counter, Megha ran the water, testing it with her fingers every few seconds until she was satisfied with the heat level. Then she used the spray nozzle to wet down Ella's short crop of hair and rinse off the excess color.

"Hey, Mama. I have one last question," she asked after Megha had draped one of the black towels over her head to catch any drips and she was allowed to sit up.

"Okay. One more. But that's it." Not that

she would have an answer to it either. In Noah Jeopardy, Penelope had a negative score.

"Will you un-cancel the Festival of Fate so that I can drink the hot chocolate and wish that Noah will stay in town?"

That was the last request she expected to get. Even though Penelope didn't believe in the Kismet hot chocolate anymore, the idea that her daughter wanted to use it to keep Noah in their lives sent a jolt of panic through her. "You wouldn't really use your wish on that, would you?"

Ella jerked forward, sending the towel flying to the tiles below. She only stayed in the chair because Megha grabbed her shoulders and held her in place. "Mama, you saw what my necklace did around Noah. You know he's supposed to be with us. I have to do something to make him realize he belongs here."

"You can't use magic to make other people do things they don't want to do."

"That's not fair." Ella's elbows poked the cape as she slumped back into the chair and crossed her arms over her chest.

Penelope leveled her gaze on her daughter. "No, what's not fair is taking away someone's choice just because you don't like the other options."

Crap. That was exactly what she'd been trying to do with the festival. Good intentions or not.

Sighing, she said, "You'll just have to have faith that everything will work out the way it's supposed to." *And try not to blame yourself if it doesn't,* she added silently.

Before Ella could argue more, Megha switched on the hair dryer. Ella glared at her as if she knew Megha had done it on purpose, but she turned back around to let Megha finish. Megha brushed Ella's hair out, the purple streaks clearly visible against the wet brown. Then she gave Penelope a look over Ella's head that said she had some questions of her own for Penelope before this conversation was through.

Penelope would take a little needling from her best friend about what was going on with Noah any day over trying to explain to Ella why wanting him in her life was a bad idea.

Penelope leaned her elbows on the table and mouthed "fine." Then she watched the thick purple chunks of hair get even more vibrant as they dried. The look was so perfectly Ella—all playful and bright—she hated that she had waited so long to agree to it.

As soon as the dryer clicked off, Ella said, "Can I see?" Her excitement over her new hair momentarily overshadowed additional questions about Noah or the festival.

Penelope fished the mirror out of Megha's bag and handed it to her.

Ella's shout of delight filled the kitchen.

"My hair's even purpler than River's mom's!" Jumping from the stool, she raced over to give Penelope an up-close look.

"I think it's purpler than anything," Penelope joked as she ran her hands through Ella's soft strands.

Megha paused washing her hands in the sink and looked at them over her shoulder. "Too much?" She unspooled a bunch of paper towels from the holder, transferring watery purple smudges from her skin to the paper before she'd actually started to dry her hands.

"No." Ella twisted around to face Megha, but kept her head tilted back so Penelope could keep playing with her hair.

Before Ella had gotten sick and her hair still fell down to her shoulders, she'd loved to have Penelope run her fingers through it as she fell asleep. But since her hair had grown back in wavy and thinner than before she'd lost it due to the radiation treatments she'd had, she usually nudged Penelope's hands away. Now maybe this one thing could go back to the way it was before.

Penelope tipped her head forward and kissed one of the larger purple sections. "It's actually pretty perfect."

"Pretty Perfect Purple. That's what I'm going to tell everyone the color is. 'Cause it's true," Ella said.

"I'm so glad you like it," Megha said.

"I love it!" Ella pulled away from Penelope then and rushed to wrap her arms around Megha's waist. "Thank you, thank you, thank you!"

"We should have done this months ago," Megha said to Penelope, her eyes the tiniest bit wet.

Penelope had to blink back her own tears at the happiness radiating off her daughter. This was exactly why they had started the list in the first place. All of the good moments they made couldn't erase the bad ones, but at least it evened out the score a little.

"No kidding," Penelope said.

She snapped a few photos with her phone at Ella's insistence and had to promise not to post anything to her Facebook until Ella could show her grandmother, River, and Noah her hair in person. Then Ella made a show of checking the activity off her list with a purple pen she scrounged for in the kitchen junk drawer and holding it up so Penelope could take a picture of it too.

"All right, Ella," Penelope said when she was done. "I think it's time for bed."

"But—"

"Nope. Girls with purple hair don't get to make the rules."

"River's mom has purple hair and she makes the rules," Ella said.

She had Penelope there.

"Yeah, but she's the mom so that overrules the purple." Penelope scooped her up before she could protest and carried her upstairs.

After she'd brushed her teeth and Penelope had tucked her into bed, Ella stared up at her with a solemn expression replacing the joy she'd had a few minutes before. "Mama, don't dye it back when I die, okay? I want to have purple hair when I go to heaven. Then everyone there will just think I'm this cool girl with purple hair who probably had lots of friends when she was alive. Then maybe they'll all want to be my friend too and you won't have to worry that I'm lonely there without you."

And just like that, the sadness flooded Penelope's chest, constricting her lungs and stabbing her heart like hundreds of small needles. She took a few shallow breaths. "You are a very cool kid, purple hair or not. But I promise not to change it back."

Megha handed Penelope a glass of wine when she returned. "This was going to be happy wine, but with the way you look right now, it might have to be drown-your-sorrows wine. You okay?"

"Ella wanted to make sure I didn't dye her hair back to normal after she died so she could be the cool new girl in heaven." Penelope took a long sip of wine to stave off Megha's hug. Refusing to have the comfort she wanted to offer shrugged off so easily, Megha squeezed Penelope's knee. "I don't want to think about that right now, so please distract me."

"That I can definitely do. So, what's with the twenty questions about Noah?" Megha leaned forward on the stool she had moved back into place at the island and pinned Penelope with a curious look.

"Oh, don't get me started," Penelope said.

"No, seriously. How does she even know him?"

Oh, you know. Apart from being his secret love child? Penelope managed to keep the truth locked inside. "His niece is in school with Ella and we ran into them after he got back to town. And Ella fell instantly under his spell like the rest of you. It took all of two seconds for him to win her over and nothing I say about him sways her."

Megha sipped her wine and smiled into her glass.

"What?"

"So you're still pretending he has no effect on you?" Megha asked.

"He doesn't."

"That is clearly a *liar, liar, pants on fire* statement if I ever heard one."

"Fine. You want me to agree that he's still hot? He is. And yeah, maybe he knows how to look at a girl to make her brain temporarily stop functioning." And maybe he looks at his niece like her laugh is the greatest sound in the world. For a second, Penelope imagined him looking at his daughter that way too, then had to remind herself they were all better off with him not knowing Ella was his. "But I promise you falling for Noah Gregory is more trouble than it's worth."

"You say that like you have some experience in that department. But I know that can't be the case because you would've told me if something had happened between you and Noah. Because I'm your best friend and that's not something you keep from best friends." Megha set her drink aside and put both hands on the arms of Penelope's stool. Twisting her so they were knee to knee—and Penelope had no way to escape—she said, "Right?"

Penelope kept her eyes on her best friend's. She didn't even blink. "You just have to look at him to know he's a bad idea." Guilt from keeping her relationship with Noah from Megha won out and she looked away.

"We are going to have to agree to disagree on that front."

If you only knew. Penelope tapped her fingers on the stem of her glass, focusing on the ripple effect it created in the wine. "I'm serious. Nothing good could come from starting something with a guy who a) is going to return to his life already in progress down in Charlotte sooner rather than later, b) has been avoiding Malarkey and everyone living in it for the better part of a decade, and c) has no interest in being in love."

Though Penelope had to concede that maybe Noah had no interest in being in love with her specifically.

"Do you know for a fact that he has things tying him to Charlotte? I mean, if he's able to just up and move here for a few months, what's to say he can't make it permanent?"

"*Can* and *want* are very different things. And besides, even if Noah was to stay, I still wouldn't want anything to do with him."

Break my heart once, shame on you. Break it twice . . .

She wouldn't give him the chance.

24

After dropping Ella off at school and having a conversation with Principal Davis about Ella's hair, in which she made very clear it was not reverting to its natural color and the school would just have to live with it, Penelope swung across town to the mayor's office. She'd put off making a decision about the festival long enough.

Henry's office light burned upstairs. If he was looking out the window he would have seen her. Thankfully his back was to the window, and she hurried up the sidewalk. She wedged the note she'd written on the back of a Festival of Fate postcard into the doorjamb an inch above the knob where Margarete would be sure to see it on her way in.

She'd kept it simple: *Tell everyone they'll have their hot chocolate this year. Whatever good it will do them.*

The drive from the mayor's office to work took her by the Orchard Street Cafe. It was so packed for breakfast that customers spilled onto the front porch as they waited for a table.

263

It took her a second to recognize one of them as her mom. Sabina watched the road, her hand flying up every few seconds to tuck in flyaway hairs or smooth out her coat.

She wasn't just waiting for a table. She was waiting for someone.

The fact that she hadn't mentioned anything about it sent a shiver of worry through Penelope. If her mom had used the chocolates again, she would be waiting for a hallucination. And every patron in the cafe would be witness to Sabina's magic-induced high.

Penelope pulled into the first open parking space she could find. Backtracking down the street, she tried to find her mom again in the half dozen people crowded in front of the door. When she reached the cafe, and Sabina was nowhere in sight, Penelope hoped her mom had come to her senses.

She peered in the window and found her mom sitting across a table from Marco.

Her mom's nerves hadn't subsided with Marco's arrival. If anything, they may have gotten worse. Sabina had no reason to be nervous around one of her oldest friends. Unless she was trying to talk him into overruling Penelope's decision regarding Ella's treatment. She'd promised she wouldn't use magic again, but Penelope hadn't thought to make Marco off-limits too.

Marco wouldn't agree to it, of course. He'd

been the one to tell Penelope to end it in the first place.

But she had to be sure.

Penelope pushed her way past the line, murmuring her apologies but not stopping until she made it inside.

Sabina blushed when Marco reached across the table and covered her hand with his. A laugh bubbled out of her, so much like when she thought her husband was still alive. Penelope froze.

There was one other reason her mom might be uneasy with Marco. Why she hadn't told Penelope about their breakfast. Sabina was on a date.

Penelope turned before they could spot her and slipped back outside. She was halfway down the sidewalk when Zan stepped out onto the porch and called her back. "I can bring something out to you if you're not up to dealing with that many people yet."

She'd been so worried about her mom she hadn't even considered that she'd be putting herself in the line of fire. Her gaze whipped back to the front window. A couple people watched her, pity weighing down their features as they lifted their hands to their hearts. She looked away, pretending she hadn't seen them. "Oh, thanks. I was actually just checking on my mom. Looks like she and Marco are having a good time so I didn't want to bother them."

"Hey, I know you don't know me very well, but I just wanted to tell you that I'm sorry about your daughter," Zan said, her hesitant tone stretching the sentence out. "Whenever I see her, she always seems so happy and full of life. It just breaks my heart that she's so sick."

It wasn't just heartbreaking. It was tragic. Unfair. Cruel. But Penelope was biased.

She smiled to force some of the awkwardness out of their way. "Thanks. Ella's optimism is what keeps me going most days."

"It makes sense now. Why you've been so certain that what I dreamed about my ex will come true. I've kinda been hoping he wouldn't show up until after the festival and I'd be able to use the hot chocolate again to make sure he didn't find me here. But that was never going to work. And you tried to get me to see that."

"I'm sorry, Zan. I wish more than anyone that there was a way to change our fates. Everything with Ella has made me realize if something is supposed to happen, it will find a way no matter what we do, so I might as well accept it and figure out how to deal with it."

Zan puffed out her cheeks then released a cloud of white into the cold morning air. "So you have to watch your daughter die and I have to either leave the first place in forever that's felt like home or risk my ex finding me and ruining my life here anyway. That just plain sucks."

"I'm not saying it's easy. But that's what I have to do because otherwise I don't think I would get through it in one piece," Penelope said. She bit her lip to keep from saying anything more. She'd agreed to help with the festival and should probably act like she supported it even when she didn't. "But most of the town still believes in the festival and the magic of the Kismet hot chocolate. And I'm done trying to convince them otherwise. My mom and I will make the hot chocolate for the Festival of Fate like always and people can drink it or not. So if the idea of drinking possibly magical but possibly not hot chocolate makes you feel better about what's coming, just ignore me. Everyone else is."

"What changed your mind about helping with the festival?"

"Fighting it was getting me nowhere. And you know, if it's what they all want, who am I to tell them they can't have it?"

"But you still don't think it will work?" Zan asked.

"It didn't work for me. But maybe what I wanted to change was just too big," Penelope said.

25

Noah had worked three doubles in a row. By the time he got back to his brother's house each night, all he wanted was a cold beer and a hot shower. Preferably together. He swiped a double IPA from the minifridge in the laundry room and popped off the cap on the opener screwed into the wall by the light switch.

He guzzled that one without taking a breath. The bitterness of the hops was a perfect match for his mood. He grabbed a second one before heading to the guest room.

The television whispered from the family room and threw patterns of light on the cream carpet in the hallway. He paused, ducking his head around the jamb. His brother slouched on the sofa with his socked feet propped on the coffee table. Tucker's eyelids drooped so only a sliver of white peeked through. Noah stepped back and accidentally knocked his beer against the molding. Tucker jerked up, cracking his good heel against the table.

"Sorry," Noah said.

"You're home." Tucker blinked a few times against the low light. He rubbed his heel on the top of his other foot and let his head fall back on the cushions. "Good night?"

"Decent. The new girl's not gonna make it, though."

"She's been there two days. Give her a chance." Noah rolled his shoulders and loud *pop*s followed in rapid succession. Just thinking about the broken glasses and spilled drinks and wrong orders at her hands had the tension tightening again. "I gave her enough chances for three people tonight. Would've been home half an hour ago if she hadn't spilled the dirty mop water all over the floor I'd just cleaned."

"That on top of a double? Man, your boss is a dick," Tucker said. He barked out a laugh and cradled his broken ribs with an arm. "Finally decide you want to make a move on your dream girl and then spend every waking hour at work so you can't even try."

"Just remember I'm here doing you a favor. You keep this shit up and you're on your own," Noah said, letting some of his bad mood rough up the edges of his words enough to get his brother to back the hell off.

"Doubtful. For one, you're too decent of a guy to bail on me now. If you didn't want to put up with my shit, you wouldn't have come in the first place. And two, if you do, you'll never get the love note River brought you from Ella." He flicked his eyes to a folded piece of paper wedged under an empty glass. "She wanted to wait up and give it to you herself, but it's a school night so I told her no dice and sent her packing. But she made me promise to tell you it's very important and you are to leave your response on the other side and she'll take it back tomorrow."

At least one *of the Dalton girls is interested in me.* Noah let out a long breath as he walked into the room. He whacked his brother's good leg with the back of his hand when Tucker made to move the note out of his reach then leaned over him to wrench it from his fist.

Written in very serious print were the words: *Plees com to dinr tomoro at the BEST piza restrot in town?*

He read it through twice to make sure he understood what she was asking. Two lopsided check boxes sat underneath the question.

"Shit, I was kidding about it being a love note," Tucker said, reading over Noah's shoulder.

Smiling to himself, Noah dug a pen from one of the cargo pockets on his pants and scrawled an *X* in the "yes" box.

"What are you doing, Noah?" Tucker nudged his cast into his brother's knee and narrowed his eyes, making all of his features sharp and accusing. "Using an eight-year-old to get to her mom is pretty low. But using an eight-year-old with a brain tumor—special seat in hell, bro."

Noah had tried calling Penelope countless times

in the past week, but she was ignoring him. No one seemed to really know what was happening with Ella or how bad things were. He'd even asked Marco when he came in for bourbon one night and was told to talk to Penelope if he wanted answers. If Ella was going to offer him that opportunity, he wasn't about to pass it up.

"Ella's the one sending me notes, not the other way around. I can't help it if she likes me. And I'm sure as hell not gonna ignore her. That is a surefire way to get on Penelope's bad side."

"You've been there long enough, I'd think you'd be used to it by now."

Noah dropped onto the chair, the unopened beer dangling from one hand between his knees. "Doesn't mean I want to be there. Plus, I like the kid. She's got one hell of a personality. I mean, what other kid would have the guts to send a grown-ass man notes home from school with his niece asking him to dinner? You gotta admit, that's pretty damn adorable."

"Which bring us back to my original question. What are you doing? You don't live here. What happens in the unlikely event that Penelope and/or Ella fall for you?"

"I appreciate the concern, Tuck, but right now, I'm just taking everything one day at a time. Seeing if there's even a place for me in Penelope's life."

"Your relationship with her—or whatever this

is—is more like a Choose Your Own Adventure. Maybe you'd fit in her life in one scenario but not another. Or maybe you're not even a choice at all."

Noah leaned forward and picked at the bottle label that was already going soft from the condensation. "If you think that's gonna make me like her less, you may want to rethink that."

"You always died in those books. Then tried again, made the same dumb-ass mistakes and died all over. You being back here and going after Penelope Dalton is the same thing."

But this time, Noah was determined to make different choices. "I was an idiot back then, so it's not the same. And I seriously doubt she's gonna kill me. But if she does, just be glad that you're the beneficiary on my life insurance."

"Noah, listen," Tucker said. He cut the volume on the television and leaned forward, mirroring his brother's stance. He spoke to his clasped hands instead of Noah. "It's not that there's anything wrong with her. But don't you think it's strange that they make chocolates that tell the future and alter personalities and shit? Don't get me wrong, they taste fantastic, but who's to say Penelope isn't using them on people to get what she wants? Not to mention the fact that she's been lying to the town about Ella getting better? I mean, what kind of person does that?"

"If she wanted to use her magic on people

without them knowing, I doubt she'd make it quite so obvious by selling her chocolates right out in the open," he said. He picked at the edge of the beer cap with his thumbnail. The nervous feeling he'd been fighting since he'd last seen Penelope returned to gnaw on his stomach. "And I don't know why she lied about Ella. What they're going through can't be fun. I don't blame her for wanting to keep it from everyone for a while."

"Okay, I can see your point about Ella. That's a shitty situation and having everybody all up in her business right now probably isn't making it any easier. But the chocolate thing is still weird. I mean, she's got this magic at her fingertips and yet she's raising her kid on her own with no sign of the girl's dad, like ever. You'd think she'd have tied her life up in a pretty little fucking bow by now if that's what she wanted. So what makes you think she's going to suddenly change her mind just because you've rolled back into town for a few months?" Tucker asked.

She had been interested in him once. She'd calmed the restless part of him that was always pushing pushing pushing to find something more, something bigger. She'd given him a reason to want to stay in Malarkey. And he'd screwed it all up in five seconds flat. No wonder Penelope had trust issues with guys.

Noah shoved out of the chair, smacking the

bottle against his knee. "You really are a dick. So, I'm going to chalk this conversation up to you being tired and pissy, take my beer, and go wash your damn bar off of me." He grabbed the note off the table to leave on River's nightstand. The paper stuck to his clammy hands. "If this all blows up in my face you can say 'I told you so.' But if I somehow manage to win Penelope over, you will owe me the biggest fucking apology."

He went upstairs and left his response to Ella next to his niece. He still had a long way to go to earn back Penelope's trust. But with Ella on his side, he might have a real shot.

Penelope waited for the hostess to clear a table for them. The restaurant was half-empty, but Ella had insisted on a table by the window. She'd said it was so she could wave to people as they passed on the sidewalk, but she scratched her nose as she'd said it, which usually meant she was lying. But she'd smiled and said please, and Penelope couldn't think of a reason she would lie about it.

She looked up when she heard her name. The pleasure in Noah's voice sent a rush of nerves racing along her skin. How was she supposed to get Ella to drop her matchmaking crusade when he showed up everywhere? Her daughter was already too attached to him, and each new interaction was just going to make it harder to let him go in the end.

She ignored the voice that said she was getting a little too used to his presence too. She caught herself staring at his full lips, remembering what it had been like to kiss him all those years ago, and looked away.

"I heard this is still the best pizza in town," Noah said as he shrugged out of his jacket and stood next to her.

"It's still the only pizza place in town. And you don't have to wait to be seated. We're waiting on a specific table," she said.

"Yeah, uh, Ella kinda invited me to have dinner with you."

Clearly, Penelope needed to lay some ground rules for Ella where Noah was concerned. And top of that list would be not inviting him to things without getting permission first. "Of course she did. I guess you both forgot to tell me?" she said after a moment.

His mouth tugged to one side in amusement. "Huh. Guess we did."

"You knew she hadn't cleared it with me, didn't you?"

"You've been avoiding me. And everyone else, based on the talk in the bar every night. People are worried about you two. *I'm* worried about you. What you're going through with Ella can't be easy. You don't have to do it alone. So if ambushing you for dinner is the only way I can get you to talk to me, then that's what I'll do."

She wanted to tell him they were fine. That she appreciated all of the concern and sympathy and was sorry for making everyone worry more by hiding from them. But the words wouldn't come. It was so much easier to lie to him—to act like he didn't matter—when he treated her the same way. But this new Noah, the one who seemed determined to win her over, was throwing a wrench into her plans to keep him at arm's length.

"Plus, it's damn near impossible to say no to that kid. She's too cute for her own good," he said.

"Tell me about it."

Penelope followed his gaze across the restaurant where Ella had gone to show off her purple hair to the waiter who always brought her free ice cream. As if she sensed them watching her, Ella looked up, saw Noah, and almost tripped as she rushed back to them.

"Does this mean I get to stay?" He held up a hand to give Ella five when she reached him.

"You came!" she said, curling her hand into his after slapping it.

"Um, excuse me, kiddo. No running inside. You know that."

"Sorry, Mama. I was just superexcited to see Noah."

"It seems somebody couldn't wait to go on her first date," the waiter called across the restaurant.

"It's not a date for me," Ella threw over her shoulder and then sent Noah a conspicuous wink.

Penelope rolled her eyes when he winked back. Songs from the fifties and sixties redone in Italian played softly from the speaker system, and she hummed along as they waited. When their table was ready, Ella scooted into the far side of the booth and motioned for Noah to follow. He didn't hesitate as he slid in next to her. She walked him through the menu as if he'd never ordered pizza before, reading out the words she knew and making up ingredients for the rest based on the photos next to some of the specialty pizzas. Then she told him he was going to eat two slices of plain cheese, like her.

"Let him order what he wants, Ella," Penelope said. She shot him an apologetic look and smiled when he shrugged like it was no big deal.

"I'm good with most pizza," he said. He slipped his arm around Ella on the back of the seat and tapped his fingers on the top of her head, making her whip her head around and giggle. "Except mushrooms. They're a great way to ruin a perfectly good pizza."

Ella rolled out her tongue and scrunched up her face in disgust. "Don't worry. There will be NO mushrooms on our pizza."

"My kind of girl," he said.

Ella scooted closer to him, resting her shoulder against his side. Her smile was quick but instead of beaming up at him, she tucked her chin into her chest and grinned to herself.

Penelope's pulse stuttered. She might be willing to risk her heart with Noah, but Ella's was a whole other story. Getting her heart broken was not an experience Penelope wanted her daughter to have.

For once she was thankful that Ella took after Sabina in the chatterbox department. Their constant stream of conversation gave her time to wrangle her nerves into something resembling calm by the time their food arrived.

Noah wiped the grease from his fingers onto a napkin and sat back into the cushion. He stretched his legs underneath the table, brushing Penelope's calf. He caught her eyes and smiled, leaving their legs touching. Ella wiped the hair back from her face and streaked pizza sauce across her temple. Penelope reached for a napkin, but Noah beat her to it. He rubbed it on the side of his glass to dampen it and dabbed it on Ella's hair. She jerked away from him, twisting her mouth into an annoyed scowl.

"Hey! Why'd you do that? That was cold!" she said. She grabbed his hand and held it in her small fist.

"Well, if you hadn't gotten pizza everywhere I wouldn't have to do it. So really it's all your fault, not mine," he said.

He fought to keep his smile from spreading

when she opened her mouth as if to argue but ended up grinning at him instead. She closed her eyes and let him pull her back to wipe the remaining sauce away.

"Thanks," she said when he released her.

"No problem, kid." He snagged a bit of discarded crust from Ella's plate and popped it in his mouth.

Ella transferred the other crust to his plate. "My mom usually eats my crusts, but you can have them tonight." She cupped her hands around his water glass and slid them up and down to soak up as much of the condensation on her hands as she could. Then she scrubbed them clean with an extra napkin.

"Hey, now. You're giving away all my crust?" Penelope asked.

"Sorry. I forgot you like them," Noah said. Ripping the piece in half, he held one out to Penelope. "I'm willing to share. At least with people who agree to have dinner with me again 'cause those people make me happy and people who make me happy deserve half-eaten crusts."

Laughing, she said, "I'd hate to see what people who don't make you happy get." She held on to the end of the crust, her fingers overlapping the tips of his. "Will you accept a maybe?"

"How about we talk about it after I get back?"

"Where are you going?" Ella asked, snuggling closer into Noah's side and pulling his arm down around her other side as if that would keep him from ever leaving.

"Sweetie, you know he's just here for a little while. He has to go home and get back to his life."

"But he can't," Ella said. Turning her face into Noah's chest, she mumbled against his shirt. Her fingers fumbled with the necklace around her neck and closed it in her fist. "You can't go."

Noah stiffened. After a few seconds, his fingers stroked down Ella's hair and he said, "I've gotta go back at least for a little bit. My cat's still at my apartment and I bet she thinks I abandoned her and is plotting to kill me if I ever return."

"I hope you left her a big bag of food. She's probably hungry if you didn't. That would definitely make her want to kill you if you let her starve."

"I've got a friend taking care of her for me. But I still want to go see her myself just to make sure she's okay and tell her that I still love her." His smile faltered.

Penelope pictured him as she had in her dream, lying on a couch with a cat snuggled on his chest in place of Ella's zebra. She forced herself to look away. It would be way too easy to fall for him if she kept thinking like that.

"Why don't you just bring her here? Then you wouldn't have to leave again," Ella said.

"I wish I could, but Fish is allergic to cats, so Bombay's banned from their house," he said.

"I've been trying to find a cat. It's on my list and everything." Ella pushed off of him but left her hands plastered against his ribcage. She smiled so wide her gums showed. "Hey, maybe I haven't found one because I'm supposed to get yours! We could keep her for you. I'd feed her twice a day and give her water and pet her until she purred. And you could come over and see her anytime you wanted."

Yep. Ground rules were a must. Number two on the list: No offering to take in Noah's cat without asking permission.

"I think we need to take a step back there, Ella," Penelope said.

Noah ruffled Ella's hair like he always did with River. "As much as Bombay would love that, I'm not sure your mom wants to take on my kid too."

"She's not your kid. She's your cat."

"It's close enough to the same thing," he said. "It's a little pathetic how much I miss that cat. She has these big sapphire eyes, and when she looks up at you, it's like she hypnotizes you and the next thing you know you've lost an hour just scratching under her chin and between her ears."

"I want to lose an hour that way," Ella said. She poked a finger into his side, making him squirm. "Will you bring her back with you, Noah?"

He flicked his eyes to Penelope's as if looking for a clue as to how he should respond. "Maybe on one of my trips I will."

Penelope held his gaze and asked a question of her own. "Are you planning on making a lot of them, even after Tucker's back to work?"

"I guess that depends on you," he said.

Her stomach lurched. Did what she wanted really matter to him now? "That's not a lot of pressure or anything."

Noah's lips tugged to one side. "Don't worry, it's not *only* on you. I already promised Fish I would come visit more often. But knowing you want me around too would definitely factor into the frequency."

"I don't know what I want," she said.

And the not knowing scared her almost as much as Ella's certainty that he should stay.

26

Penelope beat her mom to work and was grateful for the quiet. There was something magical about the shop in the early morning, when the scents of the candies had been shut up together for the night, blending together and creating a perfume so sweet and engulfing she couldn't imagine anything more perfect.

In the third drawer down, second row over, where she normally found the dried anchos, sat a leather pouch the color of burning butter. The thin straps formed a knot at the neck of the bag. The outline of some kind of flower had been branded onto the top side. Penelope traced her finger over the soft leather as she removed it. The knot unraveled with minimal effort and she lifted out a metal tin of black salt crystals and an airplane bottle of an Irish whiskey she'd never heard of before. She reached back in for the recipe she knew would be waiting. Ink so dark it almost looked wet covered the crisp, white card.

Truth Drug.

Holding the card by the edges, she read the rest of the elegant script that flowed onto the back to complete the directions.

She glared at the dark whiskey. The gold-and-black label shimmered in the light as she carried it to the work table. "Of course the recipe for truth is based on alcohol. Could you have been any less subtle?" she asked the table.

She gathered the remaining ingredients but couldn't make herself combine them.

"What is that?" her mom asked when she came in twenty minutes later and found Penelope still staring at the paper.

"A new recipe," she said, not looking up.

Sabina unwound her scarf and hung it up along with her coat in the alcove by the office. "Yes, I can see that, honey. I meant what is it for?" Her usually dreamy voice held a hint of worry that sharpened it.

Penelope heard her mom's unasked question: Will it help Ella?

She flicked her finger on the thick paper. "It's for salted whiskey caramels that force you to tell the truth."

"Well, the table doesn't offer up gifts just because. Do you think someone's been lying to you?"

She pinched the base of her neck to relieve the tension that knotted in her muscles. Sabina still hadn't mentioned her date with Marco. But that was a truth to tackle another day. "No. I think it's more that I want answers to questions I'm not ready to ask."

"Are you afraid you won't like them?"

I'm afraid I will. After her conversation with Noah the night before, Penelope was pretty sure she already knew some of the answers. Despite her resolve to remember why she shouldn't like him, some buried-deep part of her yearned for them to be true. And she didn't yet know what to think of that.

"If I know the answers then I'll have to do something about them. And I've gotten really good at ignoring this particular situation. I'm not sure I'm ready to change it," she said.

"Sometimes you don't get a choice." Sabina uncapped the salt, plucked out a few chunky crystals, and dropped them on her tongue. "And sometimes you're just too stubborn for your own good. At least when the table tells you something, you listen."

"Will you let me test them on you?" Penelope asked.

"I doubt I'd have anything interesting to tell you."

Not true. But she let it slide. "Don't worry, you're not the one I'm trying to get information out of. Just be my guinea pig. I need to see how they work so I know what I'm looking for when I give them to Noah."

Shaking her head, Sabina said, "If you want to know if he's the one, you could just drink the hot chocolate. You don't need to charm the boy."

She wanted to tell her mom it wasn't about that, but the lie wouldn't form. Instead she said, "I know you want me to settle down and be happy, and some days I think I want that too. But it's not that easy when it comes to him, Mama." She rapped her knuckles on the table, the sound echoing in the silence.

Everything Noah had done since he'd been back in town suggested he was interested in starting something with her again. And at dinner the night before, he'd said where things went from here was up to her. Now she just had to figure out what she wanted.

"That's all I get?"

"Until I know what to do about him, yes. If there's more to tell at some point, I promise to tell you whatever you want to know. For now, can you just trust me to handle this on my own?"

"I don't really have a choice, do I?" Sabina snatched the recipe off of the counter and read it, her mouth moving with each silent word.

They worked in relative silence for the next half hour, with only Sabina's soft whistling filling the air. Penelope measured each ingredient with a preciseness she'd honed over the years. Eyeballing it and hoping it was close enough was not an option. Her mom stood to the side, reading the recipe again over her shoulder as Penelope worked. They were so used to each other's movements in the kitchen, it was like a dance.

When Penelope shifted to melt sugar on the stove, her mom turned in the opposite direction to line the bar pan with parchment. When they came back to the center worktable, their arms never crossed as Sabina held the pan and Penelope poured the bubbling golden liquid into it.

A few hours later, when the caramels had finally thickened into a semihard, pliable state, Penelope turned them out onto the cutting board and sliced them first into strips and then into squares. Then she tempered the chocolate and dipped them one by one, until the dark chocolate settled into an even, shiny coat. She sprinkled three crystals of salt on each caramel before the chocolate cooled.

Her mom had a sixth sense about candies and instinctively walked into the kitchen as soon as Penelope finished. "Ready?" Sabina asked. She reached for a caramel, but Penelope snatched it out of her reach.

"Are *you* ready? I don't know how these'll affect you. You could just be compelled to answer my questions or you might spill everything unprovoked. Is there anything you don't want me to know before we start this?"

"Does it matter?"

"Maybe not, but if I can steer clear of certain topics, I will."

"Just promise me you won't probe too deep if you don't have to and we'll be good."

Penelope kissed her mom's cheek. "I promise. And thanks."

Sabina took the caramel Penelope handed her, her long nails sinking into the still-soft sides. She bit it in half and let the chocolate and sugar melt on her tongue instead of chewing. Her pupils darkened, contracting for a few seconds, and then returned to normal.

"How do they taste?"

"The whiskey's got a bitter kick, but the chocolate mellows it some. It almost feels like it's coating my throat, making it smoother. I can feel it in my lungs too, like a warm tingling, almost a tickle." Sweat glistened on Sabina's brow and beaded on her top lip. She lifted the mass of curls off of her neck and fanned her hand around her neck.

Shit, this was a bad idea. What if it was too much for her? What if there's a limit to how much magic one body can take before it breaks? Penelope poured a glass of tap water and pressed it into her mom's hands. "Come sit down, Mama." She led her by the elbow to one of the cushy wingback chairs out front.

A few of the customers sitting at tables and on the couches smiled at them before averting their eyes. Her mom had served them all while Penelope worked on the caramels. If she was lucky, no one else would come in until her experiment was finished.

"I'm fine," Sabina said, straightening her skirt around her ankles once she sat. "It was just a tad strong there for a minute. I'm okay now."

"Are you sure?"

"No." She pressed her fingers to her lips, the bright-red nails almost an exact match to her lipstick. She sipped the water before setting it on the table. "Looks like the recipe works."

Penelope gripped her mom's shoulders and forced her to meet her scrutinizing stare. Sabina's eyes contracted again, the brown of her irises marbled with flecks of gold and green. "Yeah, that's not comforting at the moment. If you're not okay, I need to figure out how to fix it. Do you want to go see Marco?"

"Oh, for heaven's sake, no. It's just a hot flash. These chocolates aren't going to kill me, so you can stop worrying about that. And, for that matter, the others aren't either. I know what I'm doing. I never take too much."

Now that the truth was out there, she couldn't ignore it. "So, it's always on purpose?" she probed.

"Don't act surprised. You and I both know you've thought it for years. You just didn't want to know the truth so you didn't ask outright. That seems to be a recurring theme for you, doesn't it?" Sabina paused and patted the armrest. "Oh, my, I think these chocolates might work a little too well." She kept her voice low, conspiratorial.

When Penelope sat, her mom's arm snaked around her waist to hold her in place. She rested her head on top of her mom's and hugged her back. "Would you have told me the truth without these chocolates?" she asked.

Her mom stiffened and mumbled something under her breath. "Probably not," she said louder.

"Why not?"

Sabina released Penelope and shifted to the far side of the chair. She was small enough that the move put a few inches of cushion between them. "I know it upsets you. But sometimes I can't help it. Sometimes reality is too much to bear."

Penelope knew that struggle all too well. But happiness was a choice, and she was determined to be grateful for each day she got to spend with her daughter. "It doesn't have to be. I had really hoped your date with Marco would help you to see that."

"How do you know about that?"

"I saw you at the cafe. You looked happy."

Sabina shook her head as if to deny it. "I was," she whispered.

The sadness in her voice broke Penelope's heart. "Why do you say that like it's a bad thing?"

"How is it fair that I get to have something to look forward to when Ella is so sick? At least with the Bittersweet chocolates I don't have to feel guilty about being happy because everyone knows it's only temporary."

Penelope took her mom's hand and laced their fingers together. "There's not a person in this town who would blame you for finding something good in the middle of all this. Not one."

"I would blame me," her mom said.

"Well, you'd be wrong."

Sabina gave a small laugh. "I feel a little sorry for what Noah's about to go through with these chocolates. But I hope you find out what you want to."

"Me too," Penelope said. Though suddenly she wasn't so sure she could go through with it.

27

Rehab was only a few blocks down the street, but Penelope was shivering by the time she reached the carved wood front door that had been salvaged from a church. She'd called in a to-go order to keep from chickening out. Curling her fingers tighter around the bag of chocolate, she went inside. Tucker waved her over to the bar where he sat with his cast propped up on the lower rungs of the stool next to him. A pair of crutches leaned against the dark-stained bar top on his other side.

"Well, this is a surprise," he said, his mouth tugging hard to the left in an amused smirk. Shifting his attention away from her, he said, "You might not be as rusty as you think, bro."

"Being flirted with by high school girls is not what I was hoping for," Noah said from somewhere behind the bar.

Penelope sat on a stool two down from Tucker and said, "Oh, c'mon, I thought that was every guy's dream."

Noah stayed crouched, restocking the beer on the lower shelves of the cooler, his back to her. His gray thermal rode up an inch or so, revealing a smooth strip of skin above the top of his jeans. "I'm not looking to go to jail, Penelope."

She heard the smile in his voice even though he didn't turn around. She didn't want to think about what it meant that he recognized her voice immediately. "Smart move."

"Yeah," Tucker said, running a hand over his close-cropped hair that was a few shades darker than Noah's. "I'm not bailing your ass out if you do something that stupid."

"Man, the double standards in this family." Noah stood, shaking his head, and pointed a bottle of beer at his brother. "I guess taking your bike out in the sleet and plowing it into a ditch is the mark of a genius then, huh? And me coming home to cover *your ass* is just what's expected?"

"Oh, bite me, Noah." Tucker leaned on the counter to hold his weight as he lifted his broken leg from the stool and reached for his crutches. He hobbled a few steps, lifting his hand and flipping his brother off.

Noah's laugh followed Tucker all the way to the door.

"Well, now that we've got the place to ourselves," he said, despite the dozen or so customers eating at the booths and tables, "what can I do for you?"

"Call-in order," Penelope said. She glanced at the bag she'd set on the seat beside her. Moving it to the counter, she took a deep breath and hoped he didn't see her hands shaking. "And I brought you something."

Noah unrolled the paper bag and inhaled. "That smells amazing. What is it?"

"Salted whiskey caramels. Seemed like something you would like."

"That sounds exactly like something I'd like." He eyed her over the open bag, eyebrows raised in concern. "Is there anything else in it?"

"You mean, is it charmed? Yes. But it won't hurt you."

He tipped the bag again and peered inside. "What will it do?"

Penelope twisted her hands together in her lap. She couldn't back out now. She squared her shoulders and met his stare. "It'll tell me a few things I need to know about you. Like whether it's worth letting you try to change my mind." Her chest didn't automatically tighten at the thought. She couldn't decide if that was a good thing or not.

"It's very worth it. But if eating some magic-laced chocolate can convince you, I'm all for it." He pulled a tap handle made out of a barrel stave and filled a pint glass for an order one of the waitresses called out as she passed a ticket back to the kitchen. "You know, considering how much effort you've put into hating me over the years—"

"I don't hate you, Noah," Penelope said.

He went on as if she hadn't spoken. "I'm surprised you told me the truth about these. You could've just let me eat it none the wiser." He kept his eyes on the beer, though with all of his years as a bartender she figured he could pour a beer with his eyes closed without spilling it.

"That wouldn't have been fair. Apart from being entirely unethical."

"So it's really the ethics part that got to you, huh?" He smiled when he said it and slid the glass to the end of the bar.

She rested her elbows in front of her, letting her fingers play with the strands of hair that had slipped loose from her handkerchief. "It was both. Whatever my feelings are toward you, you deserve to know what I'm doing. And to tell me if you're not okay with it."

"Those feelings—whatever they are—are present tense, right?"

"I didn't say they were *good* feelings."

"Yeah, but you didn't say they were bad either. And if you're even considering letting me try to change your mind about me, that means you're at least on the fence. Tipping you onto my side just got a little easier."

Noah stroked his finger in the air, adding an imaginary tick mark to his column. He winked at her and crossed his arms on the bar. With his long sleeves shoved up to his elbows, the thick muscles in his forearms flexed as he tapped his fingers on his biceps.

"Just eat the damn chocolate already." Penelope flicked the paper bag with her finger.

Noah's quiet laugh morphed into a low moan when he bit into a caramel. His tongue darted out to remove a black salt crystal that clung to his top lip. "If you wanted to know if chocolate was a turn-on, I can tell you for a fact that yes, yes it is. Holy shit this is good, Penelope. I don't care what kind of magic is in it. I would eat these every day regardless of what it makes me tell you." He popped the other half into his mouth and licked the melted chocolate from his thumb and forefinger.

"Well, it's not working yet. Wait until it kicks in before you say that."

"How do you know it's not working? Does it take time to get into the blood or something? Like a time-released drug?"

She gave him a sheepish smile. "These make you tell the truth."

"Huh." Noah scratched his ever-present stubble, letting his eyes close for a few seconds. When he looked at her again, his eyes were bright with amusement. "Well, this could be interesting. Hope you know what you're doing."

"Honestly, I don't really know what to expect out of this. But the recipe showed up this morning while I was thinking about what to do about you and I figured it was a sign. I mean, what can it hurt, right? We talk, I find out a few things I've wanted to know for longer than I should admit, and maybe we can find a way to be friends."

"You are really not helping your case here. Telling me that you've not only been thinking about me but you've been doing it for a while now. I might start thinking you like me. But maybe that's just the chocolate talking."

"Guess we'll find out," Penelope said.

The low murmur from the other patrons buzzed like a current through the air. She focused on the liquor shelves made from rafter beams bolted to the wall behind the bar. She thought she could almost smell the subtle scent of curing tobacco from the barn where the beams had been before. One shelf contained nothing but tequila. Broken, angular shards of mirror created a mosaic pattern on the back wall, reflecting light off the colorful bottles and liquids.

Noah slapped a metal bottle opener against his palm, drawing her attention back to him. "So, uh, are you gonna ask me anything? Or will I just start babbling like a thirteen-year-old girl and never be able to show my face in public again?"

"I don't want this to be awkward. It's not an interrogation," she said.

"I'd probably be better at that."

"Do you get interrogated a lot?" She shot him

a smile to ease the tension that pressed on her chest.

"No, but it's kinda freaking me out a little that you know where this conversation is headed and I have no clue. I'm normally really good at reading people, but not you. Never you."

"I can leave if this is too weird."

"No. I want you to stay." He reached for her hand but drew back before making contact. Curling his fingers into the wood, he added, "I agreed to this. I'll tough it out. But just remember that payback's a bitch."

Penelope nodded and traced the wood grain with the tip of her finger. There were so many things she wanted to ask him. But everything came back to just one question. "Have you ever been in love?" she asked after a moment.

"Wow, no shallow water with you, huh?"

"What, should I have asked your favorite color?"

"Green, if you must know."

That was one of the things Ella had wanted to know while Megha was dyeing her hair. Penelope would have to remember to tell her. "Okay. Now will you answer my first question?"

"Just once. Most of my relationships are more lust than love. Don't get me wrong, there's some strong mutual liking going on, but not in the way that would lead to it being anything real."

Is that what she'd been to him? Lust and mutual like?

Penelope avoided his eyes when she asked, "What happened with the one girl you did love?"

"I'm fairly certain my need to do things my way, consequences be damned, is entirely to blame," Noah said without hesitation. He waited for her to look at him, his whole face tight with an emotion she couldn't quite place. "If you want to know if I regret how I treated her, yes. Every damn day. She deserved so much better."

She took a deep breath and let it out slowly. She couldn't bring herself to ask him if he was talking about her. If the answer was no, she would never be able to look him in the eye again. "Why haven't you been back to Malarkey more than a handful of times since you left for school?"

"I'm a bartender. Not many options around here to do that as you're currently sitting in the one and only bar." He shook his head, as if arguing with himself. He clenched his jaw and swore. Stepping up on something behind the bar, he leaned farther on the counter so their arms almost touched and continued. "Okay, so you said you wanted to do this to learn some new things about me. Here's one very important thing: When I want something, it'll drive me insane seeing it every day and knowing I've screwed up any chance of ever having it. It'll eat away at me until all my nerves are raw and I'll do very stupid things just to numb myself to it, which only pushes the thing I want that much farther away.

It's a vicious, destructive cycle and the only way to stay out of it is to stay away from here."

"To be clear, that thing you want here is not so much a thing but a person?" Her voice was just above a whisper.

"To be clear," he said and grinned at her.

She saw the intent in his eyes and froze, unsure if she should let him kiss her or if she should bolt. Then he wrapped his hand under her jaw, with his thumb pressing lightly against her ear, and fit her mouth to his, making the choice for her. His lips were demanding and urgent and desperately soft as he coaxed hers open. The sweetness of the caramel was still on his tongue. Penelope pressed her feet against the bottom rung of the stool to get closer to him. She braced one hand on the bar as the other gripped his shoulder. He slid his free hand over to cover hers, and their fingers twined without conscious thought.

When he released her a moment later—or it could've been an hour, she wasn't sure—she dropped back onto the stool out of breath and fuzzy-headed.

"Does that tell you what you want to know?" he asked. His voice was ragged, his smile smug.

Penelope wasn't entirely sure which question the kiss answered. All of them maybe. She rubbed her arms to ease the goose bumps rioting on her skin. "I'm beginning to think this was a very bad idea."

"I tried to warn you. But from where I'm standing, it's not looking that bad 'cause now at least you know how I feel about you. How I've always felt."

"I seriously doubt you've just been sitting around pining for me all these years." After all, he'd been the one to leave her.

"Not constantly, no. But I thought about you often enough for the feelings to still be here."

"Noah—"

He waved her off with a quick flick of his wrist. The waitress slid behind the bar, trying to contain a smile as she interrupted them to place Penelope's to-go bag on the counter. She waited for Penelope to sign the credit card slip despite Noah's insistence that he would take care of it. She lingered at the end of the bar, still well within earshot, and only went back to the kitchen when Noah shot a sharp whistle at her and jerked his head in that direction.

"Listen, I was prepared to come home, help out for a few weeks, and leave without talking to you at all. Just to prove to myself that I could do it and maybe convince myself to finally forget about you. Obviously the universe had other plans. And since you're the one who initiated this little experiment today, the least you could do—you know, apart from kissing me back—is to give me a chance to make things up to you. Have dinner with me. Like a real date."

"Maybe I could bring Ella over to play with River once they're out on winter break and we can see where it goes from there?" she suggested.

"Not that I mind having Ella around, but I was thinking just the two of us." He sprayed ginger ale from the dispenser into a to-go cup and handed it to her, completing her order.

No matter what kissing him may have stirred up inside her, stealing even one minute of her remaining time with Ella was a deal breaker. "We're a package deal, Noah. You don't get one of us without the other."

"I know, I know. But this," he motioned between them, "is nice. One dinner with us and then however many more you want with Ella too."

Penelope raised an eyebrow at him. Looping her hand through the handles of the food bag, she said, "You're assuming I want more than one date." She slipped off the stool but didn't walk away.

"Exactly. Now can I ask *you* something?" Noah asked, not giving her a chance to protest his date request.

It also saved her from actually agreeing to go out with him. And at the moment she couldn't trust herself to make the right decision. Whatever it was. "It's only fair," she said.

"Did you love Ella's dad?"

She'd spent years convincing herself what

she'd felt for him had just been a side effect of the hot chocolate and teenage hormones. It hurt less that way. But the truth was there, closer to the surface of her heart than she expected.

"So much," Penelope said.

And it terrified her to think she still might.

28

Megha stalked into the kitchen of the Chocolate Cottage. She'd replaced her contacts with skinny rectangular glasses that accentuated her sharp cheekbones and wore a baggy hoodie with the words IN CASE OF HAIR EMERGENCY, RAISE HOOD printed across the front. "I'm pretty sure you owe me like twenty bucks or something," she said.

"I don't recall making a bet." Penelope finished counting the bags of marshmallows she'd already boxed up for the festival and marked the number down on the checklist.

"No, you just said you had no intention of seeing him. Which you blew pretty much immediately, might I remind you. So how in the world do you go from that to making out with him in the middle of the lunch rush?"

"We did not make out. It was one kiss, and he kissed me. Mostly to prove a point."

"I thought we were friends, Pen. Friends don't let friends find out about supersteamy kisses with superhot guys from Adi freakin' Della Lana halfway through her dye job. I was so not expecting it that I dropped the brush and left a red streak all down the front of the smock. It looked like I'd stabbed her with my shears. She wasn't as amused as I was."

"Shit. Adi knows?"

That's what she got for letting the chocolates distract her. For letting Noah distract her.

"Apparently her sister works at Rehab and called her almost as soon as it happened. His tongue still might have been down your throat, actually," Megha said.

"Oh my God, it wasn't like that."

"So what was it like?"

Penelope had thought about the kiss in every quiet moment she'd had since it happened. Part of her wished he hadn't done it. Part of her wished he'd done it again. "Surprising," she admitted after a moment.

Megha stepped aside to let Sabina enter the room. But she didn't let Sabina's presence derail the conversation. "As in he just randomly attacked you with his mouth or what?" She raised one perfectly arched eyebrow, as if daring Penelope to cut the conversation short now that her mom had heard what they were talking about.

Catching the smile her mom and friend shared, Penelope sighed. Better Sabina got the story firsthand instead of from one of their gossiping customers. "As in I enjoyed it a lot more than I expected to. Also, I don't think he planned on doing it, but I kinda provoked him."

"How do you provoke a grown man into kissing you?" her mom asked, curiosity giving her voice a melodic lilt.

"Actually, Mama, this might apply to you. Apparently you just have to feed him some truth-telling chocolates and get him to admit he's had feelings for you for a long time."

Her mom held her hand over her heart, index finger thumping in time to her heartbeats. "But what if you aren't ready to hear that kind of truth?"

Penelope hung an arm over her mom's shoulders and tipped her head so their temples pressed together. "Then you throw yourself into a festival you want nothing to do with so you don't have to think about it."

Haywood Lane had already been closed to traffic for two days. Now thick strands of globe lights zigzagged overhead, strung up between the buildings to create a canopy of light for three blocks leading to the park in the center of town where the Festival of Fate would kick off that weekend. The oak trees dotting the park had been wrapped in lights as well, and on the night of the festival, white paper lanterns would hang from their branches. The whole town would shine bright for a few hours as the residents gathered to celebrate their futures. And to try and change them.

Penelope wouldn't have been out there helping get things ready for the festival if Ella hadn't begged her to go. But it was hard to be upset about it when her daughter was having so much fun. They were on marshmallow-stick duty, which involved filling gallon-sized metal pails three-quarters of the way up with sand and adding long sticks people would use to roast marshmallows.

A flatbed truck piled high with firewood was already parked at the end of the street. Two more days and it would all be over.

Just as Penelope filled what felt like the millionth bucket, Ella gave a shriek of delight and ran to meet River ten feet away. When they reached each other, they locked hands and started spinning in dizzying circles.

"Those two," Layne said when she stopped next to Penelope. They watched their girls collapse into a tangle of splayed limbs and laughter. "It's like they've been friends their whole lives."

They probably would have been if she and Noah had made different choices. If she'd told him she was pregnant. Or if Noah had actually loved her back. But at least Ella would know that kind of friendship before . . .

She couldn't finish the thought.

"I'm happy they finally found each other," she said.

"At least they're making the most of the time

they have. I think Ella has even replaced Noah as River's favorite person." She tugged on her ponytail to tighten it, the purple streaks that Ella's hair now mimicked on full display.

"How does he feel about that?" Penelope asked. She emptied the last of the sand in the current bag into a pail, adding the gritty plastic bag to the pile she'd started stuffing in her messenger bag so they didn't blow away.

"I'm not sure he's even noticed, being pre-occupied with someone else and all," Layne said, unable to contain her overly bright smile.

The truth chocolates were definitely a bad idea. Before the weekend was out, the whole town would know she and Noah had kissed. And suddenly her mom's fears about being happy when they should be focused on Ella's well-being instead seemed not only logical but right.

"It's not like that," Penelope said.

Most people would have rolled their eyes at her response, knowing she was lying. Thankfully Layne just said, "Okay. So, what can I do to help you with festival prep?"

Together they hauled buckets around the park, depositing them where the girls dictated. And the girls ran to the firewood truck, loaded their arms with sticks, and walked faster than their mothers would have liked to the nearest stickless bucket to jab half a dozen sticks into the sand. While they worked, other volunteers erected a canopy tent and lined up folding tables beneath it where the hot chocolate and marshmallows would be passed out.

Someone strung up a banner full of glittered cursive that was so fancy it took Penelope two tries to realize it said YOUR FATE AWAITS. The girls made up guesses for what it said, each one sillier than the last, until they once again ended up rolling on the ground laughing.

When they finished with the sand and sticks, Penelope was content to just let the girls play. She and Layne sat on the top step of the gazebo where the sun shone strong, and while not exactly warm, at least it wasn't as chilly as in the shade.

"Okay, I've been trying not to ask, but I can't ignore it anymore," Layne said. She stretched back, resting on her elbows. "Does your kiss with Noah mean you've changed your mind about him?"

Penelope's stomach tightened at his name. Of course she wouldn't get off that easily. "Not yet." Instead of meeting the hopeful look she knew Layne was giving her, she kept her eyes trained in front of her. She hated that one kiss could make her forget she was supposed to keep him as far away from their hearts as possible. "But I'm thinking about it."

"Thinking is a slippery slope, my friend. At least when it comes to a Gregory. I'm pretty sure I thought about Tucker for a good month before he finally wore me down. Granted, I honestly didn't think he was serious about wanting to go out with me because what motorcycle-riding loudmouth looks at the introverted fangirl and thinks, 'Yep, I wanna hit that'? But for whatever reason he did think that and after all my thinking I realized he was pretty great."

"I hate to tell you, but it's talk like that that's making me want to run in the other direction. I'm not sure I'm ready for all that letting him into our lives entails."

Layne jerked up, her hand flying toward Penelope as if to physically stop her from running away. Shaking her head, she said, "Oh, no. Please don't say that. He'll never forgive me if I chase you off."

Penelope laughed and said, "It's not you. Don't worry. I'm just not—"

"Wow. I think I've just reached a whole new level of awkward if you're giving me the 'It's not you, it's me' excuse in regards to your relationship with someone else."

"What I was trying to say," Penelope started with a pointed look at Layne, "was that I'm just not sure I'm ready to believe Noah's as great as he seems. Because even if he is a perfectly lovely human being and also not bad to look at, there's still the issue of him not living here and me having a daughter who is already falling for him. That requires a massive amount of thinking."

Not to mention his history of breaking her heart, which required its own massive amount of thinking.

In the end, whether she decided she wanted Noah in her life or not, she had to be absolutely sure. Regret was not an option.

Layne took the girls for a hot chocolate break while Penelope got roped into a discussion with Ruth Anne about whether or not Penelope and her mom had enough time to make the amount of Kismet hot chocolate needed for the festival.

Like making hot chocolate wasn't their full-time job. Penelope's face stung from holding her smile in place for so long in the cold air. "I've got it covered. Don't worry."

"Well, *I'm* not worried, honey. But you know how other people get. When Delilah said you might just be pretending to go along with all of this so you can wait to ruin the festival until it's too late for any of us to do anything about it, I told her she'd been watching too many crime shows and it had made her paranoid."

"I said I would make the hot chocolate. Same as always. And I'm out here decorating, aren't I? What more can I do to show that I'm doing what everyone wants?"

Ruth Anne waved to someone behind Penelope, as if signaling them that she didn't need reinforcements. The half a dozen bracelets on her right wrist jingled. Smiling at Penelope again, she said, "Just wait a few more days and it'll all be over."

"No, it won't," Penelope said. She licked her cold-chapped lips. "Because when the hot chocolate doesn't work, everyone's going to blame me."

"Well, maybe last year's was just a bad batch or there were too many of us wishing for the same thing and we overwhelmed the magic somehow. Who knows? But I'm counting on things to work out right this year."

Penelope wouldn't hold her breath for that.

She managed a halfway sincere goodbye when Ruth Anne went jogging off across the park, hand waving high over her head to flag down someone she needed to talk to more than Penelope.

On the walk over to the Chocolate Cottage, Penelope kept her hat pulled low and her eyes trained on the ground a foot or two in front of her. In a few minutes she could hide in her shop to avoid the sympathetic smiles and skeptical stares. And she'd have the added bonus of proving to the people in town that she was doing exactly what she said she would.

Half a block away, she walked right into someone else on the sidewalk.

Rubbing her head where it had connected with what she assumed was the other person's elbow, Penelope swore.

"Sorry. I thought you saw me," Zan said.

"No, it's my fault. I wasn't paying attention," Penelope said. The pain in her head was already retreating. Zan appeared to be unharmed, though she was clearly rattled. Her fingers picked at one of the buttons on her coat as she stayed directly in Penelope's path. "You okay?"

"He's here."

Zan hadn't been able to outrun her fate.

Penelope reached for Zan's arm and tugged her a few feet farther down the street where they would have some privacy. "Your ex?"

"Yeah. He came in the cafe and sat there smiling at me just like in my dream. It was pretty surreal."

"Are you okay? Did he do anything to you?"

Zan smiled for the first time since Penelope had plowed into her. "That's the really weird part. He apologized. For everything. And not in the way that meant he just wanted me to forgive him so he could keep me placated and under his thumb. But like a real apology. No strings attached."

That was the thing with magic. The hot chocolate showed people a glimpse of their futures, but without the full context, the drinker would have to choose whether what they'd dreamed was good or bad.

"I can't tell you how happy I am that it wasn't what you thought it was," Penelope said. She allowed them both a silent moment of victory, then she added, "Do you think you can trust him?"

"For the day or two that he's in town? Yeah. I can manage that much."

"He's staying?"

"It's the festival. He overheard people in the cafe talking about it and now he wants to stay and check it out," Zan said.

And of course nobody bothered to tell him it wouldn't do him a damn bit of good. Penelope caught Zan's gaze and held it. "And after that, he's just going to leave?"

"That's what he said." Zan shrugged. "And he asked if that was okay with me. If he stayed, I mean. I think he would've left right then if I'd told him to."

"Why didn't you?"

"Because I'm sick of being scared of him. He can only hurt me if I let him, so I decided it was way past time to stop. It's what I wished for at last year's Festival of Fate. I figured it's fitting that's where it will come true."

Penelope hoped for Zan's sake it would work out that way.

29

Between the festival preparation, hours laughing with River, and her body simply not being able to keep up, Ella had worn herself out. When Penelope checked on her on the way to bed herself, Ella was buried under the covers, her hair sticking out the top of her cocoon the only visible part of her. Penelope watched her for a few minutes, grateful that they'd had more good days than bad lately.

Just as she turned away, Ella's bucket list caught her eye on the nightstand. Ella's favorite stuffed zebra, Pierre, guarded it, with two bean-filled legs holding it in place. Penelope hadn't seen it since they'd checked off dyeing her hair a couple of weeks before. In fact, she hadn't heard her daughter mention it in days. That did not bode well for either of them. The last time Ella had been so quiet about what was on her list, she had added "get a tattoo" and then spent two full days ignoring Penelope after she'd vetoed it.

There was something to be said for respecting a child's privacy. But preparing for the potential fallout from another crushed dream had its merits too. It only took her a second to choose.

And even then it wasn't so much a choice as a foregone conclusion.

Penelope tiptoed into the room. She stepped on something that, in the dark, could have been a dropped fruit snack or a bug. Either way, she didn't want to run into it again. She scrubbed the sole of her foot on the carpet to obliterate the cool, sticky sensation from her skin.

After checking to make sure Ella was still wrapped up tight, she bent to read the list. The top of it faced out, whatever Ella was keeping from Penelope hidden under her stuffed animal's rump. Pierre tumbled from the table as she tugged the paper free, and she caught him a few inches before he thudded onto the floor. She crouched down to read the note in the soft pink haze from the night-light plugged into the wall.

And there at the bottom, written twice as large as the rest of the list, were two new entries that stole her breath.

21. Fix Mama's hart.

22. Make Noah my DAD.

The list was gone when Penelope went in to wake Ella up for school. She'd wondered, for just a moment, if she'd made up what she'd read the night before. If maybe her head and heart were no longer on the same page about Noah and her subconscious was trying to push her in a new direction. Then she saw the corner of the paper sticking out from under her daughter's pillow where she'd tried to hide it. Which meant that those two new items were real, and it was in fact Ella, not her subconscious, who was trying to redirect her.

She waited until Ella was dressed and had stashed the list in her backpack, then she said, "We need to talk about your list."

Ella hugged her bag to her chest. "I'm not gonna show it to anyone, Mama. I just like to have it with me in case I come up with a new idea and need to write it down so I don't forget."

"I'm okay with you taking it to school as long as you don't bring it out during class. But that's not what I meant. I know you added me and Noah to your list."

"Oh."

"Yeah, 'oh.'" Penelope patted the unmade bed for Ella to sit next to her. "You know those things are probably not going to happen, don't you?" And by *probably* she meant *definitely*. There was no fixing her heart as long as Ella was still sick. And Noah would only ever be Ella's dad in the biological sense of the word. Actually being in her life day in and day out, helping raise her and love her like a dad should—that was never in the cards.

Ella took Penelope's hand and traced big, lopsided hearts on her palm with her finger.

317

"They might. If your heart wasn't broken any-more then you could fall in love with Noah and he would want to stay with us. And he could stay with you after I'm gone to make sure you're not too sad."

Penelope closed her fingers around Ella's and squeezed. "My heart is not broken, Ella. And I'm not going to fall in love with Noah." *Not if I can help it*. Though that was getting harder by the day.

"But Grams said the table gave you a recipe to fix your heart."

"Grams should not have told you that. But any-way, it's not for now. As long as you're around, my heart will be very much whole so you don't have anything to worry about."

"But what about Noah?" Ella asked.

"What about him?" Penelope countered and released Ella's hand.

"If you're not going to be in love with him, I need to ask the table for a way to make him stay."

"I'm not going to argue with you about him, Ella. If he's supposed to stay in Malarkey, he will. You can tell him you don't want him to go, you can show him how good things could be if he stayed, but you cannot use magic to make that happen. It doesn't work that way. Do you understand?"

"Yes, ma'am." Ella hopped off the bed and shouldered her backpack. "But I can still check the table, right? You know, not for something that will make Noah stay, but for something to show him that I want him to."

"You don't need a recipe to do that," Penelope said.

"But what if the magic is the only way he'll believe that he belongs with us?"

Penelope shook her head. Reasoning with her daughter was pointless. But she tried anyway. "If he really does belong here"—she couldn't bring herself to say that he belonged with them—"then he'll know it all on his own."

Ella wrapped her arms around Penelope's neck. With their foreheads pressed together, she said, "But can I at least try to find something? Just in case."

"You can try," Penelope said.

But fate had already made up its mind about Noah. Not even Ella's stubbornness would change it.

After seven drawers, Ella's high-pitched squeak reverberated through the kitchen at the Chocolate Cottage. She shoved her fist in the air, a white card clutched in her fingers. Her stunned smile and wide eyes lit up her face.

"It's cookies!"

Penelope took the offered recipe and skimmed it. A standard recipe with ingredients and measurements and bake times. But no magic mentioned.

"Dark chocolate with white chocolate chunks. Sounds yummy."

"But what do they do? I couldn't read that part."

Sabina looked up from the mound of pretzels she had yet to submerge in chocolate. Her sleek eyebrows, still as dark and unmarred by gray as the rest of her hair, arched in question.

"These don't seem to do anything," Penelope said. She waved the recipe card in front of her, attempting to deflect any criticism for letting Ella use the table for personal gain.

"It's just cookies?"

"Yep." Penelope whispered a silent *thank you* to the universe for not feeding into Ella's desire for a magical intervention.

Ella yanked the card away, slicing the skin between Penelope's thumb and forefinger. She inhaled an audible breath at the quick stab of pain.

"Why would it do this to me?" Ella asked, her voice teetering on tears.

Sucking on the paper cut, Penelope leaned into the table next to her mom. She nudged her shoulder. "Maybe the table's trying to tell you the same thing as I have been. Magic won't make him stay."

"But how will cookies make him stay? He can get those anywhere."

"No, these he can only get from you," Sabina

said, hugging Ella to her side. Then she pressed a kiss to Ella's head. "That's what makes them special."

"Can we make them today? Maybe if he eats them before the festival, he'll want to use his wish on us!" Her fingers automatically wrapped around her necklace as she pulled away from her grandmother and bounced with excitement.

Even after what Noah had told her when he'd eaten the truth chocolates—even after their kiss—Penelope couldn't imagine him staying. Not when the happy future she'd once promised him no longer existed. She flicked a finger on the recipe and said, "These are going to have to wait until after the festival. Grams and I still have a lot of work to do before tomorrow night. We can make them while you're out of school next week." She took the recipe and hid it in the back pocket of her jeans.

"But, Mama—"

"No, ma'am. The only butt here is yours and it's going to sit patiently on the sofa out front while I figure out a plan for today," Penelope said.

If only figuring out what to do about Noah was as easy as making a list.

30

Layne was a godsend. She stopped by the shop with River that afternoon and ended up taking Ella home with them so Penelope and her mom could finish all of their prep for the festival. With the influx of customers wanting an extra boost of magic before the festival, they were still working nonstop. And they had yet to make the Kismet hot chocolate.

Penelope knew the recipe by heart, but she still searched the table until she found it hidden underneath a block of chocolate. The lavender she needed, however, was in the first drawer she opened, as if once the table knew what she was making, it couldn't wait for her to complete it.

"I'll need to make at least one batch," Sabina said.

Penelope crushed the lavender petals she'd measured out into a bowl with the pestle, releasing the flowers' oils. "It's okay. I don't plan on drinking any, so I can make all of it."

"You're not even going to try this year? You're just giving up?"

"If you consider accepting your fate—meeting it head-on—giving up, then yes. I guess I am."

She didn't see any other option left. "Plus, after all the fuss I made about the hot chocolate, I would be a hypocrite if I drank it expecting anything to change."

Sabina smoothed a hand over the handkerchief covering Penelope's hair. "Of course the magic won't work if you don't open yourself up to it."

"I believed in it for so long, Mama. With all my heart. It didn't make any difference."

"She wasn't dying last year. You didn't believe with all of your heart. This time is different. You not only want the magic to work, but you need it to as well."

What Penelope needed was a miracle. And the most their chocolates were capable of was a temporary fix that tricked the mind into seeing what it wanted. She used her finger to scrape the lavender out of the stone mortar into the mixing bowl with the powdered milk and salt. "How can you say that? I had the entire town make an extra wish for Ella to get better. I couldn't have wanted anything more than I wanted that."

"But a part of you always thought she would be okay. That we wouldn't really lose her. I thought the same thing. She was too young, too loved, too important to die so soon. We didn't trust that we needed the magic to heal her, so it didn't. But now we know we were wrong. We can save her this time."

"I want you to be right. So badly. But what

happens when it doesn't work again? When we've tricked ourselves into believing she has a second chance and she dies anyway? At least my way we all have a chance to say goodbye on our own terms. That's all I can hope for at this point."

"Well, I don't want to say goodbye at all," Sabina said.

Neither do I, Penelope thought. But not everyone got what they wanted.

Late in the afternoon, Noah texted her saying he would bring Ella by the shop sometime "later." Which was a huge help and not near enough all at once. Because once Ella was there, Penelope's focus would shift from the massive batch of hot chocolate she needed to complete to Ella asking to go home every five minutes because she was bored. Even knowing that, she hadn't been able to ask Layne or Noah to keep Ella all night.

Penelope's stomach had been growling for the past hour. She thought about having something delivered, but she didn't have time to spare to make the call, much less time to eat food when it arrived. Instead, she chugged a bottle of water and hoped that would tide her over for another few hours.

A car door slammed on the street. She turned as Ella flung open the front door and ran in with a paper bag clutched to her chest. Noah was a step behind with another two bags. The scent of fried rice and spice overpowered that of the chocolate, filling the room for a few seconds.

"Ella said you'd probably be too busy to eat on your own so we should bring you something. I said you'd be smart enough to take a break, refuel so you'd have enough energy to make it through the rest of the evening. But she was right, wasn't she?" Noah asked.

"She's lived with me her whole life. Gives her an advantage," Penelope said.

"No, dinner was Noah's idea," Ella said, interrupting them. "But I told him what you liked. And he said he was gonna make me try an egg roll because it's a travis-tree that I haven't had one before. Whether I wanted to or not." She set the bag down on the side bar and began digging through it.

"A travesty?" Sabina asked, hugging Ella, who repeated the word in a whisper a few times so she'd get it right the next time. "Well, I guess you're gonna have to then since he's the one who bought us all dinner."

"Is this it?" Ella asked. She held up the small white bag by one corner pinched between her forefinger and thumb like it might eat her instead of the other way around. Grease stains ranged over the thin paper in large splotches.

Before Penelope could tell her to be careful, Noah stepped in, holding a plate under Ella's outstretched hand and stuffing a napkin into her free one.

"You eat, you sit," Noah said. "That goes for y'all too. Every time I passed the shop today you had a line to the door. You both need a break while there's no one in here."

"We can take ten minutes," Sabina said when Penelope started to protest about how much work they had left to do.

He pressed a takeout container into Penelope's hand. "Take twenty. I'm here as long as you need me. Either to give an extra pair of hands or to entertain the kid and keep her out of your way. Now eat."

Penelope shot a glance at the sidewalk. It remained empty for the moment. She settled onto one of the couches, tucking a leg underneath her to make enough room for Noah to sit beside her, and rolled her tense shoulders, which popped a couple times. Instead of sitting, Noah moved behind the couch and splayed his hands across her shoulders. First food, then a massage? How was she supposed to resist that? Her head dropped forward, giving him better access, and he worked his fingers into the knots on her upper back, dipping his fingers underneath the neckline of her shirt and increasing the pressure a bit.

"Is it always like this for the festival?" he asked.

"No," Penelope said.

"Yes," Sabina said.

Noah chuckled. "Okay."

Sabina blew on a forkful of pineapple and fried rice, holding it steady while she answered. "Most people come in a day or two ahead of time wanting to increase their chances of making the festival magic work. But this year we've had considerably more interest than in the past."

"They're worried Penelope might be right about the hot chocolate being a placebo?" he asked.

Penelope forked up some rice and let it hang in the air as steam wafted from it. "No. They're all convinced I'm wrong and want to prove it."

Ella gave an affronted little huff. "But Mama, the magic has to work. I need it to make sure I finish all the things on my list." Her greasy fingers slipped off the compass necklace she'd unearthed from her shirt. Despite Penelope telling her repeatedly that she was only allowed to wear it if she asked first, Ella had taken to wearing it almost every day. But especially on the days she was going to see Noah.

"So, what's on this list that's so important you need magic to make it happen?" Noah asked.

Ella set her uneaten egg roll back on her plate. "I'm trying to make my mom—"

"Ella," Penelope warned.

"What?" Ella asked, a guilty smile curling her lips.

327

"Eat."

"But he asked me a question."

A question Penelope did not want answered. Especially not when Noah was the one asking. He did not ever need to know how much power he had over her heart. Then or now. She frowned at her daughter. "And you're using it as an excuse not to eat your egg roll. It'll be a whole lot better if you eat it hot."

Noah took the other roll out of the bag and took a bite. After he swallowed, he said, "They're not bad cold. But if I were you I'd eat it now."

"You're really going to make me do this?" Ella asked, eying the egg roll as if she could make it disappear with her mind.

"You can put it on your list afterward," he said.

Ella twisted her face into a disgusted look. "One bite. That's all."

"I'll bet you a dollar you want more than one bite." Noah bit another inch off his roll and grinned at her despite his overfull mouth.

When Noah won—and Ella polished off the whole thing—she had to ask Penelope for a dollar to pay him.

"You'll have to earn it," Penelope said and sent Ella into the back to throw away all of their trash.

After a few minutes, she called Ella's name to make sure she wasn't finding some sort of trouble to get into back there by herself. With Ella's obsession with the table, Penelope could never be too sure what her daughter was hoping to get out of it.

"Can we go home now?" Ella asked when she came back out. Clutching her necklace in one hand, she smiled at Noah. As if he had any say in how long Penelope and Sabina would stay at work preparing for the festival.

Penelope had already returned to the front counter where she marked off items on her checklist. "Not quite yet. Grams and I still have a few things to get done before tomorrow." She'd put off making the hot chocolate mix as long as she could. If she was going to keep her promise to the town, she had to make it tonight.

"Noah can take me home and stay with me until you're done, right Noah?" Ella's state of awe when it came to him had doubled in the past half hour as if the egg roll had entranced her just as easily as one of Penelope's chocolates.

"Yeah, sure. I can do that," Noah said.

Penelope waved him off. "You don't need to do that. She'll be fine here. We won't be here too much longer anyway."

He leaned on the counter so his face was only a few inches from hers. As if he knew the thought of him roaming free in her house set her on edge. "It's really not a problem. I'll probably be more help there than here anyway. And it'll get her out of your hair."

"Hey! I'm not in her hair," Ella protested.

"That's not helping the cause here, kid."

Ella clapped a hand over her mouth. Then she spread her fingers wide enough to say, "I'm definitely in your hair, Mama. Noah should take me home now."

Somehow they convinced her that she had no other options. Penelope couldn't figure out where she lost the argument, only that she had.

31

A layer of cocoa powder coated the kitchen. Noah didn't have a clue how it had gotten everywhere. It followed Ella wherever she went no matter how many times he wiped it off her hands, face, hair, clothes. His only explanation was that it came out of Ella's pores like fairy dust. His shirt was covered too, but that she'd done on purpose, pressing a powder-covered hand over his heart and telling him she'd gotten the recipe for the cookies they were making from the magic table at Penelope's shop when she'd asked it for a way to make him stay.

So there wasn't any way he could be annoyed at her for the disaster that was currently the kitchen. She was just too damn cute.

Checking the recipe to make sure there wasn't anything magical he had missed, he asked, "What's so special about these cookies anyway?"

"Nothing," Ella said, poking out her bottom lip in a pout.

"Then why was it so important that we make them?"

"I was looking for something to make you stay but the table gave me a recipe for regular cookies instead of magic ones and my mom said it's up to me and not magic to show you that you belong here. With us."

He didn't know whether to be impressed or worried that Ella might have charmed him into staying if the table hadn't given her a nonmagical recipe. Not that he'd mind a little magic pushing Penelope over onto his side. But the idea that he might not have complete control over his life where Penelope and Ella were concerned lurked in the back of his mind.

With two cookie sheets full, Ella dropped the spoon back into the bowl of dough with a loud clang. "How long do they have to bake?" she asked, bouncing in front of the loaded cookie sheet on the island.

"Nine minutes," he said.

"Okay, I'll set the timer and you put them in the oven 'cause I'm not allowed to do that. I burned my hand once and my mom said I wasn't allowed to use the oven until I was in double digits. Sometimes, though, she'll let me hold the door open when she puts the tray in and out. As long as I stay off to the side." Ella whipped the door open with a dramatic wave of her hands and stepped aside so Noah had room to maneuver around her.

"Timer?" he asked.

"Oh, right," she said and ran behind him and around the island to the other side of the oven.

She jumped when she got there, snatched the timer from the back of the counter, and landed back on the floor with enough force that the baking sheets clattered against the oven racks. "Nine?" Ella asked. He nodded. She twisted the knob on the owl-shaped timer and carried it back to her seat at the island.

While the cookies baked, Noah poured two glasses of milk and settled into the chair next to her. Ella mirrored his position, slouching with elbows propped on the counter and chin resting on linked hands. She flicked her eyes to the side without turning to look at him, her lips sliding into a smile.

"Do you know what you're going to use your festival wish for?" Ella asked.

"I thought your mom said the hot chocolate didn't work?" he asked.

"She's wrong. It does. The magic didn't fix me last year, but that's okay. I know it still works."

He wanted Ella to be right more than he realized. "You sound awfully sure about that, kid."

Ella's expression turned serious, her eyes narrowing and locking on his. "I am. My grams says you have to believe in something if you want it to work. And my mom's too sad about me being sick to believe right. So I have to believe enough for both of us."

If anyone could make magic work from sheer

willpower, Noah would put money on it being Ella. "Then I guess you already know what you're going to wish for, huh?"

"Yep. And then my mom will know that everything worked out the way it was supposed to." She lifted his arm over her head and snuggled into his side. "And we'll all be happy. Together."

Maybe if he believed hard enough too, they could make it a reality.

When the timer went off, Noah removed the cookies from the oven, transferred them to the wire cooling racks, and waited a good two minutes before determining that was long enough. He broke one open, trails of steam escaping the still-gooey middle, and popped a hunk in his mouth. Wincing, he breathed through his mouth to cool it off then chased it with a long gulp of milk. He barely managed to stop Ella before she burned her mouth like he had.

"They're still a little hot. Why don't you run upstairs and change into your pajamas while these cool and we can watch a movie before bed?"

She dropped the cookie back onto the cooling rack and said, "I'll meet you in the living room when I'm done. Don't forget to bring the cookies with you. And don't worry, we're allowed to eat in there. I do it all the time. We just can't leave any food or dishes in there because my mom doesn't like when things are messy."

"Then we better not leave a mess," he said.

When she raced out of the room, Noah scanned the disaster area that was the kitchen and decided he'd attack it after he put Ella to bed. He plated half a dozen cookies, balanced the plate on top of one of the glasses of milk, and carried them to the living room. Not a minute later Ella's feet pounded in the hallway above. She skidded at the bottom of the stairs in her sock feet, the tail of a blanket trailing behind her. Her other hand gripped a black-and-white-striped stuffed animal to her chest. She climbed onto the couch and burrowed into Noah's side. He wrapped his arm around her, gripping the blanket she had draped across both of them.

"I like you babysitting me, Noah. If you lived here, we could do this every night," Ella said a while later as she leaned over to get her third cookie.

"I don't think you need a babysitter every night," he said.

Crumbs clung to the corners of her lips. "No, I mean if you lived in the house with us. And then you wouldn't be a babysitter, you'd be like my dad or something."

He handed her a napkin when she ate the last bite. "Whoa there, kid. I can't even get your mom to go out to dinner with me without you tricking her into it. I think we're a ways off from her asking me to move in."

"She's just being stubborn."

"That seems to run in the family."

"What does that mean?" she asked.

"It means that you're stubborn too." He laughed and pressed a kiss to her temple. Her hair smelled like chocolate and he realized he probably should've made her take a bath after they had finished baking. "But for what it's worth, I can be pretty stubborn too, so I'm not giving up on her just yet."

"Can I tell you a secret? One you have to promise not to tell anyone. Not even my mom." Ella whispered the last part as if Penelope could somehow hear her.

Noah dipped his head toward her, meeting her stare, and pressed his lips together to keep from laughing at her seriousness. "Must be pretty important if I can't even tell her."

"It is. And I'll tell her after the festival, but I don't think she's ready to know it yet."

"But you think *I'm* ready?"

She shoved up onto her knees, wrapping her small, but surprisingly strong, hands around his arm. When she grinned at him, her tongue poked through the gap in her teeth where two had come out. "Yep."

"Well, I can't argue with that." He steadied her with his free hand so she didn't topple off the couch. "Spill, kid."

"I didn't know we were going to make the

cookies tonight. My mom said we'd do it next week, but I really needed something before the festival so that you didn't waste your wish on something else. So I went to ask the magic table for help and it gave me this." Ella lifted up her pajama top and removed a photo she'd held in place with the elastic band on her pants.

There was no way the picture could exist. Not without the help of Photoshop anyway. Or magic. In the photo, he, Penelope, and Ella made silly faces at the camera, smooshed close together so they all fit in the shot. And there cradled to Ella's chest was his cat, Bombay.

"What is this?" he asked.

"It's a picture of me, my mom, my dad, and my cat."

Noah snapped his head up, tearing his gaze away from the photo. *Dad?* The sudden pressure in his chest tightened until every heartbeat throbbed in his ears and drowned out whatever else Ella had said. He swallowed hard, the dryness in his throat making it difficult for him to say more than, "You mean I'm going to be your stepdad?"

"No. You *are* my dad. As soon as my necklace went nuts around you like it does with my mom, I knew you belonged with us. I put you on my list and everything, though she said I shouldn't. And tonight I asked the table for proof that you were my dad so you would believe me and

337

stay. And there you are, right in my picture like you're supposed to be. And I have a cat too. It's everything I wanted all in one."

"There I am," he said. It was too much to wrap his brain around. Sure, it was definitely possible. He and Penelope had gone that far on a couple occasions. But if he'd gotten her pregnant, she would have told him. She would have tried to stop him from leaving town.

Unless she hadn't known yet.

He dropped the picture to his lap and nudged Ella's side with his forearm. She turned, the hopeful smile freezing on her lips when she finally looked at him. "Ella, listen to me. I need you to tell me the truth about how you found the picture, okay? I won't be mad if you're making it up, but I need to know if you are. It's really important. Did you ask for a picture of your dad or just a picture of who you *wanted* to be your dad?"

She circled his face on the photo then did the same to Penelope's, linking them together in a sideways figure eight. Infinity. "My dad. My *real* dad. I'm not making it up. Cross my heart."

His breath escaped in a long, slow exhale as his fingers fumbled in his pocket for the empty cigarette pack he'd been using to trick his mind into thinking he'd had a smoke. The crackling cellophane slipped between his sweaty fingers. He fisted it in his hand and clenched his jaw to keep from saying the dozens of things that fought to come out.

The doubt and the anger. The confusion and the excitement.

He sat like that for a few minutes, the cartoon voices from the movie they'd been watching jabbering on in the background while Ella watched him with her bottom lip caught in her teeth.

"Noah, is it okay that I told you?" she asked after another minute or two.

"Yeah, of course it is," he said. He sat up and ran a hand over her messy hair. The smile he gave her felt too big, too fake. But she smiled back. "I'm just surprised, that's all."

"Happy surprised or you're-going-to-send-me-to-my-room-because-that-was-so-not-funny surprised? I've only gotten the bad-surprised from my mom once, but it was enough to make me never want it again."

He laughed because there didn't seem to be any other kind of reaction to Ella. "Definitely happy."

"Good. Me too," she said and popped a kiss on his cheek. "Now we just have to convince my mom to be happy about it too."

Noah flinched.

If Penelope had wanted him to know he had a kid, she would have found a way to tell him anytime in the past eight years. Thinking she'd be happy that he finally knew was too much to hope for. Hell, he'd be lucky if she even copped to the truth.

He had the photo, though. And Ella was on his side. So he had half a chance of this not blowing up in his face.

32

The kitchen was a disaster. Measuring cups, eggshells, an ice cream scoop, and three baking sheets littered the island. A massive pile of cookies were stacked on a plate. Those, at least, Noah had remembered to cover with plastic wrap. What Penelope assumed had once been dough was dried in a crusty river on the stove top.

Too tired to deal with the mess, she switched off the light and headed into the living room to confront the culprits. The glow from the TV illuminated the room. An animated movie played with no sound. Penelope went to shut it off and stopped halfway across the room. Noah was stretched out on the couch, asleep. He had one hand splayed out on his chest, cementing Ella's favorite zebra, Pierre, to him. Three-quarters of the blanket had slipped to the floor.

This was her dream come to life.

She watched him for a minute. The familiar tingle moved from her fingers up her arms. She'd felt that way the first time she told him she loved him. When she thought he loved her back.

"No, you don't get to do this again," she murmured to the air. "I'll decide if I want him to stick around or not, thank you very much." She shook her hands then ran them through her hair. She let out a ragged breath. Resisting the urge to readjust the blanket, she clicked off the television and went upstairs.

Noah had turned back her sheets and left a few sprigs of lavender on her pillow. The sweet scent lingered in the air. She found a half-eaten cookie in the sheets. She laughed, imagining Ella sneaking in behind Noah and thinking no one would notice.

Fate or not, she was afraid she'd already made up her mind about Noah. And she wasn't sure how she felt about it.

It took her until she'd changed into her pajamas and climbed into bed alone to give in to what she wanted.

Penelope crept back downstairs, her bare feet padding a subtle rhythm on the dark wood. She sank to her knees in front of the couch. Noah's deep breaths ruffled the downy fur on the stuffed animal's head. His T-shirt stretched tight across his broad shoulders. The screen-printed ink on the letters spelling out their high school's name had faded or been rubbed off of half of them. She'd seen him in that shirt when they were younger too many times to count, but something about seeing him in it again set off sparks along her skin.

Inching closer, she trailed her fingers over the

soft hair at his temple. The stubble along his jaw scratched at her fingers as she traced the sharp line toward his chin. His lips parted and a sleepy sigh escaped. His eyelashes fluttered, but his eyes remained closed.

She leaned in and fit her mouth to his. Just a whisper of a touch.

But it was enough.

Noah's arm snaked out, winding around her back so his long fingers cupped her neck and hitched her closer. He blinked a few times. The haze of sleep cleared a little more each time his eyes met hers. His lips moved faster, his fingers gripped tighter. Penelope pressed her hips into the cushion and fisted her hand in his hair. His tongue teased her bottom lip until she opened for him. He tasted the way he had in her dreams. Like chocolate with a hint of spice. Like forever.

She closed her eyes against the thought, refusing to let it take hold. *Wanting him and loving him are not the same thing.*

It was such a fine line between the two, would she even know if—when—she crossed it?

He slid his hand underneath her shirt, his palm stretching over her stomach and fingers grazing her ribs.

"Noah," she managed between kisses. "Wait. Not down here."

Stepping over the stuffed zebra that had fallen to the floor, she led him up to her room. Penelope willed her hand not to shake in his. She cast a quick glance at Ella's room then slipped inside her own and locked the door behind them.

Her mouth found Noah's again, even in the dark. They stumbled to the bed, all hands and lips and need.

They were breathless. Delirious. Drowning in each other like they had the first time.

She shifted to straddle his hips, two layers of fabric the only thing holding them back. But as she leaned down to kiss him again, he said her name. The desperation of a moment before replaced with hesitation. She straightened, and his heart pounded under her palm on his chest.

"Why didn't you tell me Ella's my daughter?" he asked.

"Noah—" When had he put it together? How? Penelope slid off of him and tucked her knees beneath her. Tugging her shirt down, she attempted to cover her exposed thighs. Like that would make this conversation any less awkward. She kept her hands holding the thin fabric in place. "What makes you think," she said, taking a stuttered breath, "that she's yours?"

Noah gave a humorless laugh. "Besides the way you're looking at me right now like you might need to breathe into a paper bag for a few minutes?" His eyes narrowed and cut right through her.

He had her there. She forced a slow breath in,

attempting to prove him wrong. But as her heart rate showed no signs of returning to normal anytime soon, she had to let it go to suck in another quick breath.

"Ella showed me a photograph of all of us together. In the future. Apparently your magic table gave it to her tonight. She said she already knew I was her dad and that the picture was just the proof to convince me."

"There's no way she could have already known. I never told her. I never told anyone." Unable to look at him directly, Penelope stared at the few inches of space between her knees and his hip.

"I get it. We weren't together very long, and then I left and never came back." His voice dropped to a coarse whisper. "But my brother was right here all these years. You could've found me if you'd wanted to."

"You're right. I could have. But I didn't."

He sat up so his legs bent in front of him and rested his wrists on his knees. His hair fell across his face when he tilted his head to look at her. Tension spread from his clenched jaw down his body, tightening his muscles until he looked ready to explode. "Did you think I wouldn't come back if I knew?"

"No. I worried that you would." All of the hurt and rejection and soul-crushing sadness she'd kept buried for so long came rushing back strong as ever. She released one side of her shirt to press her fist to her chest where her heart threatened to burst. "And at some point you would have felt like I'd trapped you here. With me. With the future you didn't want."

"You really think I wouldn't want this? A life with you and Ella?"

A flare of anger supplanted her heartache. Penelope pushed up onto her knees and shuffled back a few inches until her toes peeked over the edge of the mattress. Then she dropped to the floor, putting the whole bed between them. "Do you remember what you said to me when I told you I dreamed about how you were my future?"

Noah flinched. "Not in exact words, but I know the general gist." He turned and hopped off the other side of the bed but made no move to round the end to get closer to her.

"Well, I know the exact words, Noah." They were permanently carved into her heart, and no amount of scar tissue had been able to hide them. "So I am beyond confident when I say this life was not something you ever wanted." She spoke just above a whisper to keep from waking Ella. Not even the low volume could stop the pain from seeping into her words.

"Maybe not back then. We were so damn young, Penelope. And there you were, telling me that was it. That my life was already decided for me and I had no say in the where or the how or the why." He dragged a hand through his hair, sending it into disarray. The hard lines around his mouth smoothed out when he flashed his eyes to hers. "That scared the shit out of me. *You* scared the shit out of me."

Penelope scooped her pajama pants off the floor and pulled them on. "I scared you? I wasn't asking you to drop everything and marry me right then and there, Noah. But I was in love with you and thought you were in love with me. And I stupidly thought you'd want a life with me one day." The words scraped her throat raw on their way out. She'd held them in for so long their edges had been honed into razors. She looked down, half-expecting to see her heart thumping on the floor at her feet with her confession.

"God, it was so easy to picture the rest of my life with you, Penelope. It was never a question of whether or not we'd be happy together or if I loved you. I knew they were both true."

"But you still left," she said.

"But I'm here now," he countered.

He said it like it made everything easier, better. Like it wasn't a temporary living arrangement. But her heart could only handle losing one person in the near future and Ella already had claim on that position.

Penelope crossed her arms over her chest and forced herself to ask the question that he didn't want to acknowledge. "I know, but for how long?

Because this amazing little life Ella and I have has an expiration date. You missed all the good stuff, and a lot of the bad too. But the worst, that's still coming. And I can't see you sticking around for that."

Noah's expression hardened, his jaw clenching again and his eyes narrowing into unreadable slits. "Wow. Nice to see you think so highly of me."

The bite in his voice sent a chill up her arms. She shook it off, refusing to let her feelings for him cloud her judgment.

"With our history, what else am I supposed to think? I thought you were going to be my future. I wanted you to be. And you couldn't run away fast enough. You've been that other guy for so many years, a month or two of good doesn't erase that."

"I was only that guy in your head. If you'd given me a chance to be Ella's father from the start, you would've seen a very different version of me."

Neither of them really knew how their life together would have played out, though. And just because the hot chocolate made her dream of him didn't mean they'd live happily ever after. Just that they would love each other, and that wasn't always enough.

"Maybe," Penelope said, the only concession she was willing to make. She walked to the door and twisted the lock. The loud click shot through the silence.

"So that's it, just a 'maybe'?" He met her at the door and stood close enough for her to feel the heat radiating off his skin. He didn't touch her, though, and she tried to make herself forget how he'd felt beneath her a little while before. "Why did you bring me up to your bedroom then?" he asked, as if reading her thoughts.

She avoided his eyes, looking instead at the hollow at the base of his throat, the frenetic rise and fall of his chest. "I don't know. Momentary lapse of sanity. I saw you sleeping there and logic went right out the window."

Noah braced his arm against the doorjamb above his head, blocking any attempt she might have made to open the door. "You're unbeliev-able. You know that, right?"

"For being honest with you?"

"I don't know what this is. But it sure as hell isn't honesty."

Penelope couldn't tell him that she'd dreamed of him twice. Not when he'd just admitted her initial dream was why he'd left her in the first place. She might be falling for him again, but she wasn't stupid enough to confess it a second time.

"I don't know what you want from me," she said after a moment.

"I want a chance. With you. With Ella." Noah didn't bother to whisper this time. His voice was steady, sure. "Even if it's just for a little while."

And there it was. The confirmation she'd been waiting for. No matter what the hot chocolate wanted her to believe, whatever future they had together, it wasn't forever. She wrapped her arms around her waist, as if that could protect her from the painful truth. "And then what? You'll go back to your life already in progress while I have to pick up the pieces of mine alone. It's hard enough knowing that I'm losing Ella. I can't risk what's left of my heart too."

"Who said I was going back?"

"Um, everyone."

"Not me."

"You don't have to say it. Not when you're going home every other weekend to keep from losing your job," Penelope said.

He lowered his arm and reached for her. She backed away, her eyes flashing an angry warning at him to keep his distance.

"Not that it's any of your business, but I would've told my boss to piss off by now, but he's a buddy of mine and I don't really want to burn that bridge if I don't have to."

No. He'd need that bridge to get the hell out of town when he realized this wasn't what he wanted after all.

She stepped forward, hand already twisting the doorknob. "Well, it's a good thing I'm not asking you to then, huh?"

"It doesn't mean I'm leaving," Noah said.

"It doesn't mean you're staying either." She ignored the way her heart protested by thumping hard in her chest. "If you want a relationship with Ella, I'll support it one hundred percent. You both deserve a chance to have that while you still can. But any sort of relationship with me is not part of that deal. No more of whatever we've been doing for the past few weeks. That's done."

Penelope opened the door and tilted her head up to face him. The disappointment and hurt etched in hard lines on his face sent a wave of regret coursing through her. But she couldn't give in. She couldn't let herself want anything more than what he was able to give. And that would never be enough for her.

33

He had a kid.

Shit.

He had a kid.

Not only had one, but wanted to have one. Wanted it as much as he'd wanted Penelope before he'd shot that chance to hell by reminding her that she hadn't wanted him in the same way—despite kissing him like her life depended on it. And while she dug in her heels about not wanting to start anything with him, at least she hadn't made Ella off-limits too.

Whatever time Ella had left—and God it better be more than Penelope acted like—he would spend it making up for everything he'd missed. With Ella and her stubborn mom.

"Must've been a good night if you're just getting home," Tucker said when Noah walked in.

"It was enlightening, that's for sure," Noah said, the words coming out hot and jagged edged. He continued toward the stairs without stopping to see his brother's reaction.

"Whoa, hold up a minute. You can't say that and just walk away."

"God, you're such a girl. Can I at least take a shower before you beg for gossip?"

Tucker struggled with his crutches, dropping one as he tried to stand. His arm flailed and somehow he managed to hobble his way into Noah's path. "No, because then you won't come back out of your room tonight. I'm not letting you leave until you tell me what she did to put you in such a piss-poor mood. And you can call me a girl all you want, but have you forgotten how fast things spread in this town? Everyone'll know within a few days if something happened between you and Penelope, so you may as well just tell me so I can help do damage control if needed."

"Damage control won't be necessary." At least Noah didn't think so. The people in Malarkey were a weird bunch, though. They could blame him for not being around for Ella's whole life, for leaving Penelope to raise their daughter on her own. If he'd known, he would've been there. And now, well, now he just had to prove to Penelope that he wasn't going anywhere. "But since you're insisting, no, we didn't hook up. And yes, I'm probably in love with her. The kid too. So before you can ruin it by being your usual asshole self, I'm going to shower. Then I'm coming back down so we can talk about a few things. Do you think twenty minutes is enough time for you to come up with something halfway supportive to say?"

"If it's closing the deal you're having trouble with, maybe you should lay off the 'probably' shit when you throw out the word 'love' to a girl."

Noah flipped off his brother without turning around. He wasn't going to let Tucker's dickishness derail his hope for a future with Penelope and Ella. Not even Penelope had managed to do that and she'd put in considerable effort.

He caught a hint of Penelope's perfume clinging to his clothes as he stripped. He tossed the shirt onto the floor. He couldn't decide if he wanted to scream at Penelope or kiss her the next time he saw her. The one thing he was sure of was that he wanted there to be a lifetime of next times. No matter what Penelope had said about them not having a future together. This was the universe pushing him where he was supposed to be. And he was supposed to be in Malarkey with Penelope and Ella.

As he showered, he ran through the epic to-do list he was now faced with tackling. It would be worth it, though. To finally get the life he wanted.

When Noah went back downstairs, he didn't waste any time getting to the point. "I'm gonna move back."

"Just like that?" Tucker asked.

Dropping into the chair opposite his brother, he leaned forward, propping his elbows on his knees to keep from bouncing them. "You know I've wanted to come home for a while. Offering to help out while you're out of commission was just a convenient excuse."

"Let me guess. This has nothing to do with wanting to be around your family and everything to do with getting in Penelope's bed."

"It has everything to do with family." Noah ran a hand through his damp hair and flicked the droplets at Tucker. "Ella's my daughter. There's no way I could go back to my old life even if I wanted to."

Tucker jolted forward, his cast thumping hard against the floor. He swore and readjusted in his seat so that he faced his brother. "I'm sorry. You do realize how kids are made, right? There's no way you slept with the girl of your dreams and then just walked away. Not with how hung up on her you still are."

"Yeah, I know. And yeah, I did."

"You've got to be kidding me. So you slept with Penelope and she just decided not to tell you that you knocked her up? I don't buy it. It's not like you were some random one-night stand she couldn't look up afterward. To me, that's a clue that you weren't the only guy she was sleeping with and the kid isn't yours."

Noah scrubbed a hand over his face, unable to look at his brother. "I know how it sounds, but you're wrong. She used one of her hot chocolates, and when she told me what she'd dreamed about I acted like a complete jackass. I don't blame her for wanting nothing to do with me." It wasn't entirely the truth, but there was nothing he could do to change the past, so continuing to blame Penelope for all the time he'd missed with them didn't help anyone.

"Shit."

"I know it's a lot to take in, but this is a good thing. I have a kid, Tuck. A kid I'm already crazy about. And I have a chance at making a life here with her and Penelope."

However many days Ella had left, he was going to be in them. And if fate was on their side, they'd have her for the rest of their lives. He just had to keep believing that.

"So a girl and a kid all in one fell swoop?" Tucker asked.

Noah blew out a breath and raised an eyebrow at his brother. "Pretty much. I came back looking to prove to myself I was over Penelope and found two people I'm not sure I can live without."

Now he just had to convince Penelope she felt the same way.

Penelope was still in bed, though not asleep, when Ella crawled under the covers with her the next morning.

"Where's Noah?" Ella asked.

She stared at her daughter. The smattering

of freckles on her cheeks. The enviously long eyelashes. The hope lighting up her big brown eyes. She hated that her answer would snuff it out. "He went home."

"But we were supposed to make you breakfast. I had it all planned out. Chocolate chip waffles and bacon and half hot chocolate, half coffee to drink. Full hot chocolate for me, though."

"That sounds yummy, sweetie. You and I can still make it if you want."

Ella rolled over so they were no longer facing each other. Her fingers twisted in the chain of the compass necklace as she huffed out a sigh. "No. It's not the same without Noah."

"It's the same as it's always been," Penelope said. And the truth of that sat heavy in her chest, like something important was missing, despite her life never feeling incomplete before.

"I know. But now that we found him, he should be here. He wants to be here. He told me."

If he'd wanted to stay, he would have fought harder last night. He wouldn't have walked away. Again. Even though she'd told him to. "I know you want him to be your dad, Ella."

"He *is* my dad. You know he is."

"Okay, technically, yes. Noah is your father." Father, not dad. Dad implied reading bedtime stories and kissing scraped knees and compromising on how many bites of food were enough to warrant dessert. But try explaining those differences to a girl who had never had either one in her life.

"Then why did you make him leave?" Ella packed a lifetime of accusation into that one sentence. She side-eyed Penelope, keeping her face directed at the ceiling while she glared.

"Sometimes wanting something isn't enough. Everyone carries around baggage with them from all the things they've experienced, and sometimes it's just too big to get past."

"But why don't people just set it down? Or get a wagon to pull it on?"

If only it were that easy. Penelope stroked a finger down Ella's cheek, wishing she could erase the hurt in her daughter's eyes. "Some things are hard to let go of, even if it would make life easier."

Ella scrunched up her face and pouted. "Maybe you should both try harder," she said after a few heavy breaths through her nose.

"Ella," Penelope warned.

"What?"

"You know better than to talk to me like that."

"I just want us all to try and be a family, okay, Mama?" The desperation in Ella's voice made it quaver. "It's already on my list and everything."

"You can still see him, Ella. I already told Noah that too." Penelope's voice was harsher than she'd meant. She closed her eyes and counted to five.

"That's not the same as being a family. He should be here with us all the time. He's already missed too much. If he misses much more, I'll be gone."

Gone. The word sounded so final coming from her daughter's lips. "Sometimes people can't always be here when you want them to be. But that doesn't mean they can't still be important to you."

Ella sat up and rearranged the covers around her so there was a thick barrier between them. Her small hands bunched and pulled on the fabric before smoothing the wrinkles out again. "If you hadn't been fighting with him he would have stayed last night and everything would be okay now."

"No, he wouldn't, sweetie. That's why we were fighting. This life, this town, it's not for him. No matter how much you both think it might be right now."

"That's not true. Noah belongs with us." Ella shook her necklace. Something rattled around inside, as if a piece that made the compass work had come loose. She looked up at Penelope, face flushed and eyes wide. "He's supposed to be with us. Sleeping in this house and walking me home from school and laughing with you when I snort milk out of my nose at the dinner table. That's how it's supposed to be. So you have to be nice to him and make him see that he wants to be with us too. Because if he doesn't know we want him too, we're going to mess it all up!"

"It's not that simple."

"Yes, it is!"

"That's enough, Ella. I wish I could give you everything you wanted, but Noah is never going to be what you want him to be. He had a chance to choose this life and he didn't. I'm sorry."

Ella sat up, throwing the covers off of her. "That's not true. He would pick me but you made him go away! And you broke my necklace. It was working last night when he was here but now it won't move at all. Not even for you. You broke everything!" She stood on the bed, one hand on her hip, the other clutching her necklace, and stared down at Penelope. Her eyes filled with tears.

"Stop yelling and sit down before you lose your balance and fall off the bed," Penelope said.

"Not until you make him come back! Call Noah. Tell him I want him here for breakfast like we talked about. He'll come over. You just have to call him."

"You can see him, but not right now. And if you keep arguing with me, you won't get to go to the Festival of Fate tonight." Penelope hooked her arms around Ella's knees and dragged her down, releasing her only once she stopped kicking.

Ella jerked away from Penelope, the chain of her necklace catching on Penelope's hand and ripping free from her neck. "You're ruining everything!" She leapt from the bed and raced to her room. The walls shook with the force of her door slamming.

Penelope picked up the pendant. It was still warm from being wrapped in Ella's fist. She shook the compass and the red dial that always spun like mad when she was near gave a feeble shudder, then froze.

She dropped face-first onto her pillow. The sound she let out was caught somewhere between a scream and a sob.

The compass's magic was supposed to lead Ella to the people who loved her. Now it was gone, and her daughter's heart was in pieces.

She really was ruining everything.

34

Ella wasn't in her room.

Or in any room in the house.

Or even in the yard.

As far as Penelope could tell, Ella wasn't anywhere.

35

Noah lurked by the hot chocolate tent even though Penelope and her mom wouldn't be around to man it for another hour or so when the sun went down. But with this being the shortest day of the year, sunset would come early and he'd be able to set the first of his plans in motion.

Since his plans relied on Penelope giving him another shot, he needed her to show.

More than half the town had already crowded into the park. The bonfire had been going for hours and people rotated spots in front of it. Others set up camp with lawn chairs and blankets and thermoses of soup and coffee and something stronger to keep the cold at bay.

He caught a flash of purple weaving through the crowd. Five seconds later, he was being mauled. Or at the very least, hugged with the ferocity of a lion cub.

"Hey, kid." *His* kid. Damn that was a crazy thought. He wrapped his arms around Ella when she clung to his waist. Scanning the park and not finding Penelope, he asked, "Where's your mom?"

"She's being stubborn." Ella stepped back,

fisting her hands on her hips, and gave him a squinty-eyed, tight-lipped look that was 100 percent Penelope.

"That happens sometimes."

"It happens a lot lately. But if I can get my future to come true because of the festival hot chocolate, I think she'll be better," she said. "You're going to put your future in the fire with me tonight, right?"

"You bet I will." He smiled down at her, noticing how unprepared she was to be outside for the next few hours. "Where are your gloves?"

"I forgot them."

Noah rubbed his hands up and down her arms to warm her up. "Let's get you over to the bonfire before you turn into an Ella-cicle."

"Yeah, that would be bad. If I froze right in the middle of the festival people would just shake their heads and say 'Why didn't somebody thaw her out?' And you'd be really sad."

"Yes, I would. And so would your mom." He tugged on one of the purple hunks of her hair to get her to look at him. "Do you think we should go find her and get her to warm up with us?"

"I might freeze before we find her," she said. Her teeth clanged together when she shivered.

Noah knew she was exaggerating to avoid answering the question, but as sick as she was, he didn't want to take the chance of making her worse somehow. But that didn't mean he had to let the kid get away with manipulating him. He tilted his head toward the fire and set off in that direction.

Pulling out his phone, he asked, "So if I call Penelope, she'll tell me you are allowed to be hanging out with me?"

Ella scurried around in front of him, raising her hand to stop him. "Don't. You can't call her yet." She tried to tug the phone out of his hands. He tightened his grip and lifted it out of her reach.

"So what you're not telling me is that I'm going to be in even more trouble with her when she finds out about this?"

"It'll be okay. She won't find out as long as I'm home before she comes to get me for dinner."

That little sneak. Forget about her not being allowed to hang out with him, Ella wasn't even supposed to be at the festival, period. "Whoa, hold up, kid," he said. Noah latched on to the hood of her coat as she walked toward the fire without him. She jerked to a stop, throwing a glare at him over her shoulder, but couldn't hold back the smile that threatened to undermine her attitude. "Your mom doesn't know you're here? She thinks you're still at home?"

Ella turned to face him. "We had a fight and I went to my room."

"And you don't think she'll notice you're gone? 'Cause I'm pretty sure she will, if she hasn't already, and she's probably going to lose her sh— She'll be really worried about you." He dialed Penelope's number and listened as it rang and rang. Just as he pulled the phone away from his ear to end the call, she answered.

"Penelope, I—"

"I'm sorry, Noah. I can't do this right now." Her voice was raw with panic.

It looked like she'd already discovered Ella's empty room. Noah frowned at Ella. "Ella's with me. She's fine," he said before she could hang up on him.

"Oh, thank God." Penelope's sigh rasped through the speaker. "Are you at the house or the bar? I've been looking for her for over an hour. I can't believe you just now thought to call and tell me where she was."

"She just found me at the festival. Like two minutes ago. I figured she was here with you and that you just wanted nothing to do with me after the way things ended last night and that she came over to hang with me on her own. She only told me you had no clue she was even here when I wanted to go find you. And now she's giving me this really impressive death-glare for calling you." He raised an eyebrow at her, silently asking if that was the best she could do. "Sorry about her sneaking out, by the way. She definitely gets her rebelliousness from me."

"That's not funny, Noah."

"Oh, c'mon. It's a little funny."

Whatever Penelope was doing on her end of the phone blocked out the first part of her response. The only part Noah could make out was, "I'm coming to get her."

"That might be kinda difficult. I already promised to do my wish with her at the bonfire. She said it was important to her completing some of the things on her list and that I had to help her. Of course, this was before I knew she ran away. But I still promised, so you can come join us, but you can't take her home yet."

"Did you seriously just tell me what I can and can't do with my own kid?"

He shrugged, forgetting she couldn't see him. "All I'm asking for is a few hours with her. With you. I've missed out on her whole life. I just want to spend time with her while I still can."

Penelope said, "That was a low blow, Noah." Then she hung up.

But it worked, he thought. And he meant it. He wasn't going down without a fight. Noah nudged Ella to get her moving toward the fire again. "So, why'd you run away?"

"Because I was mad at my mom for making you leave. And for breaking my necklace and ruining our lives."

"I hate to have to tell you this, since you have a serious grudge going on, but that's not all your mom's fault. I don't know anything about the necklace, so you can stay mad at her about that if you want. But she only made me leave because I hurt her when we were younger and she's scared I'm going to do it again."

Ella slowed to walk beside him. Turning her gaze to him, she said, "You won't do it again."

"No, I won't. But until she believes that, things might not be the way any of us want. So you need to cut her a little slack and you definitely can't run away again. And next time you want to see me, you've gotta ask, okay? You can see me anytime you want as long as your mom says it's all right."

"What if she says no?"

"Then we'll have to wait until she's ready."

"I hope that's soon," she said.

"Me too, kid."

Penelope couldn't find a parking spot anywhere close to the park. She left her car in the middle of the street a few feet from the barriers that marked the beginning of the festival. If Martin wanted to ticket her for it, so be it.

The lights strung up overhead blinked to life as daylight faded. Tendrils of smoke wafted through the air, permeating it with the scent of the bonfire already in full burn. Downtown Malarkey was full to bursting with friends and neighbors, and Penelope pushed past every one of them without so much as a "hello" or a "sorry" in her haste to find her daughter.

Ella was fine. She was with Noah. Safe. But until Penelope laid eyes on her, her heart refused to slow from its current panic-attack speed.

They sat on an upturned wooden stump at the edge of the bonfire, Noah on the cold wood with Ella settled onto his lap like she belonged there. He'd unzipped his coat and wrapped it around her shoulders to keep them both warm in the near-freezing temperature.

Pulling Ella's gloves out of her pocket, Penelope walked the last few feet to reach them. "Do you want these?"

Not expecting Penelope to suddenly be there, Ella jumped. Noah's arms tightened around her to keep her from falling forward into the fire. He checked out the gray mittens with triangular cat ears and face sewn onto the backs as he took them from Penelope and asked, "Got any in my size?"

"Fresh out, I'm afraid."

Ella twisted around to look at him. "Next time, you should leave a pair at our house so my mom can bring them too."

He set her on the ground and leaned in so their faces were inches apart. "There's not going to be a next time, remember? No more sneaking out to see me."

No more sneaking out period, Penelope thought. But saying that out loud would probably start her fight with Ella all over again.

"I know. I just meant the next time we both go out and forget our mittens," Ella said.

Noah cocked his head to meet Penelope's stare. "Hopefully your mom will be with us from the start next time."

"And then we'll all just have to hold hands to keep warm." Ella wrapped her mittened hands around both of theirs, her smile so bright it put the fire to shame.

How could Penelope take that kind of sheer happiness away from Ella just to keep her own heart intact?

Penelope squeezed her daughter's hand. "Can you give us a minute?" she asked Noah.

"Sure. I'm not going anywhere, so just come find me when you're ready," he said.

The way he said it, the weight he gave each word, made it seem like he was talking about much more than staying at the festival. Like he was offering her the future she never thought she'd have, and all she had to do now was take it.

"Okay," she said, not certain what she was agreeing to. Then she led Ella away from the fire—and Noah—to talk without the distraction he was proving to be to both of them.

With the entire town out for the festival, no place in the park was private. Penelope ended up walking the few blocks to the shop so their family drama wasn't on display for everyone to see.

Sabina had already closed up for the day. She

had wanted to go out and look for Ella too, but Penelope convinced her to go set up the hot chocolate for the festival to keep the crowd from revolting. A trace of guilt seeped into Penelope's thoughts for abandoning her mom at the last minute. Now that she had found Ella, she'd have to make it up to Sabina.

"Mama, please don't be mad at Noah," Ella said once they were inside.

Penelope hugged Ella from behind, curling her body protectively around her daughter's. She pressed a kiss to Ella's chilly forehead. "Maybe you should ask me not to be mad at *you* for leaving the house without telling me."

Ella's shoulders slumped. "Am I in trouble?"

"You probably should be, but right now I'm just happy you're okay. But if you ever do anything like that again, I will—" The unfinished threat hung in the air. There was no punishment Penelope could think of that she would actually go through with.

"I won't. Noah made me promise too."

"Good." Penelope relinquished her hold on Ella. "I know you want everything to be the way you want right now, but I need some time to figure out what's going to be best for us where Noah is concerned."

"How much time?"

"I'm not sure. But I promise you'll be the first to know when I figure it out, okay?"

Ella thought about it a moment and nodded. "Okay. But I'm still mad about my necklace."

Penelope fingered the compass she'd had in her pocket since realizing Ella was missing. "Sweetie, we don't know how the necklace worked. For all we know, it was just supposed to point you in Noah's direction. And once you found him it had done its job so it stopped working."

"I don't think so."

"Why not?"

"Because I found Noah weeks ago, and it was still working last night. When he tucked me in bed, it went nuts. Like it knew he belonged there with us. But then you made him leave. Noah said it was because you were scared of him breaking your heart again, but he won't do that. He promised. But I think that's why my necklace is broken too. So maybe if you let him un-break your heart, the necklace will be fixed too."

Was that really a promise he could keep?

Penelope wanted to believe it, to believe him. But she couldn't. Not yet. "Un-breaking a heart isn't as easy as it sounds."

"It is if you use a magic recipe," Ella said.

She still had the recipe for curing a broken heart despite throwing it away half a dozen times. It always reappeared in the top drawer of her dresser where she'd first stashed it to put it out of her mind.

Maybe the key to getting everything she wanted was within reach after all. She just had to be willing to take a risk.

"Wait," Ella said as they stepped outside to go back to the festival. "I forgot my mittens. Be right back." She ran back in, disappearing into the dark store. She reemerged a minute later, mittens on and a mischievous glint in her eyes.

Tucker, Layne, and River had arrived at the festival while they were gone and were squeezed in around the fire with Noah, who, true to his word, had stayed. He smiled at Penelope, his surprise giving way to an expression she couldn't quite place when she and Ella joined the group.

Not just a group, Penelope thought. *A family.*

Hers and Ella's if she wanted it.

Layne pulled Penelope into a hug and whispered, "Forget anything I ever said about Noah wanting to leave town, okay?"

"I'm trying," she said.

The girls offered to hand out hot chocolate when word spread through the park that people were anxious to put the magic to the test. Penelope left them under Sabina's supervision and—at her mom's insistence—waited with the others in the line that snaked out from the table a few hundred people deep.

Noah cupped her elbow and held her back when the line moved forward, putting a foot of distance between them and Layne and Tucker in front of them. "You and Ella work things out?" he asked, his voice barely audible over the hum of people in the park.

She wrapped her fingers around the necklace in her pocket. The metal was warm against her skin. "We reached an understanding of sorts."

"No more running away?"

"That and she has to be patient when it comes to what happens next."

They shuffled a few feet forward. Noah shifted his hand from Penelope's arm to her back, leaning in close so his breath rushed over her neck. "So, where does that leave us?"

Nothing had changed since they'd argued the night before. Figuring out what role Noah would play in their lives wasn't a decision she could make lightly. Stepping forward to break their contact, she said, "I don't know yet. Ella's obviously willing to fight for you, so you don't need to worry there."

"Which means you still don't trust that I'm in this. What will it take to convince you?"

Penelope turned to face him, well aware that so many pairs of eyes were on them. "Honestly, I don't know. Can't we just leave it alone tonight and watch our kid having a good time?"

"Anything that means I still have a chance, I'm all for."

"I'm not making any promises."

374

"That's okay. I'll make them for both of us."

She closed the gap in the line. When they reached the front, Ella grabbed a full cup from the table behind her and handed it to Noah.

"Why was it sitting over there?" Penelope asked.

"I made it a few minutes ago and saved it for him," Ella said, sharing a guilty look with River.

River gave her a not-at-all-subtle thumbs-up. "Yeah. We were making them for all of you but then we got busy and had to stop. That one's yours." She pointed to another cup set apart from the rest.

"Right," Penelope said. At least they were bad enough at lying that it was easy to spot when they were. Turning to Noah, she said, "Don't drink that."

But the cup was already pressed to his mouth.

He licked the chocolate foam from his top lip and said, "What's wrong with it?"

"I have no idea," she said.

"Nothing's wrong with it," Ella said. She handed the other cup to Penelope and watched as she took a sip. "Sheesh."

Penelope held the hot liquid in her mouth, identifying each flavor to make sure the girls hadn't doctored the drink. It tasted exactly as it should. "Okay. It's fine. Drink away."

She still didn't know if the hot chocolate would allow anyone to alter their fate, but when it was her turn to write down how she wanted her life to turn out and toss it in the fire along with the rest of the town, she looked at Ella and Noah beside her and couldn't think of anything she wanted more than a long, happy life with them both.

36

Noah called Penelope the next morning, asking her and Ella to meet him at the school playground after breakfast. He led Penelope to the swings while Ella and River ran to the merry-go-round and latched on to the handles without stopping. Their momentum set the ride in motion, and after three spins, they both jumped on, wrapping their legs around the blue metal bars and dipping their heads back into the wind. Penelope sat on the cold, curved rubber. Nerves danced in her stomach and she kicked the gravel beneath her to get moving. She slid her eyes to him and quickly looked away, unsure of how this conversation would go.

"Are you okay?" she asked.

"I had a dream about you last night. I mean, it didn't feel like any dream I've ever had before, but it wasn't real either."

She spun around to face him. The swing swayed beneath her, and she grabbed the chains to keep steady. "What did you dream about?"

"You and Ella." He walked backward a few steps and swung out in a slow arc. He kept his legs straight in front of him, the heels of his boots scraping a trench in the pebbles beneath him. "We were having breakfast in your house, except it was our house because we were married. Ella was a few years older too—not quite a teenager yet, but so damn close—and she was walking her little sister around the kitchen in circles, the baby clutching her little hands around Ella's fingers for support. It was just this normal, everyday kind of breakfast, but it was perfect. And I woke up with this absolute certainty that that was where my life was headed."

She'd hoped so long ago that he dreamed of having a future with her. But now, it seemed, he'd done it in a very literal sense.

Goose bumps that had nothing to do with the weather crawled over Penelope's skin. She toed the ground, drifting a few inches back and forth but not actually swinging. "The hot chocolate Ella gave you last night at the festival, was it hot? Like spicy peppers hot?" she asked.

"Yeah. Was it not supposed to be?"

"No, it should've tasted like lavender and dark cocoa." She focused on the ground instead of him, staring at a heart-shaped pebble with a deep crevice down the center. She couldn't tell if it was dirt or just the light that made it look black in the center. She flipped other stones on top of it until she hid it. There was no room for broken hearts in this conversation. "Ella must have given you our Corazón hot chocolate to make you dream of your true love instead of the Kismet hot chocolate we use for the festival."

No longer kicking, he gradually slowed. "Wait. What are you saying?" he asked and rested his forehead against the thick chain.

It was almost too good to be true. But she said the words anyway, hoping that would somehow make it true. "I think your dream was real. It just hasn't happened yet."

Noah's laugh vibrated in the air between them as he drifted past her. When he walked his feet back to gain momentum, his smile was wide, delirious. "So that was our future? We get married and have another baby and Ella is still with us years from now?"

Penelope twisted her swing so she could watch him. His leather jacket hung open, revealing the toned muscles in his chest that strained against his cotton tee as he leaned into the movement. "If that's what we want, we could make it happen."

His shoes scraped the ground as he slowed again, spitting pebbles over their feet. He turned to face her and hooked his fingers around the chains of her swing to pull them closer. One knee slipped between her legs while the other pressed against the outside of her thigh. Her breath caught at his closeness. All she had to do was lean forward and their lips would touch.

"Does this mean you're back to not hating me? 'Cause I'm about to kiss you, and it will work out much better if you don't want to punch me in the face."

She dipped her head forward, resting her forehead on his, and laughed. While his hands still held her swing in place, she shoved her fingers into the hair at the base of his neck and brought his mouth to hers. His breath was hot and sweet against her skin, his scratchy stubble scraping against her chin.

The first thing she noticed when she pulled away was that her feet weren't touching the ground. Noah had pulled her so close she was practically sitting in his lap. The second was that the playground was silent. She whipped her head to check on the girls. The merry-go-round was still, and they lay with their feet pressed against the center post and their heads under the handlebars, oblivious to Penelope and Noah's kiss.

He eased her back into her space, but didn't let go of the chains. He played with her fingers, loosely threading his with hers and rubbing his thumb over the space between her thumb and forefinger. She took a deep breath and let it out slowly.

Noah traced the tattoo behind her ear with his fingertip like connect the dots. The touch was light, but she felt it all the way to her toes.

"A constellation?" he asked.

"How can you tell that? It's just dots."

"But they're strategically aligned dots." He laughed when she rolled her eyes at him. "I don't know which stars they are, but I know you. Fate, astrology, horoscopes. It all kinda fits together, right? Seems like if you were going to get something inked into your skin, it'd be something you love."

"It's Pisces. Ella's zodiac sign."

"I didn't peg you for the tattoo type," he said, trailing the path of the tattoo again. "Even one as subtle as this."

She shivered again. "Yeah, well, I'm full of surprises."

"Got any more?"

"Tattoos or surprises?"

"Either. Both."

"Wouldn't you like to know?" She grinned at him then pulled him down for another kiss. "What about you?" she mumbled against his lips.

Noah broke their contact and braced his feet in the gravel to keep his swing from moving too far away from her. He lifted his shirt and exposed his ribcage. The face of a compass was drawn in black and gray across his skin. A larger version of the one on Ella's necklace, covering a space the width of her hand with her fingers spread.

She pressed her shaking fingers to his warm skin, and his muscles contracted. Touching the *N* at the top of the sharp point, she had a quick flash of it meaning Noah instead of North. That Ella's compass was somehow tuned to him, pointing to him because he belonged with them. Her breath hitched, and a wave of heat washed over her.

"When did you get that?" she asked, her voice nothing more than a whisper.

"A few years ago. Why?"

Penelope dropped her hand, curling her fingers into her palm to keep from touching him again. "Have you seen the necklace Ella found? The one she says is proof that you belong with us?"

"Not really? I mean I know she's been wearing one, but I haven't gotten a good look at it since it's always clamped in her fist so you don't take it away from her." Noah inspected his tattoo as if trying to see whatever she had, then, finding nothing that explained the change in subject, he smoothed his shirt back into place.

"It's that, Noah," she said and pointed to his side. "Exactly that."

He raised an eyebrow at her. "You mean it's a compass?"

"No, it's *this* compass. The size and shape of the starbursts in the background and the style of the letters and the words between the cardinal points, whatever language it is. All exactly the same."

"It can't be the same. This is based off of a photograph of a compass my great-grandfather had custom made. There was only one, and it's been lost for half a century." Noah took her hand, opening her fist and linking her fingers with his. He pressed their joined hands to his chest and smiled when she lifted her gaze to meet his. "Do you know what it says? The lettering?"

Penelope shook her head.

"When it is love you seek, keep this close to your heart—"

"And love will reveal itself," Penelope finished for him.

His eyes widened in surprise. "How do you know that?" He lowered their hands but didn't let go.

"It was on a note that came with Ella's necklace." She closed her eyes and took a steadying breath. "Did your great-grandfather's compass work like a normal compass?"

"Yeah, I think so. He was a fisherman so it was as much for practicality as it was my great-grandmother's way of reminding him she loved him while he was gone."

Penelope's fingers itched to touch his tattoo again. To trace that part of his family's history permanently on his skin. But her hand was still locked in his. "Why'd you get the tattoo?"

"Why'd you get yours?" Noah countered with a half smile.

"I asked first."

"Okay. I got mine because I missed my family and home and just fucking everything. Tucker was so damn happy about starting his life with the girl he loved and I guess I wanted that too. Not like I was ready to settle down, but I wanted to know that I could, that there was a girl out there I'd want that with. An uncle or someone had mentioned the compass and what it said in a toast at Tucker and Layne's wedding and it stuck with me. So I asked my dad about it and he said it had been lost after my granddad's death but he had a picture of it. And, I don't know, it just felt right making it a part of me. Now, your turn."

She glanced at Ella, her throat tight from all the things she wanted to say. After a moment, she settled on the simplest, yet truest, explanation. "I needed something that would always be with me even after she's not," she said.

"If my dream was really what's in our future, that means she's not going to . . ."

"Die?" Penelope finished when he didn't. "That future's not a guarantee. If we make different choices then what you dreamed might never happen."

Noah's fingers tightened around hers. He glanced at Ella and River then turned back to Penelope, his expression unreadable. "But if that's what we both want, to be together, with Ella and another kid to boot, we could make it happen, right?"

"Yeah, if that life is really what we both want."

But if there was doubt on either side, they could lose it all.

• • •

There was only one way Noah knew how to prove to Penelope he was all in. After his shift at Rehab ended, he borrowed his brother's car and drove the two hours home and the two hours back to Malarkey, stopping just long enough in between to pick up what he needed from his place.

When he pulled into Penelope's driveway, he rubbed at his eyes to make sure the house wasn't just a sleep-deprived hallucination. All the lights were off, which shouldn't have been a surprise considering it was just shy of 6:00 a.m. But after being awake for almost twenty hours, he'd lost track of time. And he needed to see Penelope more than he needed sleep. Needed to make sure she had no doubts about what he wanted them to be.

Noah glanced at Bombay curled up on his jacket on the passenger seat, tail twitching and eyes round and alert. He typed out a quick text to Penelope and tapped his fingers on the phone's screen while he awaited a reply.

I'll be right down, she wrote back less than a minute later.

"You've gotta make her love you, okay?" he said as he shifted Bombay off his coat. He couldn't open the door and risk the cat shooting out past him into freedom so he struggled into the coat behind the steering wheel. After zipping the front most of the way, he tucked the cat inside and added, "If she says no, we're screwed. Both of us. So let's make this good." He hugged her to his chest and got out. She kneaded her claws into his shirt, content to be bundled up with him.

Shit, I hope this is a good idea.

"Everything okay?" Penelope asked as she cracked the door and blocked the entrance. She shivered as the cold air rushed in to flutter the bottoms of her pajama pants.

"Yeah. Sorry," he said, shifting to block the wind. "I went home to pick up a few things."

"Did you even sleep?"

He closed the gap between them and twirled a strand of her hair around his finger. "It was important."

Bombay struggled against his one-handed hold. Then she gave a pissed-off, warbly cry that made Penelope jump away from him. He unzipped his jacket an inch so the cat's head could poke out.

"Oh, Noah. What are you doing? Please tell me you're just bringing that cat over here to show it to us," Penelope said, shaking her head. "If Ella sees her, you're in so much trouble."

"Damn. I was kinda counting on Ella helping sway you to my side." He held up Bombay, lifting her paw out of his coat in a wave. She shook in his hands, her heart hammering against his palm at the unfamiliar surroundings. Rubbing his thumb under her chin, he tightened the grip on his other hand to keep her from bolting. "I don't want to rush you, but I need you to know I'm serious about staying."

"I can't see anything with the way you're holding her. She's so small. Give her here." Penelope cupped one hand under Bombay and stroked a finger down her back. After a few passes, the cat started purring and Penelope eased her away from Noah's grip to nuzzle her cheek into the cat's fur, ruffling the black and white markings on her neck. "How old is she? She doesn't look like a kitten, but she can't be full-grown."

"She's about two, I think. You should've seen how tiny she was when I got her. She fit in my palm but she's always been feisty. It's a hard combo to resist." Noah slid his eyes over Penelope again. "So, can we come in?"

Penelope held the door open for him and carried the cat into the living room where she set Bombay on the back of the couch to get a better look. "What happened to her ears?"

Laughing, Noah ran the tip of his finger over one of the short, folded ears. "She's a Scottish Fold. That's the way they're supposed to be. Gives her extra personality."

"Can't argue there. And I can see why you thought wooing me with an adorable ball of fur was a smart idea. But I thought you said River is allergic to cats," she said.

"She is."

"So what are you planning to do with her?"

"I'm working on it," he said and fought the smile that threatened to give him away.

"We can't take her, Noah. I know Ella offered, but we don't even know what this is yet," Penelope said.

"Did I ask you to take her?"

"No, but you're going to. I can see it in your eyes." She leaned over and picked up Bombay again. Holding her almost nose to nose, she said, "He's going to ask me. Just you wait."

But Penelope hugged Bombay closer. A dead giveaway she had no intention of making Noah or his cat leave.

The end of the Festival of Fate always triggered an influx of customers to the shop, all wanting an extra boost of luck or to drink the Enlightenment hot chocolate to see if their wish had changed their futures yet.

Penelope had been carrying around the recipe card for curing heartbreaks in her apron pocket for days. Her fingers sought it out, needing reassurance that there was still a chance for everything to work out. When the shop finally showed signs of slowing down, she invited Noah over to help them make it.

Ella tackle-hugged him when he walked in the door. With his hands clamped on her skinny waist, he flipped her into the air and carried her upside down with her knees bent over his shoulders and her bubbling laugh filling the shop.

Penelope didn't hesitate to kiss him when he reached her.

"So, what are we making?" Noah asked, setting Ella back on her feet.

Penelope led him to the kitchen where she had the ingredients already laid out on the work table. "Chocolates to cure heartbreak."

"And you think we need those because?"

"Because our daughter's dying. And I'm really not okay with that," she said. Saying *our* instead of *my* was still a conscious choice, but one day she hoped it would feel natural. She fanned the recipe card through the air between them. "So maybe my mom was right and this recipe will stop the heartbreak before it even happens."

"I'm all for trying anything that might save her. But I thought we couldn't eat or drink anything we make ourselves. Won't the magic mess us up?"

"That's why we're all making it. I've split the recipe so we can each make a fourth and then we swap."

"I get to make them too?" Ella asked as she and Sabina entered the room, each carrying two mugs of hot chocolate.

"Yep."

Sabina set her cups on the counter and wrapped

an arm around Penelope's waist and squeezed. "Do you really believe it will work?"

The magic working was the only option she would accept. Penelope pressed a kiss to her mom's temple, and said, "It has to."

And they set to work, each on their own small batch of chocolates.

With every truffle she made, the tension in her shoulders receded a little bit more. And as the feeling of undiluted happiness washed over them all, Penelope laughed for the simple pleasure of it.

They all needed more of that in their lives. Laughter and love and the unshakable belief that fate worked in mysterious ways.

ABOUT THE AUTHOR

Susan Bishop Crispell earned a BFA in creative writing from the University of North Carolina–Wilmington. Susan lives and writes near Wilmington, NC, with her husband and their two literary-named cats. She is the author of *The Secret Ingredient of Wishes*.

Center Point Large Print
600 Brooks Road / PO Box 1
Thorndike, ME 04986-0001 USA

(207) 568-3717

US & Canada:
1 800 929-9108
www.centerpointlargeprint.com